Pepper Pot Farm

K.T. DADY

Pepper Pot Farm
K.T. Dady

A partner who is your best friend is a blessing from the beginning to the very end.

Prologue

Tessie

Tessie had finally settled Daisy after ten minutes of the eight-year-old girl constantly crying in her arms. The child fell asleep completely exhausted, and Tessie felt as though she could easily join her. She removed herself from the single bed and tucked Daisy in. She really wished she could provide what the child had asked for, but Daisy wasn't her daughter. She knew she had no right to pick her up and carry her out the door of Pepper Pot Farm.

I'll just have to talk to Nate. Tell him how sad his daughter is. I'm not sure he is going to listen to me. He's so loved-up with Dana bloody Blake, he's not seeing how miserable that woman makes Daisy. What am I supposed to do? Daisy begged to come and live with me.

She watched the sleeping girl for a moment longer. Her heart was aching so badly.

I could just take her. He'll fight me, but this isn't about him. Daisy is suffering. I could just punch Dana in the face for the way she has been talking to Daisy. She thinks Daisy hasn't told anyone. Well, she's told me. I hate that woman so much. It seems like a good plan. Punch Dana in the face, carry Daisy to my car, and tell Nate to sod off.

Tessie sighed inwardly. She knew she couldn't take away someone else's child, even though Daisy was her own daughter's cousin. She had to talk to Nate about Daisy's wishes. The chat alone might wake him up.

I'll go and talk to him now. Get it over and done with. He's outside in one of the barns, which is good. I can't talk to him in front of that woman. I need to calm down and go about this sensibly. If I start off aggravated, he will just close down on me. That's what I do when someone shouts at me, and I really want to shout at him right now.

She took one last look at Daisy and quietly left the bedroom to stand at the top of the stairs for a moment to compose herself before heading down. She knew what she had to do, but thinking about it and acting it out were two different things, and she had a feeling the conversation with Nate wasn't going to end well.

The moment he started going out with Dana Blake, Tessie had become almost invisible to him. She had watched over time as their friendship faded away to next to nothing. Once he got engaged to the woman, he was gone, but Daisy remained close to Tessie, calling her often, asking to live with her, crying a lot.

Tessie couldn't sit back any longer. It was time Nate knew exactly how his daughter was feeling, whether he liked it or not.

She quietly walked down the stairs and practically froze when she heard Dana's voice coming from the living room.

Oh great, she's back. Maybe I should just have it out with her instead. No, Tess. Just calm yourself. This is not the time for... Why is she whispering?

Tessie tilted her head, trying for a better angle to overhear Dana's muffled conversation.

'Don't rush me. It's all in hand. I've got this far, haven't I?'

There came no reply, and Tessie realised that Dana was on the phone. She moved down to the hallway and stood alongside the wall next to the living room door. Dana was

6

keeping her voice low, but she sounded annoyed about something.

'I'm the one doing this, not you. You can come to this dump and sleep with him if you feel you can do a better job than me. No? Thought not.'

Tessie frowned with confusion.

What is she talking about?

Dana's voice seemed closer as though she had moved towards the opened doorway.

'He's not here. He's in the barn, being the good little farmer he is. I don't care about that. Look, it's not long to wait now. I'm going to move the wedding forward. The sooner I can sell this place, the sooner I can get out of here. Do you know how much this place smells of cows? I can't live like this much longer.'

It took every ounce of willpower Tessie had to hold herself back. She wanted to slam her hand on the door and push it back into Dana's face, but she knew she had to remain perfectly still and listen. There was more to learn. Dana had more to say to whoever was on the other end of the line.

'He won't know what's hit him. I'm not bothered. He'll get his half, won't he? This land is worth a small fortune. I've already spoken to an estate agent. I have a fair idea what this farm will go for. I just need a few more months. Of course I haven't fallen in love with him. I know he's hot, but he's a farmer, for crying out loud. I can do so much better than him, and I will once I have divorced him and sold his home and business. Oh, I'm sure he'll recover. He can do something else with his life. I'm actually doing him a favour, when you think about it.'

It took a moment to process Dana's spiteful words. She was only marrying Nate so she could get a hold of his farm and then sell the whole place to the highest bidder, and Nate had no idea. Tessie could feel her blood starting to boil. She had to do something.

Dana was mid-sentence when she saw Tessie Sparrow slowly push the living room door fully open. 'I have to go.'

Tessie glared at her.

Dana calmly placed her phone down on the old rustic coffee table, then she straightened and flicked her long dark hair over her shoulder.

Tessie answered the question bouncing in Dana's eyes. 'I heard every word.'

The corner of Dana's mouth twitched into a small smirk. 'He'll never believe you.'

Just for a moment, Tessie knew that to be true, but she had to at least try to help him. He had been her friend since childhood. She turned on her heels and headed for the back door in the kitchen.

'We'll see,' she called over her shoulder.

Dana's body thumped into Tessie, causing Tessie to slump over the large kitchen table with such force an 'Oof' sound whooshed out of her mouth. Her wild locks of red hair were suddenly scrunched inside Dana's hand. A pain ripped through her head as her hair was yanked away from the table, then her head was slammed back down onto its solid pine surface.

Tessie saw sparkles, then darkness that lasted seconds. She quickly turned her body and swung her arm straight up, connecting her fist with Dana's right cheekbone. As soon as her hair was released, she straightened and swung a second punch.

Dana was taller than Tessie, but that didn't stop the smaller woman from striking out again. The two women stumbled into each other and hit the floor, rolling around on the cold stones. Tessie scrambled on top and banged Dana's head on the leg of the table. Suddenly, she was almost flying through the air, and it took her a moment to realise that she was in Nate's huge arms.

'What the hell is going on here?' His angry words spat out through clenched teeth over her shoulder as she wriggled in his strong hold.

Dana put on the crocodile tears as she sat up on the floor and cuffed her bleeding lip. 'She just attacked me, Nate. She's crazy.'

Nate wasn't releasing Tessie from his grip anytime soon, and Tessie knew she had to calm down if she was ever to be free, but she was struggling with that emotion. All she wanted to do was rip Dana's throat out with her bare hands.

Dana was going for an Oscar. 'She told me she's in love with you, Nate. That she plans to ruin our wedding, because you should be marrying her instead. She said she was going to make up lies about me.'

Tessie's slowing heart rate had accelerated again. 'I'm going to kill her.'

Dana flopped her head into her hands and continued to sob quietly.

'I'll deal with this.' Nate carried Tessie outside onto the pathway that led to the barns.

Tessie felt the cool air fill her flaring nostrils as Nate dropped her, blocking her from re-entering his home. She pointed her finger out towards the back door. 'She's lying, Nate.'

He pointed his own finger. 'You need to leave.'

She could tell how angry he was at her for fighting with his so-called beloved. There was little chance of her side of the story entering his brain. Dana Blake had him wrapped around her perfectly manicured little finger. Still, she had to try, if not for his sake, for Daisy's.

'Nate, you need to listen to me.'

He shook his head and took an obvious calming breath. His taupe eyes softened a touch, and he lowered his hand. 'Please, Tess, just leave.'

'Not till I tell you.'

He grabbed her arm and marched her off to the driveway where her dad's old estate car sat, cold and dusty. He let go of his hold and gestured towards the end of his drive. 'You're not welcome here anymore, Tess.'

Even though his words were spoken quietly, she felt as though he had slapped her in the face with them. Tears pricked, glossing over her green eyes.

I'm not going to cry. He has to listen. I need to tread softly.

'Please, Nate. Why won't you give me a chance to speak?'

She watched his body relax and felt his heat as he closed in on her. He lowered his head and gently kissed her damp cheek where a tear had fallen, taking her by surprise.

'Don't speak to me again, Tess,' he whispered close to her ear.

She shivered at his closeness, his soft words, and his goodbye. It was over. Years of friendship. Just like that. He wasn't even going to fight for it. Something shifted inside of her, and before she had time to think about her actions, she reached out and grabbed his checked shirt, balling it tightly into her hand and pulling him back down to her eye level. He was a huge muscular man, so she knew her grip was only in place because he was currently in shock from being unexpectedly grabbed by her. But she was fuming and wasn't thinking about anything other than getting through to him somehow.

'You listen to me, Nate Walker. I just overheard that bitch on the phone telling someone how she was only marrying you so she can divorce you and get her hands on this place. She plans to sell the farm from under you, and you're not going to let her. Do you hear me, you stupid sod. I do not love you. I'm not jealous. This is me telling you what I heard.'

Nate ripped her hands away from his top and pulled himself up, towering over her tiny frame. His eyes were filled with fire, and his outstretched hand was shaking slightly, which was something she had never witnessed before.

'I don't know what you think you heard, Tess, but it wasn't that. You're wrong, and we both know that you are jealous and that's why you're here saying these spiteful things to me.'

She felt like smacking him in the mouth. 'I'm not bloody jealous. I'm trying to help you.'

His shaky hand flapped in front of her face, then slammed into his pocket. He lowered his eyes to the ground and took a breath. 'Please go, Tess. There's nothing left to say.'

'Don't make me kick you in the shin, Nate.'

His eyes shot up to glare into hers.

'I've just told you something major, and you're not even going to entertain the situation. What's wrong with you, Nate? You never used to be this stupid.'

'I'm not stupid, and the only thing I'm not entertaining is you. Now, get off my farm.' His pursed lips and creased brow told her he wasn't playing nice anymore.

Tessie opened the car door whilst steadying her breathing. Thanks to Dana, she had a splitting headache, and now she had a crushed heart from the weight of her fallen friendship with Nate Walker. She took a moment, balancing one foot inside the car and the other still on the driveway. His eyes were boring into her back, she knew that much. There really wasn't much else to say. If he wouldn't listen to her, she couldn't help him. He was going to lose his family home, and that fact only seemed to be hurting her. She turned her head to face him. There was something she could try.

'Nate, ask Wendall James if Dana has been asking questions to anyone about this place. He's not just an estate agent, he's your friend. He'll tell you the truth.' She knew her words had come out as broken as she felt, but maybe if she wasn't shouting at him, he might take that piece of advice on board.

He didn't reply or even move, so she got in the car and turned the key. She didn't move for a second, trying to focus, clear her head, and remove the deflated feeling that had consumed her and refused to disappear.

Nate was kneeling down at her side. His hand resting on the inside of the opened window.

She didn't feel as though she could look at him to say their final goodbye. It was too much.

Why are you staring at me, Nate? Why are you here with me? You hate me. You want me gone. What are you doing? What are you going to say now?

His fingertips brushed lightly across the top of her arm, causing a flush of heat to run through her.

'I'm sorry it's come to this, Tess.'

She swallowed hard and rolled back her tears before facing him. His eyes were gentle now, recognisable. The stubble just growing on his face felt warm under her fingers as she slowly brushed along his jaw.

'I do love you, Nate. You're my best friend.'

12

Her breath caught as he took her hand and softly kissed her knuckles. 'I love you too, Tess, but I really bloody hate you right now.'

She snatched her hand away and drove off, checking on him one last time through the rear-view mirror.

Please, Nate, believe me, not her.

1

5 Years Later

Nate

Nate Walker sat at his kitchen table with his head slumped into his hands. He'd had a rough night worrying about how he could afford to repair his rundown farmhouse.

Pepper Pot Farm had been in his family for many years, and it looked as though no one had done any work on the old white-washed building in any of that time. The house was in need of some love and care, and the farm equipment needed updating. Business had taken a dive on his dairy farm in the last few years, and he was starting to see his family home fade before his eyes.

He had more than money worries on his mind that morning. All he wanted to do was talk to Tessie about the unexpected phone call he had just received.

Hurry up, Tess. You only dropped the girls to school. I need to talk to you. Oh, why is this happening now? I really don't need this in my life. I need Tess, that's what I need.

He raised his weary head as Tessie opened the front door. He got up to put the kettle on, opened the cupboard door, looked at it drearily as it came off its hinges, placed it on the worktop, and sat back down.

Great! This house is falling apart. I can't think about that right now.

Tessie was tying back her long red curls that had spiralled out of control in the strong wind outside. She kicked off her brown ankle boots and placed her feet into the pink slippers that were by the door. She stopped in her tracks as she saw Nate's muscular frame taking up the kitchen doorway.

His face said exactly how he was feeling.

Tessie didn't speak. She just walked up to him and wrapped her arms around his built waist. Her five-foot height took her head straight into his firm chest.

Nate hugged her back and sighed.

Oh, Tess. I really don't want to have this conversation with you, but you have to know.

Tessie looked up at him and smiled warmly. 'What's wrong?'

He immediately felt a bit better. His mouth curled slightly at the beautiful moss-green eyes gazing up at him with compassion.

If there was anyone in the world who could cheer him up instantly, it was Tessie Sparrow.

He felt her shiver in his arms. 'Go in the living room and sit by the fire. I'll bring you in a cup of tea.'

Her arms left his body. 'I'll call Jeff Mills about that boiler, shall I?'

Nate shook his head. 'I've already called him. He'll be here after lunch.'

'Daisy was all right about having a cold wash this morning, if that's what's playing on your mind.'

He thought about how much his thirteen-year-old daughter had to put up with sometimes. He knew exactly what growing up on his dairy farm in Pepper Bay was like. He had taken over the running of the family business when he was in his early twenties. It wasn't too much of a hardship for him, as he was used to it. He hardly ever left the Isle of Wight and was happy to stay in the small bay he grew up in. He hoped he never had to move.

Tessie was still looking up at him. 'She can stay at the pub with me if the boiler doesn't get fixed today.'

He nodded. 'Sit on the sofa. I won't be a minute.'

She walked into the cosy living room.

Nate poured the tea and joined her.

'I called you because something's come up, and we need to talk.'

Tessie's eyes were wide. 'You're worrying me now.'

He moved closer to her on the old brown sofa and placed his hands over hers, swallowing them whole. 'After you and the girls left for school, my phone rang. It was Tori.'

He felt her hands tighten beneath his.

'What did she want?' Her voice was low with a hint of nerves.

'Her parents sold the flat above Dolly's Haberdashery. They want to give the money from the sale to Daisy and Robyn.'

Tessie frowned in annoyance. 'Hope you told them where to stick it.'

'I said I needed to talk to you first.'

She removed her hands from his and sat back, shaking her head.

Nate caught the light from the open fire flicker across her face, highlighting her cute freckles.

'I know.' He sighed. 'It's a bit of a shock.'

'A bit of a shock! That family hasn't had anything to do with either of our children since they were born. My Robyn wasn't even born when they left for Australia. You would think they would want to know her, seeing how she's all they have left of their Henry.'

'We've talked about this before, Tess. We can't judge them. Their son died. Grief can do funny things to a person. Everyone knows that.'

16

'Funny things! My boyfriend had just been killed down the beach by falling rocks from the cliff. I was pregnant with his child. Tori had just given birth to your daughter. His own twin sister upped and left to go across the other side of the world without even saying goodbye to any of us. Daisy doesn't even know her. We haven't heard anything from that lot in thirteen years. Why now, Nate? Why now?'

Wish I knew.

'I don't know, Tess. I don't want you getting upset.'

'I'm not upset, Nate. I'm angry.'

Nate slumped backwards. 'I'm still in shock, if I'm honest.'

'They sold their own shop in Pepper Lane and the flat above it when they left. I always understood why they wouldn't sell Dolly's flat while she was living there. They were happy to keep renting it to her. I know all about Dolly's niece taking over the shop and buying that flat above it from them, but what I don't get is why they have decided to involve our girls all of a sudden. They don't even send birthday cards. Why are they offering money now?'

Nate shrugged. 'Maybe they want to start having contact. I don't know. Tori didn't say. She didn't actually ask after Daisy at all. She just told me about the sale.'

He watched tears well in Tessie's eyes. She moved closer to him, and he knew that she needed a hug. He placed one hand on her hair to soothe her as she snuggled into his jumper.

'Don't cry, Tess. I won't let anyone tear our family apart. You know that. I'll never let anyone hurt us again. I made that promise to you five years ago, and I intend to keep it.'

Tessie's muffled words rumbled into his chest. 'I'm upset for our Daisy, Nate. Her mum called after all this time, and she didn't even ask after her.'

'You're her mum, Tess, not Tori. Daisy only sees you as her mum.'

Tessie's green eyes flashed his way. 'We can't tell her. She'll be devastated.'

'Yeah, maybe. I don't know how it would make her feel, but I'm not willing to take the risk. I won't be telling either of our girls anything.'

'Have we got the right to refuse money on their behalf though?'

'I could tell Tori to put it in a trust, and then when the girls are older, we can let them know, and then it will be up to them if they touch it or not.'

Tessie sat up. 'Bit like me with my gran's money just sitting there untouched.'

Nate sighed. 'Why are there so many strange people in the world?'

'I don't know, but I wish they'd leave us alone.'

'Are we in agreement then, Tess?'

She nodded. 'Okay. Tell her to do that.'

He could tell that she wanted to say more. She was hesitating, and it was making him nervous. 'What's on your mind?'

She gave a half-shrug and curled back into his chest.

He hated not knowing what was in her head. 'Tell me, Tess.'

Silence filled the air for a moment.

'I was just wondering if you will start talking to Tori again now. You know, calling each other.'

Nate sat her up so that he could look her straight in the eyes. 'Listen to me, Tess. That won't be happening. I don't need any complications in my life. I'm happy with how things are around here. I know we're not a couple, but as far as I'm concerned you and Robyn and Daisy are my family, and that's all I need. Obviously, I have my sister and gran, but you know what I mean. I let someone break our circle once before. It'll never happen again. I'm never dating anyone ever again. You know that. I've got this place to worry about, and two daughters to look after. I haven't got time to have women in my life. So, no, Tess, she won't be invited back in.'

Tessie took a deep breath that was obvious to them both. 'I'm not against you seeing anyone, Nate. I just worry it will... well, you know.'

He nodded. 'Yeah, I know.'

'I'm just happy with the way we live our lives.'

'So am I, Tess, but you know what, one day you might meet someone else, and as long as he is decent, I'll be all right with that.'

What am I saying? I'd hate it. The thought of another man holding her. I can't think about that. I want her to find love and happiness, even if that's not with me.

'You know I haven't been with anyone since Henry. I don't think I ever will. I'm thirty-two. I don't think anyone is going to want me now.'

He breathed out a laugh. 'Yeah, you're well past your sell-by date.'

She nudged him. 'You know what I mean. I still live with my parents in their pub. I have a thirteen-year-old daughter. I pull pints when I'm not running around after her or hanging out with you and Daisy. Half the time my hair's a mess, and I can't be bothered with makeup. I'm hardly what you might call window display.'

You're beautiful, Tess.

Nate shook his head to himself. 'Why do you always put yourself down? You're the cutest girl on the Isle of Wight.'

Probably the smallest, but hey, your crazy hair adds some height.'

She laughed. 'Oi!'

He dropped his smile as he watched the sadness reach her eyes. He'd seen that look so many times over the years, and every time, it broke his heart.

I know you miss Henry. I know how much you loved him. I wish I could make your heart smile again, Tess.

'How about you and Robyn come back here for dinner later. Gran said she was making a beef stew tonight. We can watch one of those soppy films the girls like and have hot chocolate. I'll make sure the heating is back on by then.'

Tessie smiled.

That's better.

'Right. Now that's settled, get back here and give me a cuddle. I'm getting cold.'

She flopped into his big arms, making him instantly relax.

2

Tessie

There was nowhere in the world to Tessie Sparrow that was as relaxing as being in the arms of Nate Walker. It was one of her favourite places. He made her feel safe. He made all the wrongs in her life right. He made her feel needed.

'Why don't you stay over tonight, Tess. You never sleep here. There's not much room in Robyn's bedroom, or her single bed, and Joey still hasn't cleared her room out properly yet since moving into Honeybee Cottage, but I have a king size, so you can share with me, if you like. There's plenty of room.'

Tessie stared forward at the rustic coffee table. He had never asked her that before. As close as they were, they had never shared a bed.

'The girls would love it if you were here first thing,' he added.

'I'm always here first thing. I have my breakfast here every day during the week before taking them both to school.'

'Oh, you know what I mean.'

Not quite sure I do right now. I'm thinking you're rattled from the phone call. Maybe more than you're letting on. Maybe you just need us all around you tonight. Are you feeling insecure, Nate? I'm not asking him that.

'Okay, I'll stay tonight.'

His arms tightened around her slim frame. 'I could do with a nap now.'

'Me too.'

He shifted their bodies so that they were lying on the sofa.

Tessie was practically on top of him, as there was little room once his large frame was sprawled out.

You're worried. I know you are. Let's clear your head a bit. What can we talk about?

'So, how is Joey settling in down at Honeybee Cottage with Josh?'

'Every time I see her, she's smiling, so that's a good sign. To be honest, I think she's over the moon. That cottage and Josh Reynolds were all she ever wanted.'

Tessie nodded into his jumper. 'Took them long enough to finally admit how they felt about each other.'

'Yeah, well, love is strange.'

'People are strange.' She paused. 'People probably think we're strange.'

'I don't care what people think.'

'They always talk about us.'

'Still don't care.'

Change the subject, Tess.

She leant up on one elbow and used her free hand to pull her phone out of the pocket of her jeans. 'I want to show you something.'

He raised his brow. 'Should I be worried? You've got that goofy look on your face.'

Shrugging away his comment, she showed him the screen and waited for a reaction.

Nate frowned with curiosity. 'Is that our farm?'

'Yep. It's an Instagram account. I've created it to help sell more of your cheese. Pretty much everyone's a foodie these days, and Instagram is a great place to showcase your business, so I've set up this business page. It has a direct link to your sales page, which means people can order online.

I've also created new packaging with the brand logo stamped on these cute stickers that go on the wrapper.'

Nate widened his taupe eyes. 'We have a logo?'

'You do now. Plus, I've added loads of info on the site so that the buyers know exactly where the cheese comes from, who makes it, and so on. People are interested in that sort of thing, you know.'

'You do know that we can't just pop a bit of cheese in an envelope and stick it in the post box, don't you?'

I did not think of that, but I'll look into safe packaging.

'Of course.'

He didn't look overly convinced. He rolled his eyes and then frowned back at the phone. 'What's that picture there? Why am I in it?'

Tessie didn't need to see him grimace or hear the tone in his voice drop to know that he would not like having his photo online.

You're built like a wrestler. You're handsome, with a warm, friendly vibe that pours from your gorgeous smile. I love your smile and your face. I could stare at you forever and not get bored. Everyone will see what I see now. This will definitely help pull in the punters.

'The buyers will want to know about the person who runs Pepper Pot Farm, Nate. It's perfectly normal.'

'Is it perfectly normal for the owner of a business to put up pictures of themselves topless?'

Oh, crap. He's going to make me take it down. Think. Think.

'It's just an action shot, that's all.'

Nate's brow wrinkled. 'What action am I supposed to be doing there? I've just come out of the barn after a workout and I'm walking back to the house.'

Yep, and you look so hot.

Tessie knew how he liked to pump weights in his makeshift gym a couple of hours a day after seeing to the cows and chickens. She had purposely waited for him to come out to get the perfect shot, knowing he wouldn't have known what she was doing with her phone. She couldn't ask permission for such a photo because she knew the answer would be a flat no.

'Life on the farm.' She quickly showed him some more pictures of Pepper Pot Farm. 'See…'

'Wait, go back. What was that one?' His head lifted from the cushion. 'Why are the Hart twins sitting on straw bales with their tops off? They look like they're in a '90s pop band poster.'

That is exactly why.

'Like I said, it's everyone who works here, and they work here. They loved having their picture taken. They thought it was fun, and they have loads of positive comments. They're well liked. Mind you, they do look like they should be in a pop band. I don't know why two lads in their twenties would want to work on a dairy farm anyway.'

'I was in my twenties when I took this place on. I've always loved it.'

'You had little choice in the matter. Your dad passed away. I bet you wouldn't have taken this place on that young otherwise.'

'I would have. My dad just wouldn't have let me. Anyway, the Hart twins love it up here. Some people actually like farming, Tess.'

She grinned. 'Well, they certainly do, and they told me to put their pictures up on the account anytime I like.'

Nate scrunched his nose. 'Well, at least they got a say in it.'

'Nate, it'll be good for the farm. Look, you've already got near on five thousand followers, and it's only been up and running just over a fortnight.'

'Is that good?'

'Yeah, Nate, that's good.'

'Have I got any comments said about me?'

Hell yeah! The word sexy has popped up the most. One lady said she'd buy anything you sold, and another said you could melt your cheese on her any day. You definitely have a fan club.

'Not really. Anyway, it's all about the cheese. That's what's important.'

'How much cheese have we sold, and why haven't I noticed us selling any, and how can we afford fancy packaging, and…'

Tessie shushed him by lightly touching his lips with her index finger. 'I've got it all in hand. The sales are a bit slow at the moment, but that's to be expected. No one knows the farm yet. Well, no one outside of the Isle of Wight, that is. Give it time, Nate. I've only just started.'

Why am I touching his mouth? Move your finger.

He looked concerned and slightly irritated. 'Did you pay for any of this?'

Here we go.

She gave a slight head shake. 'No. Your sister paid for the new packaging.'

She watched his face heat and felt his chest tighten. 'You mean that millionaire partner of hers paid.'

'No. I never said that. Josh Reynolds did not pay. He wouldn't. Well, he would, but he knows you wouldn't allow that. God forbid you allow anyone to put their hand in their pocket to help you out, Nate Walker.'

Nate's dark eyebrows furrowed. 'Don't make it sound like a bad thing, Tess. There's nothing wrong with making your own way, you know.'

Tessie huffed. 'And there's also nothing wrong with letting your friends and family help you out from time to time. You'd help them if the shoe were on the other foot.'

'That's different.'

'No, it's not. Jake Reynolds is one of your oldest and best friends. He's only uphill at Starlight Cottage. He's a millionaire coffee shop owner, and he would sell any one of his shops to give you the money to fix this place up if he knew for one minute you were struggling financially, and so would his brother.'

Nate raised himself swiftly, causing Tessie to almost fall off the sofa. He quickly caught her and pulled her closer to him, all the while not removing the scowl from his face. 'They had better not know about my finances, Tess.'

'Relax, Nate. They don't. Nobody does. I wouldn't do that to you.'

He flopped back, closed his eyes, and took a breath.

Let's wipe that grumpy look off his face.

She leant over him and gently kissed his cheek.

Why did I just do that? Ignore it. Ignore it.

He opened his eyes to look at her.

She tried for a warm smile to hide the awkwardness she was feeling. 'Please don't stress, Nate. Joey wanted to help. She used some money from her own savings. Money she had saved from before she got together with Josh. Joey wouldn't do that to you either. She's your sister. She loves you, and she knows what you're like.'

Why is he staring at me like that? He looks like he wants me. Is he going to kiss me? No, of course he's not. Maybe he's just studying my face to see if I'm lying to him. At least he doesn't look so mad anymore.

She steadied her breathing and lowered her eyes, staring blankly at her phone. 'It's going to be okay, Nate.'

'Yeah, I know,' he said softly.

I'm going to ignore the fact that his eyes just dropped to my lips.

'I really like the farm's Instagram page, Nate.' She caught a tiny twinkle in his eyes.

'It's… nice.'

She rolled her eyes to meet his.

'I'll live with it,' he added.

Tessie stretched away from him to place her phone on the coffee table. His arm held her all the way so that she didn't fall. She rested back against him and felt his fingers lightly stroke her shoulder.

His simple touch made everything better.

'Thank you,' he mumbled into her hair.

She felt her heart warm and smiled to herself. 'Does that mean I'm still invited to sleep over tonight?'

'You can move in if you like,' he whispered.

She closed her eyes, deciding not to respond to his joke.

3

Nate

A closing door woke Nate. His eyelids flickered before slowly opening. He looked down at Tessie snuggled in his arms, still asleep. His back was aching from sleeping on the soft sofa, but he didn't care. Not whilst she was in his arms.

A muffled voice came from the hallway. He couldn't see who was out there because he was facing away from the living room door.

He raised one arm in the air to grab their attention. He was pretty sure he knew who it was. 'Gran? Is that you?'

Tessie's head moved on his chest.

Nate's grandmother, Josephine, appeared in the doorway. 'That was Jeff just leaving. The boiler is fixed, but he said we really should invest in a new one.'

Nate frowned. 'He's not due till lunch. Wait, you're back early too. What time is it?'

'Lunchtime,' replied Josephine.

'Are you kidding me? I've been asleep that long?'

Josephine smiled. It did little to soften her natural hard lines and fixed stern expression. 'You must have needed it, son.'

Tessie opened her eyes. 'What time is it?'

'Lunchtime,' said Josephine. 'I'll make us something to eat.'

Nate watched Tessie look sleepily up at him.

Hello, gorgeous. I really wish we were in bed right now. Get a grip, Nate. You're just friends. Keep it that way. No

28

more dating, remember. That includes Tess. Don't ruin this. Everything's perfect as it is.

'We slept that long?' she asked.

He smiled softly. 'I think my back might be stuck in this sofa.'

Tessie lifted her head and wiped her mouth. 'Oh, I dribbled on your jumper.'

'Yeah, you seem to do that when you fall asleep on me.'

'I don't wake up like this when I'm in bed, you know. It must have something to do with you.'

He gently raised them both up to a sitting position. 'We'll see about that tomorrow morning when you do wake up in my bed.'

Shut up, Nate. That didn't sound right. Actually, it sounded perfect. I can't wait to sleep with her all night.

Tessie's green eyes smiled his way. 'You keep saying things like that and we'll be the talk of the bay.'

'We're already the talk of Pepper Bay, and next door in Sandly. Even the people there talk about us. If only I had a pound for every time someone asked me when we're going to get together.'

If only I had a pound for every time I thought about it.

Tessie sighed. 'Yeah, I know. I get asked that too.'

He felt his heart thump as her hand came up to his face to gently sweep back the front of his thick dark hair.

'I love these little grey bits at the front of your hair, Nate.'

I don't know what to say. I don't know how to respond to that. She looks awkward now too. What were we talking about? Oh yeah.

He slowly stood and stretched his aching back. 'I wish people would just mind their own business. They should worry about their own lives, not ours.'

29

'I'm not bothered anymore. It's not like it's anything bad.'

Nate reached out his hand and pulled her up to stand in front of him. He flattened down her wild hair and tucked a loose curl behind her ear whilst scanning her gentle eyes. 'No, it's nothing bad.'

She turned and headed for the doorway. 'I'll put the kettle on, and you can crank the heating up. It might be April, but it's still really cold at the moment. I hope springtime takes over soon. Winter is starting to take liberties.'

Nate laughed and followed her into the kitchen.

Josephine was leaning over the old oak worktop, making sandwiches whilst talking to herself.

'Who are you talking to, Gran?' asked Nate.

'Anyone in the universe who wants to listen to me. You should try it sometime. It's good for the soul,'

Tessie grinned at Nate as she grabbed the old cream kettle.

'Tess wants to know when the springtime air is going to kick in, Gran. Any weather predictions?'

Josephine turned her head. Her beady eyes glared over at her grandson. 'You normally tell me to shut up about my weather predictions.'

Tessie wagged the kettle at him. 'I hope you haven't been telling your grandmother to shut up, Nate Walker.'

His mouth curled as he sat at the kitchen table. 'Only when she's scaring people.'

Josephine raised her eyebrows. 'Not my fault some people can't handle the truth. All I do is say what will be. They soon come to me when their lives are a mess and they want me to read their tea leaves or cards. Don't see anyone complaining then.'

'So, nothing to report for spring?' he asked, trying not to sound as teasing as the look in his eyes.

Josephine placed a large plate of cheese-and-pickle sandwiches in the middle of the table. 'Well, seeing how you asked. We're in for a heatwave soon, so be prepared.'

Tessie switched the kettle on. 'A heatwave. I'll have to sort out my summer dresses.'

Nate glanced her way. He tried not to think about how great she looked in her summer dresses. It was his favourite look on her. 'The cows won't be pleased with that news.'

'Pepper Bay will.' Tessie smiled. 'We'll get loads more tourists if the weather is that nice, and after the winter we've had, it'll be a great start to our busy season.'

'Are you not working at the pub today?' asked Josephine, sitting down at Nate's side.

Tessie joined them at the table whilst waiting for the kettle to boil. She picked up a sandwich and took a bite. 'Yeah, but I fell asleep. Mum and Dad can cope.'

Nate grinned at her muffled voice.

Josephine frowned. 'Don't talk with your mouth full, Tessie. You need to be more ladylike for when you get a man.'

Nate joined his grandmother in frowning.

Tessie swallowed her mouthful. 'Who says I want a man?'

Josephine gave a slight shrug. 'It's in your future. You cannot avoid your destiny.'

'What man?' asked Nate, trying for indifferent rather than aggravated.

Josephine got out of her chair to get some cups ready for the tea. 'Life is no fun with spoilers.'

I want to know. If there's a man coming into Tessie's future, I want to know about it. Who is he? What does he want? He can bugger off. She doesn't need anyone. She's got me.

Tessie shook her head as she took another bite of her food. 'You're always giving out spoilers. Anyway, my Mr Destiny can get stuffed if he doesn't like the way I eat.'

Nate laughed at her. He turned to face his gran. 'Tessie and Robyn are staying for dinner tonight, and they're both sleeping over as well.'

Josephine stopped what she was doing for a second before pouring the tea. 'Okay. There's plenty of dinner. I'm still making extra at the moment, as I keep forgetting that our Joey has moved out.'

Tessie smiled into her sandwich. 'We need to start getting organised for her wedding. I can't wait to decorate the big barn. Obviously, nothing flammable, but we can have fairy lights, and fake candles…'

Josephine interrupted, 'I'm sure Josh Reynolds can afford to fly in his own readymade wedding barn for their reception.'

Nate huffed. 'Gran! Josh is happy to have the party in our barn. He loves Joey and is doing it for her.'

'Plus, they share memories in that particular barn.' Tessie grinned.

Nate shook his head. 'I don't want to know about their shared barn memories, thank you very much, Tess.'

Josephine brought over the tea, interrupting Tessie's giggle. 'They're having a double wedding in the registry office over in Sandly with Jake and Anna. I'm sure Jake won't want his wedding party in a barn. He is way fussier than his little brother.'

'Jake's already agreed.' Tessie turned to Nate. 'Anna loved the idea. She thinks it's magical.'

Josephine huffed. 'She would like anything, that girl. She was homeless, living on the rooftop of Jake's posh London building. After that experience, everything is magical.'

'It is quite magical.' Tessie scrunched her nose and shook her head. 'Not living on a roof. The barn reception, I mean.'

Nate smiled at her.

Josephine slurped on her tea loudly, gaining their attention. 'You'll make a cheap wedding one day, Tessie Sparrow.'

Tessie shrugged. 'I'm not bothered about weddings, Jo. A marriage is way more important.'

I agree.

'Take no notice of Gran.' Nate gave his grandmother the side-eye. 'She never did like the Reynolds.'

Josephine narrowed her eyes, crinkling her brow even more. 'That's not true. Edith was one of my best friends.'

'Edith was a Marshall.' Nate had only known Edith as a Reynolds, but he knew that was her married name.

'Yes, but then she married John Reynolds.'

'Well, anyway.' Nate huffed and shook his head. 'I wasn't talking about their grandmother, I was talking about Jake and Josh.'

'Don't you like them, Jo?' asked Tessie.

'I do, but it's just all that money they have and what it did to them.'

'They're no longer playboys, Gran, and Josh is good to Joey. He loves her more than anything, including money.'

Josephine placed her brown mug down on the table. 'I know my Joey is happy and loved. She has a good future ahead of her too. I'm not worried about her.'

'That's good,' said Nate. 'Now, eat your lunch, and I don't want to hear you say anything bad about Josh in front of Joey. You'll only upset her. She's still getting over almost losing him in that helicopter crash.'

'He's doing a lot better now. Joey said he only has the odd twinge, and Jake is back to normal. That was so scary to almost lose them both.' Tessie's sad expression was quite visible to Nate.

He locked eyes with her, knowing what had come to mind.

I wish we didn't lose Henry either, Tess.

Tessie smiled warmly and turned away. 'So, we've got Easter in a few days, the new Instagram business, and the craft fayre is coming up soon, and then there's the wedding. We are going to be seriously busy. The sooner we get organised, the better. We could start tonight.'

No. Tonight's family time. I just want to focus on us. You've never slept over before. I want to make the most of it.

'We'll start tomorrow.' Nate grabbed a sandwich from the pile in the middle of the table. 'Let's just enjoy our night tonight. One last calm night before the chaos hits.'

4

Tessie

The bottom end of Pepper Lane was lined with a collection of quaint pastel-coloured shops that sloped down towards a small shingle beach. Rows of flowerboxes sat along the pavement and outside the top floor windows. They were filled with the prettiness of springtime. A narrow conduit ran the full length of the shops on one side. Over the road, at the top end, was The Ugly Duckling pub. The only pub in Pepper Bay. The road was free from cars because they weren't allowed that far down, but there was a car park up the road and a tram that ran between Pepper Bay and the larger seaside town of Sandly.

Pepper Bay attracted many tourists, especially during the summer months. The top half of the picturesque Pepper Lane was lined with an array of cottages, from Starlight Cottage right at the top near the cliff, down to the newest built home Honeybee Cottage, which was where Nate's sister lived. Artists loved to paint pictures of the cottages, and visitors often took photographs of the scenery.

The shops appeared in paintings and photos too. The pastel-pink shop was Edith's Tearoom, where Joey Walker worked as a baker. She had run the place ever since Edith Reynolds told her to take over, which was a few years before Edith sadly passed away.

Tessie opened the door to the tea shop and smiled over at her friend, who was standing behind the counter serving two customers. She waited in line until Joey was finished and the two elderly women had taken their boxed-up slices of lemon drizzle cake and left the premises.

'Hey, Tess, you want some cake?'

Tessie eyed the chocolate fudge behind the glass counter. 'Ooh, I'll have a couple of pieces of fudge and a cup of tea, please, Jo.'

Joey's taupe eyes twinkled. 'Sit down, Tess. I'll join you while there's no one about.'

Tessie sat at a nearby table and placed her cold hands down on the pink gingham tablecloth. 'You on your own today?'

'Ruby's due in later, and Molly's got the day off. She's gone out for the day with Freddy.'

Tessie smiled warmly to herself. 'I'm so glad Freddy finally told everyone he was seeing Molly. I gave him a right telling off when I found out. Fancy being in a relationship with someone for two years and having to hide it, and just because he was being insecure. Oh, wait, that means Fred won't be working at the pub today. That's all right. I'm sure he's left plenty of cold dishes in the fridge for anyone who wants dinner tonight. God, I love his cooking. Molly is lucky there.'

Joey sat down with two teas and a saucer filled with fudge. 'Nate's a good cook. He just doesn't get a chance to do much because Gran likes to do everything for him.'

'I know he can cook. Your gran taught you both how to cook.'

Joey smiled her big wide smile, revealing her perfect teeth. 'Yep. Josh's gran was the same. Josh cooks our dinners most of the time. I'm surprised he's not a chef, but he prefers to draw and paint. That's his passion, really.'

'How are you getting on up at Honeybee?'

Joey tucked a fallen strand of her blonde hair behind her ear. She had the same eyes as her big brother, but where he had their dad's dark hair, she had inherited their mother's golden locks. 'We love it. And now that Josh is better, we can't wait to get married.'

'We were talking about that over lunch at the farm. I've got loads of ideas for the barn, but Nate said we'll start organising tomorrow. I was going to start tonight at dinner.'

'You up at the farm for dinner?'

Tessie nodded.

She's going to get excited when I tell her the next bit.

'I'm sleeping over tonight as well.'

She watched Joey struggle to keep a neutral expression. She could see the corners of her mouth curling up against her wishes.

'Oh, that's a first for you, Tess.'

Tessie raised her brow. 'Really? That's all you're going to say about it?'

Joey's pretty face broke out into a huge smile. She quietly clapped her hands in front of her chest. 'Okay, I'll admit it. I'm excited.'

'There's no need to be.'

'Oh, come on, Tess. It's a big step. You and my brother are finally getting closer.'

'We can't get any closer than we already are, Jo.'

Joey widened her eyes. 'You can.'

Tessie stuffed a piece of fudge into her mouth. She went to speak but the homemade confectionery was so creamy, she had to take a moment to appreciate its flavour.

Joey grinned. 'Good?'

Tessie nodded and mumbled.

Joey Walker was well known in the area for her baking skills. Pretty much everything she touched became mouth-watering.

Tessie swallowed. 'I don't want you getting excited about us, Jo, because you'll end up disappointed, especially if he ends up with another woman again.'

Joey's face lost all trace of happiness. 'Oh, please, don't talk about Dana Blake again. I know it was five years ago, but she still gets under my skin whenever I see her. Even more so since she kissed Josh just to wind me up.'

Tessie remembered the moment well. Poor Josh was just standing there minding his own business when Dana walked up to him and kissed him in the middle of the street, all because she knew Joey was looking.

Tessie hated Dana, with her long legs and sleek dark hair and flawless skin.

Joey reached forward and touched Tessie's arm. 'I'm sorry, Tess. I know she hurt you too. I don't know where Nate's head was back then.'

'To be fair, she is pretty.'

Joey scoffed. 'Pretty ugly. The woman's horrendous. She is soulless. I don't care what she looks like, she's pure evil. I don't like her at all.'

Tessie tried to lighten the mood. 'Really? You hide it so well.'

Joey smiled. 'I can't help it, Tess. Just her name annoys me. I just wonder what would have happened to my family if she had got away with it.'

'Well, she didn't get away with it.'

Joey patted her arm. 'Only thanks to you finding out her twisted scheme in time.'

'If I'm honest, the thing that hurt me the most back then was that Nate didn't believe me at first. He called me jealous.'

'I didn't know that. I'm so sorry. You were trying to save our farm from being sold from under us, and that's what he came out with? I wish I knew that back then. I would have said something.'

Tessie controlled the deep sigh that was trying to escape her. 'It's done now. He did apologise afterwards, when he finally saw her for what she really was. In fact, he has apologised for that quite a few times over the years. I think it plays on his mind.'

Joey lowered her voice. 'I know he cares so much for you, Tess. He just wants to make sure you don't harbour any hate towards him somewhere inside your heart.'

I could never hate him. He means so much to me.

Tessie waved the comment away. 'Of course I don't hate him. We grew up together. Our children are cousins. He was Henry's best friend as kids. He's a huge part of my life.'

'Yeah, I know, but I think he just worries sometimes that the hurt he caused you back then won't ever be repaired.'

'It's fine. We're fine.'

Joey looked about as convinced as Tessie knew her voice had sounded.

Joey picked up her cup. 'You know, I always believed that if it wasn't for that woman, you and my brother would have got together years ago. You started to hang out again and get really close when the girls were around three. I thought you were a perfect match. I still do. You know that.'

'I guess Nate has never seen me in that way. He's never hit on me. Ever. It wasn't only Dana he went out with. He dated other girls. He was obviously ready to start dating again after Tori left him.'

Joey shook her head. Her blonde ponytail flapped behind her. 'He did not date girls. He had that one relationship with Dana, and before that he had a couple of dates with Cara. That didn't go further than one kiss, because Cara told Nate she felt like she was kissing her brother. They decided they were actually better off as friends, which worked out all right for Cara, because shortly after, she met Brook Brown. I'm glad she ended up marrying Brook, which reminds me. I've got to pick Scruff up from Brook later on. He had to stay in for treatment. Well, I don't think he had to stay, but Brook wanted to keep an eye on him. She's such a great vet. So, you'll have Scruff for some company tonight as well. Where are you going to sleep? My bed's not there, and my old room is still a bit of a junk yard at the moment.'

Tessie twisted her mouth to one side. She really didn't want to answer. 'I'll pick up Scruff for you. It'll save you the trip. I'll just jump on the tram.'

Joey raised her brow in amusement. 'Tess? What aren't you telling me?'

Just tell her. Get it over and done with.

Tessie half-shrugged. 'Nate said I could share his bed.'

Joey slapped one hand over her mouth.

Tessie giggled. 'No, Jo. It's not like that.'

Joey mumbled from behind her closed fingers.

'I don't know what you're saying.'

Joey lowered her hand. Her face was flushed and her smile practically beaming. 'I'm not saying another word about you two.'

Tessie found that hard to believe. 'Really?'

'Well, maybe one thing. Oh, come on, Tess. You're my best friend and he's my brother. Do you know how hard it is for me not to interfere in your love life?'

Tessie raised her index finger in the air. 'I don't have a love life.'

Joey winked. 'You might, after tonight.'

'Jo. We're just friends. How many times did you fall asleep with Josh before you two got together, eh?'

'You can't compare. I was sleeping with Josh every time he rocked up in the bay, not falling asleep with him. Although, there were times when we did that too, but we're not the same as you and Nate.'

'I've fallen asleep with Nate loads of times. Being in his bed next to him won't be any different.'

Joey slowly nodded as she bit in her bottom lip.

'It won't,' said Tessie.

Joey stopped smiling and leaned closer across the table. 'Seriously, Tess, don't you have any feelings for him at all?'

'I care about him very much. You know that.'

'I mean deeper than that. Doesn't he ever make your heart flutter, your legs turn to jelly, or create butterflies in your tummy?'

Quite often.

Tessie shook her head. 'No.'

Joey sat back in her chair, with shoulders slumped and her face filled with disappointment. She appeared to have a sudden thought that made her smile. 'Well, you might start feeling those things after tonight.'

5

Nate

'Stew smells lovely, Gran.' Nate leant over the pot and grabbed a small spoon from the side.

Josephine pushed him away before he dipped the spoon in to swipe a dumpling. 'Go and tell the girls to wash their hands. I'll be serving up in a bit, and where is Tess?'

'Joey called to say that Tess offered to pick up Scruff from Brook.' He looked up at the duck-patterned clock on the wall. 'She jumped on the tram. She should be back by now.'

Josephine turned away from the oven. 'Call Artie, Nate. Check the tram hasn't got a fault in the line.'

Nate wasn't keen on the worried look in his gran's eyes. 'You got a feeling, Gran?'

'Not sure, son. Just make that call.'

Nate picked up his phone to call the man whose family ran the tram. 'He's not answering.' He hung up and steadied his breathing. His phone rang, and he quickly answered it, hoping it was Tessie.

'Oh, Joey, I thought you might be Tess. She's still not back, and I was starting…'

'Nate, I've just heard that the tram has fallen down the riverbank. Now, don't worry, Tess might not have got on it yet.'

It was too late. Nate had stopped listening to his sister. He was halfway out the door whilst putting on his boots.

'What's happened?' called out Josephine, running towards him.

'Tram's in the river.'

He heard his gran gasp as he closed the door. He jumped in his dirty old pick-up truck and sped down the long driveway towards Pepper Lane. He saw Josh Reynolds zoom past on his red motorbike, heading in the direction of Pepper River.

Jake's dark 4x4 was waiting on the road at the end of Starlight Cottage. He followed Nate all the way to the bottom end of Wishing Point, where the tram crossed the river.

All the vehicles came to a sudden halt.

The old red-and-brown tram was on its side, half in the water and half on the bank. The fire brigade were already up to their knees in the cold water, and paramedics were treating two people inside their ambulances.

Everything around Nate swirled. People were moving in slow motion. The noise sounded muffled and warped. His body felt frozen. He couldn't move from his seat. He couldn't feel his lungs. Nothing seemed real. The scene playing out in front of him was a nightmare. He felt a sudden pain surge through his throat, causing him to wake from his trance-like state.

Move, Nate. Move.

He flew out of his truck to run down the hill, quickly followed by Jake and Josh.

One of the firefighters saw Nate heading his way. He held out his arm to tell him to stop.

'Is Tessie Sparrow down there?' asked Nate, trying to get closer to the water.

'We're just getting someone else out now. Stay back.' The firefighter waved over to one of his colleagues. 'You let us do our job, Nate.'

'Can you do it quicker, Philip?'

I feel sick.

A dog barked up by one of the ambulances.

'Nate.' Jake touched his arm.

Nate turned to his friend. 'Don't stop me, Jake, I don't care what Philip says, I'm going down there in a minute.'

Jake softened his stern expression. 'Nate, look.' He pointed behind them. 'Scruff's up there.'

Nate turned to see his shaggy, old, black-and-grey dog mooching on the grass. He ran up towards him.

She's here. Where is she?

'Tess?' he shouted. 'Tess?'

He could see Jake talking to Philip, and the firefighters pulling someone from the tram. The person was wrapped in a foil blanket. A tuff of dark hair poked up through the top. It wasn't her. He looked over at Josh, who was heading towards the paramedics. A small crowd had gathered by the second ambulance, and local news reporters had turned up. Microphones and cameras filled the area, causing more chaos and disruption.

Scruff came up to Nate, sniffed his leg, and then carried on exploring the grass.

Nate didn't know which way to turn next.

Come on, Tess. Where are you?

Josh called out to him and waved him over to an ambulance. 'Nate. Nate. She's in here.'

A female paramedic stopped Nate from coming closer to the back of the vehicle. 'You wait there, sir. We're treating people.'

Nate bobbed his head around the small crowd blocking the ambulance. 'Tess? Tess?'

'Nate?' came her muffled voice. 'Is that you?'

Tess. Oh, thank God!

He felt his lungs work again. 'Yeah, I'm right here, Tess.' He rubbed the back of his neck with one hand whilst watching Josh use his bright azure-blue eyes and charm to make his way past people to get to the opened doors of the ambulance. He could see the top of his dark hair and hear his voice.

'Hey, Tess, you okay?'

Nate strained his ears over the commotion.

'I'm okay, Josh. What are you doing here?'

'Never mind me. I want to know what hurts?'

'Just my head and right arm.'

The paramedic who had spoken to Nate caught Josh in the doorway. 'Come on, sir, out the way.'

Nate watched Josh walk back towards him, avoiding the news cameras.

'She looks a bit dazed, one arm is in a sling, and she has a wound on her head, but she's sitting up and talking. She's going to be all right, Nate.'

Thank God. I need to see her. I need to hold her. Why don't these people get out of the bloody way!

Jake joined them. 'No one's been badly hurt, according to the firefighters, so that's good. That tram is having more and more problems every year. I'm going to see that it gets the update it needs.'

Nate was still trying to gain some sort of visual access into the ambulance.

Jake nudged his arm. 'What's the news on Tess?'

Josh answered, 'She's taken a knock, but she'll be okay. I couldn't get any more info. I got moved along.'

Jake grinned at his brother. 'Losing your charm there, Josh.'

Josh smirked at him. 'You try and get any closer. I'm afraid to say that the old Reynolds eyes won't work on that

45

paramedic, neither did *Old Muscles* here. That is one seriously focused woman.'

'Well, I'm glad she's focused. It's what Tess needs.' Jake looked over his shoulder. 'I'll speak to her. You know, most women tend to respond better to an actual conversation anyway, Josh.'

'Yeah, well, just try to avoid the reporters, eh, Jake. We don't need them finding out who we are. You know what they're like. They'll stick around and ruin our wedding.'

Jake nodded at his brother.

Nate watched Jake make his way through the crowd to speak to the busy paramedics. He spoke to one, and then the other, and then made his way halfway through the crowd to wave Nate over.

Nate's large frame struggled to push through. 'What is it, Jake?'

Jake pulled his arm to help drag him along. 'I told them you're her husband. They're about to take the injured to hospital now, so there's no room for you, but the paramedic said you can quickly say hello, but hurry, they need to get moving now that they've just freed the last person from the tram.'

Nate felt himself being moved to the back of the ambulance. He glanced up to see Tessie sitting up at the back.

She smiled weakly at him, and he just wanted to climb inside and hold her.

'Hi, Nate. Don't worry, I'm fine.'

He tried to hide his full concern. 'Clearly.'

'Don't tell my parents until I'm out of hospital. I don't want them worrying for nothing.'

Stop worrying about everyone else.

He nodded. 'Okay.'

'Save me some dinner, Nate. I'm starving.'

He smiled. 'Now I know you're all right.'

'Will you pick me up from the hospital when I'm done?' she asked quietly.

What is she talking about? Does she think I'm going home now?

His brow furrowed. 'I'm coming with you, Tess. I'll follow the ambulance.'

'What about Scruff? He's out there somewhere.'

'He's fine. Jake will take him back to the farm and explain what's happened to Gran. He won't tell the girls. We'll explain to them when they can see you for themselves.'

Otherwise they'll go out of their minds with worry just like I did.

'Good,' said Tess. 'Daisy will worry too much. It'll make her ill. You know what she's like.'

'It's all in hand, Tess. I promise. How are you feeling?'

Before she had a chance to respond, the paramedic was back. 'You can see your wife at the hospital. We have to leave now.'

Nate saw Tessie smile warmly at him, and it filled his heart. He returned the smile and then mouthed, 'I'll see you in a minute.'

The doors closed, and he watched as the vehicle drove away. He stood still for a moment as though unable to move.

Oh God, what has just happened? She only went to pick up the dog. She should be at home now with me, eating stew and smiling at me the way she does. I could have lost her. I don't know what to do. Wake up, Nate. Tess needs you.

He quickly went back to his truck.

Jake was putting Scruff inside his car. 'I'll drop him off, then meet you at the hospital.'

Nate shook his head. 'It's okay. You don't need to come. We shouldn't be there long.'

'Joey's already halfway there.' Josh pointed up at the road.

Nate nodded down at his feet. 'Okay. You two can go home though, but thanks for coming out.'

'We're family.' Jake closed his car door. 'It's what we do, right?'

Nate smiled weakly at him. He turned to Josh. 'Go up to the farm, Josh. Gran's made enough beef stew to feed an army. I'll bring Joey back with me for some dinner. Oh, wait. You're a vegan. Erm…'

Jake looked at his brother. 'He's all right, Nate. He can eat with me. Anna misses him and would love to have him for dinner.'

Josh grinned. 'Let's stop worrying about food. You get off, Nate. I'll call Joey in a bit. Let her know what's happening.'

Nate gave them a big bear hug each, told them he'd call once home, and got in his truck. He took a deep breath to calm his rattled nerves. His heart was pumping fast, and his head felt light and unfocused. He knew he had to steady himself before turning the key. He couldn't allow his brain to take over and start replaying the scenario.

Josh's motorbike roared.

Nate lifted his head, composing himself. He wiped away the lone tear that left his right eye.

Easy, Nate. Breathe. Relax. She's fine. She's safe. She's waiting for you.

He started the engine and headed off to the hospital before everything became a total blur and rendered him useless. He had no time for frazzle-brain.

6

Tessie

Tessie was sat on Nate's sofa in front of the crackling fire. She had a red blanket over her legs and had already been put into her grey flannel pyjamas by Joey. Her right arm was resting in a sling, and her forehead had been cleaned and stitched. She felt a bit battered and bruised but the painkillers had done a good job, and Josephine's beef stew had filled her empty stomach and warmed her soul.

Scruff was fast asleep on the rug in front of the fire. He had escaped the tram uninjured. Jake had popped him in to see the vet before taking him home, and Brook gave Scruff the all clear.

Ed and Elaine Sparrow were sitting on another sofa, both staring at their daughter with concern.

'Stop staring at me. I'm fine.'

Elaine breathed out the air she appeared to be holding on to. 'You'll be the death of me, Tessie Sparrow.' She ran her fingers through her short white hair as she turned to her husband.

Ed was a lot calmer. He smiled widely over at Tessie, revealing his one gold tooth in a row of white. The shine from the fire made his bald head glow and his diamond stud earring shine. 'Now we know you're all right, we'll head back to the pub. We called Freddy and Molly in to help out. They'll be wanting to head home soon.'

'Where you should be, young lady.' Elaine waggled a finger her way.

'Mum, I'm thirty-two.'

'Mum's fine here.' Robyn's voice boomed out as she entered the living room, making sure she was heard amongst the adults. 'Nate will look after her with me and Daisy.'

Elaine wrapped her arms around her granddaughter as Robyn sat on her lap for a hug. She moved Robyn's long strawberry-blonde hair out of her eyes and kissed her cheek.

'She'll be okay with us, Elaine.' Nate was leaning on the doorframe, with one leg hooked around the other.

Daisy poked her head around his waist. Her deep blue eyes shined over towards Ed. 'I'll help too.'

Elaine waved her over. 'You come and give us a cuddle as well.' Daisy curled up on the sofa between Ed and Elaine, and Elaine started to tidy Daisy's blonde hair.

Robyn moved her hand away. 'Stop fussing us, Gran.'

Ed tapped his wife's arm. 'Come on, love. They've got this covered. It'll be nice and quiet here for our baby to rest.' He looked over at Tessie. 'Your mother will bring you some more of your things up in the morning.'

Tessie smiled lovingly at her father. 'Thanks, Dad.'

Robyn moved to let her grandmother stand, and Elaine gave Tessie a kiss and headed for the door whilst telling Nate to call if Tessie needed anything.

Tessie was relieved when they finally left. All she wanted was a bit of peace and quiet.

Nate was back in the doorway, staring at her.

She glanced over at him.

You would take care of Robyn if anything happened to me. I know you would.

'Do you need anything, Tess?'

Daisy sat on the floor by the coffee table. She flipped open her notepad. 'I have all of Tessie's information here, and also our schedule until she's better.'

Tessie and Nate smiled at each other.

Robyn sat on the sofa behind Daisy. 'So, what's next?'

Daisy read her well-organised notes. 'Next lot of painkillers in two hours. Hot milk before bed, because that's soothing, Jake's picking us up for school in the morning, and he's bringing us home too, and… that's it, for now. Oh, and Robyn's on breakfast duty tomorrow. I have a roster that I'm working on. I'm going to enlarge it and colour-code it and put it on the front of the fridge so that everyone knows what they're supposed to be doing.'

'Sounds great, Daisy.' Tessie smiled.

'Apart from the bit where I have to do stuff.' Robyn huffed and folded her arms tightly.

Daisy turned to her. 'You have to pour cereal into a bowl, Robs. I'm not asking you to milk the cows.'

Nate sat on the other end of the sofa to Tessie. 'What's this about Jake taking you to school?'

Daisy went back into efficient mode. 'I made some calls earlier. He agreed.'

Nate looked as surprised as Tessie felt. 'Jake Reynolds on a school run.' He laughed out loud.

Tessie tried to laugh but winced.

Oh my God, that hurt so much.

Nate turned to the girls. 'Why don't you go upstairs and make your chart, Daisy. Robyn, you make Josephine a cuppa.'

Robyn frowned. 'I'm not allowed to touch alcohol.'

Nate chuckled. 'It's tea, Robs, not alcohol.'

Robyn shrugged as she stood. 'Josephine always says a little splash in her tea of a night helps her sleep.'

Nate raised his brow. 'Oh does she?'

'Leave the tea, Robyn.' Tessie waved towards the door with her good arm. 'Go and get your PJs on. We'll all watch a film in a bit.'

Daisy's shoulders slumped. 'But my roster might take all night.'

'You have your notes. You can make the timetable tomorrow.'

'Okay, but as long as we get to choose the film, not Dad.'

Tessie nodded. 'Deal.'

Nate got up and closed the living room door as the girls left. Tessie closed her eyes for a moment and took a slow, deep breath. She felt the sofa dip to her side and Nate hold her hand. She smiled to herself and then looked at him.

He looks pale. He looks tired.

'Are you okay, Nate?'

'I'm just worried about you.'

She lowered her eyes. 'I'm okay.'

'We both know that's a lie.'

I'm not going to worry you any more than I know you already are.

'I'm just tired.'

Nate glanced at the TV. 'We don't have to watch a film. I can take you to bed now.'

She grinned. 'I bet you say that to all the girls.'

He breathed out a laugh and reached over to gently check the sling. 'You're lucky you didn't break anything.'

'I don't really need a sling. It's a bit much, don't you think?'

Nate narrowed his eyes. 'No. I don't. The doctor said your arm is badly bruised. This is to help it relax while it heals. You're wearing it, Tess. You can hardly move your arm.'

'Yes, boss.'

She watched his eyes turn to her head wound.

'Do you still have a headache?'

A bit.

'No. The painkillers helped. Stop worrying, Nate. I'm just tired. It's been a crazy day.'

'You can say that again.'

She watched him for a moment. The crease lines in his brow tightened, and his breath was shaky. She dipped her head so that she was resting on him and felt him kiss the top of her hair.

'Tess, when I saw that tram…'

'I know, Nate. It's over now. I'm okay.'

I can't think about it. I can't let it keep running through my mind. It's over. I'm alive. It wasn't my time. Everything's going to be okay.

'I don't know what I'd do without you in my life,' he said softly.

Oh, Nate, if only you knew how much I struggle when you say things like that to me.

'I'm not going anywhere, Nate Walker, not while you and our girls need me.'

'We'll always need you, Tess. So, I guess that means you'll be here forever.'

Tessie smiled to herself. 'I guess that does.' She lifted her head as Robyn walked back in the living room, swiftly followed by Daisy.

The girls sat on the other sofa, staring straight at Tessie and Nate.

'What?' he asked.

'We have something we'd like to talk about.' Robyn's pale-lavender eyes revealed seriousness and maturity whilst Daisy was looking nervous, sitting back slightly from her cousin.

'What do you want to talk about?' Tessie felt a wave of worry fill her. 'Is everything all right at school?'

'It's not school, Mum.'

Nate took charge. 'Your mum needs to rest now, Robyn. Perhaps leave this till tomorrow.'

Robyn sat up straight and nudged Daisy, making her do the same. 'It can't wait any longer.'

'Well, spit it out then, because you're worrying your mum, and me.'

Robyn was clearly the spokesperson. 'We've talked about this for a while now, but we weren't sure when to ask, but after what happened to Mum, we've decided not to leave it any longer.'

Tessie was waiting patiently for her daughter to get to the point. She could tell that Nate was worried and knew he hated dithering. 'Yes?'

Robyn took a deep breath. 'If it's all right with you two, I want to start calling Nate, Dad, and Daisy wants to call you Mum.'

Silence filled the air for a moment.

Robyn continued, 'As far as we're concerned, you are our parents anyway, so, why not? Daisy is more my sister than cousin, and this is our family. We want it to be more official.'

'Official?' questioned Nate.

'I added that bit,' said Daisy quietly, bashfully raising one hand.

Robyn nodded. 'We have spoken to Gran and Pops about it, and they liked the idea and are happy for Daisy to also call them Gran and Pops. Josephine said she didn't care what I called her. She said I'm her family anyway no matter what.'

Nate tilted his head to one side. 'Oh!'

Tessie looked at Nate, then turned to the girls. 'Can you give us a minute to discuss this?'

Robyn stood as Daisy nodded. 'That's fair enough.'

'We did spring it on you.' Daisy joined her side.

'You need time to process.' Robyn led Daisy out of the room.

Tessie looked at Nate again. 'What are you thinking?'

'I'm just wondering when our girls grew up?'

She laughed, then winced.

'Hey, are you okay?'

'Yeah. It just hurts to laugh at the moment.'

Nate glanced over at the door. 'What do you think, Tess? It's one thing for Daisy to call you her mum, but Robyn's dad died, and I know I'll never replace Henry, and I would never try to do…'

She touched his arm. 'Nate. It's all right. Robyn knows all about Henry, but she never got to meet him. You and my dad have been the only father figures she has known, and the way I see it… she's chosen you to be her dad. That has nothing to do with me.'

'I still want your input.'

I think it's incredible. The way she looks up to you. How much she loves you. I know you once let me down, but I know you would never let her down.

'I'm okay with it. Now, what about you? Are you okay with Daisy calling me her mum?'

She watched Nate shrug. 'She already does, really. She loves you to the moon and back. I think this accident has knocked the girls for six.'

Tessie nodded slightly. 'Yeah. So, are we going to agree to this then?'

Nate smiled affectionately. 'I'd like that.'

Tessie felt her heart warm. 'Me too.'

'Well, it took you long enough.' Robyn poked her head around the door.

Daisy followed her inside, carrying a pillow. 'I brought this to prop up Tess... Mum for the film. She can put her legs up. Dad, you'll have to sit on the end by her feet. I don't want you squashing her.'

Nate shifted to the end of the sofa whilst Daisy arranged the pillow behind her mum's back. 'I'm starting to think I'm going to be outnumbered by you lot.'

'That's been happening for years,' said Robyn.

'Well, now that I am officially your dad. You can start helping to milk the cows, Robyn.'

A flash of horror washed across the young girl's face. 'I want to add a clause into this contract.'

Tessie frowned in amusement at her daughter. 'What do you know about clauses and contracts?'

'Daisy taught me.'

Daisy nodded as she sat down. 'Clauses are important.'

Nate grinned. 'Is that right?'

Robyn took control of the TV. 'Right, let's pick a film.'

Tessie smiled to herself as she looked around the living room at her family.

I love this. I love them.

She caught Nate smiling too, and it warmed her heart even more.

7

Nate

The spare quilt and pillows did little to cushion the hard floor in Nate's bedroom. He knew he was in for an uncomfortable night on the worn-through, thin carpet beneath him, but he daren't sleep in the bed in case he accidently knocked Tessie whilst he slept.

He had placed her in his bed, with her bad arm near the edge, and had planned to climb in next to her.

Tessie had fallen asleep during the film, and Nate carried her up to bed. She didn't wake when he carefully removed her sling and tucked her in.

He sat on the end of the bed for a while watching her. He made sure she had water and her medication by the side of the bed before he snuggled down for the night on the floor by her side.

Normally, he would fall asleep straight away, but he was staring up at the ceiling, going over the what-ifs.

What if Tess had died? What if Tori wants Daisy back? What if I lose the farm? What if Tess blames me for everything going wrong? What if the girls blame me? What if I can't make Tessie feel better? What if she leaves me because of Tori? What if... Oh, shut up, Nate. Right now, Tessie Sparrow is here, and she's safe, and she's in my bed, and I wish I was wrapped around her. This was not how I visualised our first night together.

He sat up and looked over at her.

Her mass of long red curls were splayed over his pillows. The faint aroma of lavender night cream drifted towards him. His eyes filled with emotion as he scanned her pale skin. *You're so beautiful, Tess.*

He loved her freckles, which she sometimes moaned about. He loved her crazy hair, that sometimes drove her nuts. He loved her petite frame, that she wished was taller. He loved her cute smile, and how she still managed to look gentle whenever her blood boiled and her temper flared. He loved how patient she could also be, whether it was with him and his moods or the rowdy drunks at the pub on a Friday night. She was kind and funny and brought so much to his life and his daughter's life.

They had grown up together as nothing more than friends. He was with Tori. She was with Henry. They hung out together because Tori and Henry were twins. They spent a lot of their time in Waterside Cottage, where the twins lived. They'd seen each other kissing and cuddling with their partners. Never in a million years did they see themselves ending up becoming so close. Becoming a family.

Nate wanted to reach out and remove a strand of hair from her cheek, but he daren't wake her. He knew she needed her rest.

You're perfect, in every way. I'm so glad you're with me. Christ, Tess, if anything happened to you.

He took a deep, quiet breath. He'd had a hell of a day and just needed his mind to quieten down. He decided to go downstairs to the living room and call Joey.

'Everything all right, Nate?' she asked quietly.

'I can't sleep, Jo.'

'Too much in your head?'

He flopped onto the sofa and stared at the dead fire in the grate. 'Tori called this morning to tell me they've sold the flat above Dolly's, and they want to give the money to the girls. Then there was the accident, and then tonight, the girls told us they want to call us Mum and Dad.'

He heard Joey's breathing down the phone. 'Wow, that's a big day. I can't believe Tori actually called you.'

'I know, right.'

'Is she going to call back?'

I hope not. The last thing any of us need is her coming back into our lives. Daisy is settled, Robyn's happy here, and Tess finally trusts me again. There's no way I'm letting anyone into our circle.

'I don't know, Jo. She didn't say. She didn't even ask after our Daisy.'

'I don't know what to say, Nate.'

You're not the only one.

'How's Tess tonight?' she asked. 'I'd rather talk about her.'

'Sleeping. She'll be fine. I keep thinking about how much worse it could have been.'

'You can't think like that. I've had that with Josh tonight. I'm in the kitchen getting a glass of water to take up to bed. It's the first time he's left me alone tonight. He keeps thinking what would have happened if I had gone to collect Scruff. He doesn't want me on that tram ever again.'

Nate sighed deeply into the phone. 'It does get you like that.'

'You can't think that way. We've been using that tram since forever. It's a big part of our community. Jake's going to get involved with its upkeep now, so that's something positive. Think of the positives, Nate. Robyn calling you Dad from now on. That's huge. How do you feel?'

Nate smiled to himself. 'It feels right, but I did think of Henry. I don't know what he'd make of it or the family we've created. I think that the love he and Tess had was always way more than the love between me and Tori. They were always smiling. Sometimes, I don't know what I'm doing, Jo.'

'You're doing fine. You have such a perfect happy family, Nate. You're so lucky. If you just add intimacy into the mix, you'll have it all.'

'Don't start, Jo.'

'Come on, Nate. I know you love her, but surely you must be in love with her too by now. You act like you are.'

Nate's brow crinkled. 'No, I don't.'

Joey laughed. 'Yeah, you do.'

Bloody hell, am I that obvious? I can't be. Tess would have noticed if I was. She would have said something by now.

'Joey, I'm too tired for this. I've got to be up in a few hours, and I'm sleeping on the floor tonight, so I probably won't even get that much sleep. I don't need you going on about love again.'

'I can't help it. I just want that for you and Tessie.'

It would be nice, but things are perfect as they are.

'Yeah, well, life isn't one big fairy tale, Jo.'

He heard his sister sigh, and he knew he was meant to.

'Don't you have any of those feelings for her at all? Anything?' she asked, sounding hopeful.

You have no idea.

'Goodnight, Joey. Bring some pastries up in the morning.'

Joey huffed. 'Okay. Goodnight, Nate. Love you.'

'Love you too, Jo.'

He stared at his phone for a second, then placed it on the coffee table. He put his legs up on the sofa and rested his head on the arm and closed his eyes.

60

* * *

Nate had finished his morning chores earlier than usual, thanks to the Hart twins arriving half an hour early and taking charge. Everyone had heard about the tram accident, and the lads just wanted Nate to have one less thing to worry about.

He entered the kitchen to have his breakfast to find Tessie standing by the oven, stirring scrambled eggs with one hand.

'What do you think you're doing?' he asked, heading towards her.

She glanced over her shoulder and winced. 'I didn't think you'd want Robyn's cereal breakfast, so I'm making you scrambled eggs on toast. I thought you might like it.'

'I'll love it, but you can sit yourself down.' He gently guided her over to a chair at the table. 'I'll finish this.'

Tessie went to pour some orange juice from a carton on the table, but Nate interrupted that action as well.

'Leave that alone. You stop moving. You're supposed to be resting.'

She breathed out a laugh. 'I can pour a drink.'

'No, you can't.'

I'm not letting you do anything. You can rest. I'll carry you back off to bed in a minute. Oh, Nate, don't go there. You've messed up all morning thinking about her in your bed. Just stop. Act normal. Look, you're burning the eggs now. Concentrate.

'Jake called to say the girls got to school okay. I'm not sure if he seemed pleased with himself or in a flap,' said Tessie.

Nate laughed. 'I guess it was an experience for him.'

The toast popped and he got busy making breakfast. He placed the plates on the table and sat next to her. Her gentle green eyes rolled his way, causing his need for her to surface. *Ignore it. Act normal.*

'Have you taken your meds this morning?'

Tessie tried to cut up a piece of toast with her fork. 'Yes. Daisy is the strictest nurse I've ever met.'

He leaned over her plate and started to cut her food into bitesize pieces. He stopped when he saw her grinning at him. 'What? You needed some help.'

She started to eat her breakfast with a lot more ease, which made him smile.

'After this, I'll set you up in the living room for the day, Tess, and you are going to rest today. You're battered and bruised, and you need to heal.'

'I don't mind. Joey brought up some pastries earlier on. I might have one later with a coffee and watch Homes Under the Hammer or something.'

'I might join you.'

Tessie smiled. 'I also got a delivery of flowers first thing. They're in the living room. Anna sent them. She's popping over after lunch, so that'll be a bit of company.'

Nate frowned playfully. 'You've got company. You've got me.'

'You can get back to work.'

He waved his hand over to the back door. 'Ah, the twins have it covered. They wouldn't let me do hardly anything this morning. Oh, and they send their love. They'll pop in at one point to see you.'

'We're lucky to have them.'

'Yep.'

'How are your eggs?'

He grinned. 'Hey, they're our eggs. They're always good.'

Tessie's laugh came to an abrupt halt. 'Ow!'

She's in so much pain. I just want to hold her. I wouldn't know where to touch. I might make things worse with my big arms. What should I do?

He reached across the table and placed his hand over hers. 'Still hurts to laugh, eh?'

'I'll laugh again one day. Meanwhile, I might get some work done on the Instagram account. You don't have to worry. I'll be on the sofa, with my feet up. It's easy work. I want to check the orders on the website too.'

'Hmm, okay.'

'You know, if the shoe were on the other foot, you wouldn't let me do anything for you, or tell you what to do, and you'd be out there working still.'

I can't argue with that.

They finished their breakfast in silence.

'Thank you for looking after me, Nate.'

Nate felt his heart warm at the gentleness in her voice. He stood and took her plate away, swallowing down the lump in his throat.

'I'll always look after you, Tess.'

You mean everything to me.

8

Tessie

Anna had brought a large tin of fancy biscuits with her on her visit to Pepper Pot Farm.

'Don't tell Joey. She'll only say she could have made some. I know her biscuits are nice, but these are mouth-watering. Jake introduced me to them.'

Tessie gently giggled as she nibbled on a chocolate one. 'Thanks, Anna, but you already bought me flowers.' She nodded over to the large collection of colourful blooms in the corner of the room sitting next to a vintage lamp.

Anna tucked one side of her dark bob behind her ear. 'Oh, hush. You deserve more after what you went through yesterday.'

Tessie was fed up talking about the accident. 'Let's talk about your wedding. May will be here soon.'

'We've pushed it to June now. A summer wedding will be nice. Plus, Stan will be living in the cottage that Jake had built for him on our land by then. Do you remember I told you about him. He works in the building in London where Jake's apartment is. You'll love him. He's like a father to me. I can't wait for him to arrive.'

'I'm looking forward to meeting him. He'll love living here. We'll make him welcome in no time.'

'Thanks, Tess. I only came here in November, but I already feel like this is where I belong.'

'Pepper Bay is a very homely place. By the way, am I still decorating the barn?'

Anna nodded. Her ice-blue eyes sparkled with excitement. 'Of course. We can't tell many people in case the press get hold of the news. Jake said they will ruin the wedding with their cameras all over the place if they knew.' She sighed. 'It's not easy being well known. There have been some horrible things written about his family in the past. It's all tabloid gossip. You wouldn't think people would be interested in a couple of men who inherited a coffee shop chain, but there you go.'

'I wouldn't mind a few more people knowing me, then I'd get more sales for Nate's business.'

Anna dunked a biscuit in her tea. 'Are things slow?'

Tessie explained about the Instagram account she started and her marketing ideas. She made sure she left out the part about Nate's money worries.

'I don't do social media anymore.' Anna shrugged. 'But I think my shop would probably benefit from something like that.'

Tessie agreed. 'Of course it would. The Book Gallery should be on Instagram too. You can add a link where people can buy the books and the paintings. Those paintings would sell like hot cakes. Tell Scott. He'll know how to set that up.'

'We were thinking about online sales. Scott has got his own Etsy shop where he sells his prints. Jake said he'll hire someone to do something for The Book Gallery, but we haven't got around to it yet. Can I hire you, Tess? I'd rather someone I know. You can run an Instagram account for us.'

Tessie smiled widely. 'You don't have to pay me, Anna. I'll set it up for you and show you what to do.'

She watched Anna give a slight head shake.

'Jake won't want me having extra work to do. He only let me hire Scott, because he wants to take me around the world and back again, and what with the baby on the way…' Anna gasped. 'Oh, I'm not supposed to tell anyone yet.'

Tessie's moss-green eyes were as wide as her smile. 'You're having a baby?'

Anna shushed her. 'We're not telling anyone just yet. Only Joey and Josh know.'

'I won't tell anyone. I promise.'

Anna raised her brow. 'I know you'll want to tell Nate.'

'He'll understand me keeping this kind of secret from him.'

'You can tell him. I don't want you to have any secrets between you. I'll let Jake know later on. He'll be okay.'

Tessie held back a laugh. 'I can have secrets from Nate, you know. It's not like we're in a relationship.'

Anna turned her eyes to the contents of the biscuit tin. It was obvious she was trying to avoid saying anything.

Tessie rolled her eyes. 'Oh no, not you too.'

'What?'

'You have something to say about us being together?'

Anna shrugged and sipped her tea. 'It's none of my business.'

Tessie breathed out a laugh. 'It's none of anyone's business, but it doesn't stop them going on about it to us.'

'I think it's because you two act like a couple. Not gonna lie, when I first saw how you were together, I thought you were a match.' Anna giggled into her cup. 'Jake was so jealous of Nate when he introduced us. He thought I had a crush on Nate.'

Tessie smiled. 'That's probably because most women do crush on Nate.'

'I just thought he was really sweet and very friendly.'

Tessie nodded. 'He is definitely that.'

'I was too busy falling in love with Jake to notice anyone else.'

'I must admit, it was amusing to see Jake Reynolds all loved-up. I was surprised it took you a while to notice how much he liked you. I saw it straight away, but then, I've known him since we were kids. I'd never seen him look at anyone the way he looked and still looks at you. I'm glad he found you, Anna.'

'I'm glad he found me too. I still laugh about how I was living right above him. We worked out the floorplan to his apartment, and my tent on the roof was directly above his bedroom.'

Tessie watched Anna's face warm.

'You were so brave living in a tent, Anna. I don't think I'd be very good at being homeless. I'd be too scared, and not much scares me.'

'Jake doesn't laugh about it as much as me. He tends to feel more down about my time being homeless, and how he wished he knew earlier. I tell him not to think that way, but he can't help it sometimes.'

'Henry was a bit like that. He used to lean towards the negative more than the positive.'

Anna's eyes smiled warmly. 'I'm sorry for what happened to Henry. It must have been a nightmare for you, Tess.'

Tessie could feel Henry's presence, as she often did. She could see him smiling at her, giving her a cheeky wink. She felt him when she was in the tram accident, and in the delivery room when Robyn was born. She visualised him standing at her side on their daughter's first day at school. He held her hand the time her heart ached when she first saw Nate kissing Dana Blake. He had never stopped being her best friend.

'I still miss him, Anna.'

'I don't suppose you will ever stop. Not really.'

Tessie shook her head slightly. 'No.' She swallowed down the lump in her throat. 'We were together from early teens, but we'd known each other since birth. We used to hang around with Nate and Tori. She's Henry's twin. I'm not sure how much you know. Anyway, Tori had this big happy idea about us having babies at the same time and then getting married later on in a double wedding, which we were all up for. We were lucky to get pregnant pretty much straight away.'

Anna quickly swiped away a tear. 'I'm so sorry, Tess. I guess that's another reason you get so fed up with people going on about you and Nate.'

Tessie straightened up. 'No, not at all. I'm not actually bothered by it. It bothers Nate.'

'Perhaps because Henry was his friend.'

'Maybe.'

'Whatever it is between you and Nate, from an outsider's point of view, it looks pretty special. Maybe neither of you are ready to move closer together yet, but if you did… Oh, I don't know, Tess. I just want you both to be happy.'

'We are happy, Anna.'

'I'll change that to in love then.'

'I do love Nate, you know. He means the world to me.'

Anna smiled and nodded. 'But you're not in love with him.'

Tessie gave a slight head tilt. 'Honestly, Anna, sometimes I wonder about what exactly it is that I do feel.'

'It'll come to you when the time is right. I didn't expect to have feelings for Jake when I met him. It took me by surprise. Not my dog though. Oh no, Max fell in love with Jake straight away.'

Tessie giggled and looked over at Scruff and the golden retriever curled up asleep by the fireplace. 'Maybe I should ask Nate's dog, or perhaps Max might know.'

Max raised his tired head at the mention of his name. He flopped back down again when he realised nothing was going on.

Anna laughed. 'Or you could ask the psychic, Josephine.'

'Do you know, she won't do any readings for Nate or Joey, but she's looked at my palm a few times and at my tea leaves.'

Anna looked down at her hand. 'Mine too.'

'She hasn't said anything to me about what she sees, and Nate tells her to leave me alone.'

'It's nice the Walkers are letting you stay here while you get better. You wouldn't get much peace living above a pub.'

Tessie nodded. 'Mum wasn't too keen on the idea at first, but Dad talked her round, like he always does.'

'I love your parents. They have a great relationship. Your mum told me about her past. Talk about true love conquers all. It's like a proper book. Rich woman disowned by mother for falling in love with poor publican.'

'Yeah, someone could make a TV series just about their love life.'

Anna frowned. 'It's a weird thing to disown your kid for. It's not like your dad was horrible or anything. He just wasn't rich.'

'My grandmother, who, by the way, I never got to meet, wasn't a very nice woman. I don't think it ever was really anything to do with Dad not having much. I think it was down to my grandmother not having control over my mum anymore.'

'It must have been hard for Elaine to walk away from her old life.'

Tessie shook her head. 'Mum said it was the best move she ever made. She was happy to leave. She said that being with Dad felt right, and she had never felt that way before. She called him her missing jigsaw piece.'

Anna cupped her hands in front of her heart. 'I love happy endings.'

'Yes, they're nice when you see them.'

Anna selected another biscuit from the tin. 'You'll get one too.' She wiggled her fingers over the top. 'I can see it in the crumbs.'

Tessie laughed. 'Yes, I probably would have to build mine from crumbs.'

Anna glanced up. 'Hey, I come from crumbs. Don't knock it.'

'Maybe I'll add crumbs into your wedding. Speaking of which, let's get some ideas down.'

Anna agreed. 'And then we can talk about you working for The Book Gallery.'

9

Nate

Nate's head jolted as his hand slipped from propping up his face. He opened his bloodshot eyes to see the numerous scratches in the kitchen table looking back at him. Trying to wake himself properly, he glanced up as Tessie entered from the hallway.

'You need anything, Tess?'

She shook her head and sat by his side. He was not oblivious to her thigh touching his.

'No. I was just stretching my legs.'

Nate was suddenly worried she'd been outside. 'How far did you walk?'

'From the living room to here.'

He grinned. 'As soon as you're better, I'll take you out for a proper walk. We can go up to Wishing Point. Have a picnic when the weather warms up.'

He watched her smile as she gazed at her sling. 'That'll be nice.'

He thought about the grassy area that stretched from the clifftop down to the river. It was filled with dandelion seed heads, and everyone who visited made a wish or two. He had made many himself over the years. More so as a child. It was a large place sitting between Pepper Bay and Sandly, and the tourists and locals loved it during the summer, as it was the perfect picnic spot, whether sat up high for the view over the bay or down low by the riverbank.

Nate remembered the last time he was over there for a picnic. He was with Tessie and the girls, last summer. He had relaxed so much, he fell asleep on the green-and-white checked blanket, and when he woke, Tessie was snuggled up under his arm trying to do the cryptic crossword in the local weekly newspaper. He remembered how good that had made him feel. They had started to look at each other differently by the beginning of that year. Their hugs had started to feel tighter and warmer, and they touched each other's faces and hair a lot. Everything came naturally. Every look, every touch, every moment spent together. It all felt right, and he could see how they had been slowly gravitating towards each other over the years.

I'm already looking forward to it. Just you and me this time, Tess. No kids. No noise. No injuries. You need some peace and quiet. Some rest time. I know you're in pain. I can see it in your eyes.

'You tired, Tess?'

'No. I'm okay. It's just, my neck aches a bit.'

'Do you want me to rub it?'

'I don't think that's a good idea. It's still bruised.'

Nate found he was staring at her neck for a lot longer than was necessary.

Stop staring at her neck. What are you doing? Your tongue's going to roll out in a minute like a crazy cartoon character.

'How about I set you up in bed. You can have your dinner there.'

'I'll have my dinner here.'

'Then bed?'

Tessie grinned. 'Stop trying to take me to bed, Nate Walker.'

He burst out laughing.

'Speaking of which,' she added. 'I thought you were going to sleep with me.'

What?

Nate swallowed, trying to create some moisture inside his suddenly dry mouth.

'Last night. You didn't get in bed.'

Oh, right. Yes. Of course that's what you meant.

'I was worried about knocking you in the night, Tess.'

She glanced at her sling. 'My bad arm would be away from you.'

Nate nodded at her face. 'Your head wound wouldn't.'

He watched her start to twiddle her fingers. He hated it when she acted nervous about saying something to him.

'What is it, Tess? What do you want to say?'

She hesitated. 'Perhaps, tonight, we could try the bed situation out.'

There was silence in the farmhouse kitchen for a few seconds.

'Okay,' he said quietly, after clearing his throat.

Tessie leaned over and rested her head on the side of his big arm.

Without thinking, he stroked her hair. 'You all right?'

'Yeah, just snuggling up to you, if you don't mind.'

I never mind. It's one of my favourite things to do.

Nate smiled to himself. 'Do you want to snuggle on the sofa instead? It'll be more comfortable.'

He felt her head move on his arm.

'Not yet. I was going to wait in here till the girls got home from school. They're late coming home tonight.'

Nate looked over at the kitchen doorway. 'Yeah, well, Jake's on school run duties. He's probably picked them up in his private jet and whisked them off to Disneyland for a few hours.'

The rumble of Tessie's giggle vibrated through his arm.

She lifted her head as the front door flew open and Daisy and Robyn walked in.

Daisy headed straight towards them. 'I'm taking Jake off school run duties. Josh is taking us tomorrow. We'll see how he goes.'

Nate and Tessie shared a look.

Robyn came into the kitchen. 'Jake Reynolds is sooo embarrassing. You are not going to believe what he did.'

'What did he do?' asked Tessie.

The girls sat opposite them at the table.

'Everything.' Robyn huffed dramatically.

Daisy shifted her eyes away from Robyn to look over at her parents. 'It wasn't just Jake doing the school run. He had a chauffeur, a childminder, and a bodyguard.'

Robyn was clearly unimpressed. 'And the bodyguard walked us right up to the door.'

'That wasn't the worst part.' Daisy turned to Robyn.

Robyn shook her head. 'When Jake picked us up, he asked to see our head of year. He asked her if the school needs anything new, so that wasn't too bad, but then he asked her if we were behind at all in our studies and should he get us extra help, and then he was surrounded by a load of mums all asking him stupid questions and giving him their phone numbers.'

Nate was intrigued. 'Anything else?'

Daisy giggled. 'Jake asked Zac Preston's mum if Robyn could go on a playdate with Zac. It was so funny.'

'It was not,' snapped Robyn. 'A playdate. He actually said that. Can you believe it! I'm thirteen. And he asked in front of Zac, who I hate.'

'They're going for ice-cream on Saturday.' Daisy was smiling widely.

'And Jake will probably bring his bodyguard to sit with us.' Robyn was less than impressed.

Tessie was clearly holding back her laughter. 'I'll speak to him. Let him know you're too old to go on playdates. He's new at this.'

'He's new at a lot of things.' Daisy giggled. 'He doesn't even realise that Mrs Preston wants to have her own playdate with him.'

Nate laughed out loud whilst Tessie's mouth dropped open.

'I have never been so embarrassed in my life.' Robyn's arms flopped on the table.

'You don't have to go.' Tessie reached out and tapped her daughter's clenched knuckles.

Robyn scrunched up her nose. 'Yes, I do. Otherwise Zac will think I'm a right weirdo.'

Nate was confused. 'What do you care what he thinks? You said you don't like him.'

Robyn shook her head in annoyance. 'It's not the point. I have to go.'

Daisy sighed. 'All the girls in our year would go out with Zac if he asked. Robyn's going to be hated by a lot of girls now.'

Robyn turned to her. 'I don't care about them.'

Nate furrowed his brow. 'Wait, is this like a date?'

Daisy nodded. 'Jake's the only one who doesn't see that.'

'Well, I'm glad his bodyguard will be there now.'

Robyn flapped her hands up and scraped her chair backwards. 'Great! Nobody cares how stupid I'm going to look in front of Zac Preston.' She stormed out of the room.

Daisy got up and took her schedule off the front of the fridge. 'I'm going to make the adjustments.'

'So, Josh is taking you to school now?' asked Tessie.

'Yes, I called him after I fired Jake.'

Nate couldn't stop his mouth from curling upwards.

Jake Reynolds got fired. This just gets better and better.

Tessie was more concerned. 'How will Josh take you to school? He only has a motorbike.'

You are not going on that.

'We're going in his new car.'

'What new car?' asked Nate.

'The one that's arriving tonight.'

Nate looked at Tessie.

'What kind of car is it?' she asked.

'Well, we had a choice.' Daisy was acting rather casual about the matter. 'Robyn wanted a fast car, but then Auntie Joey overheard and said no, and so we now have something that is family friendly. I'm not sure what car it is. I only know that much. Robyn wasn't impressed with Joey's input.'

'And this all happened on the ride home?' asked Tessie.

Daisy nodded. She waved her colour-coded schedule in the air. 'I'm going to my room to do this, and then I'll do my homework.' She stopped in the doorway. 'Oh, has my new desk arrived yet?'

Nate's eyes widened. 'What new desk?'

'The one Jake ordered this morning.'

Tessie slowly shook her head.

Daisy gave a slight shrug. 'Oh, well. Never mind. It should be here anytime. Don't worry, I'll put it together myself if it isn't already built, and I'll do Robyn's too. You know she won't do it, or her homework. Although, when our new laptops arrive, she might.'

'Laptops?' questioned Nate.

Daisy glanced over at the front door. 'Yes, listen out for the delivery, please.'

Nate looked blankly at Tessie.

76

Tessie turned back to Daisy. 'What else have you asked Jake to buy you?'

'I didn't ask him to buy me anything. He offered.'

Nate was having a hard time holding back his growing annoyance. 'You should have said no.'

Daisy shied her eyes away. 'But I need a desk in my room to do my homework, and my laptop hardly ever works, Dad.'

He opened his mouth to say something but closed it again when he felt Tessie's hand rest on his arm.

'Okay, Daisy. But you're not to accept anything else from him. Is that understood?'

Daisy nodded. 'Yes, Mum.'

'If you need anything, you ask us.' Nate was still agitated but keeping calm.

Daisy raised her eyes, going straight for the tried and tested puppy-dog look. 'We only mentioned it because Jake was asking us about school and homework and stuff.'

Oh, those two hooked him in all right. I'm surprised that's all he bought.

'I'll call him later to say thank you,' said Tessie.

'I did already say thanks.' As Daisy walked away, she glanced back over her shoulder. 'You might want to talk to him about the pony Robyn asked for though.'

Nate's mouth gaped as Tessie's eyes widened.

10

Tessie

Joey had helped Tessie into her pyjamas the first night at the farm, so getting dressed that morning by herself was an awkward, painful task that had brought tears to her eyes and a desperate need for her mum.

Tessie sat next to her nightclothes on Nate's bed. She sighed deeply as she glanced down at the sling keeping her arm nicely relaxed.

Oh, come on, Tess. Just get it over and done with.

She started to remove the sling and stopped when a gentle tapping sound hit the bedroom door.

'Are you decent in there?' asked Nate softly.

'You can come in.'

His head entered the room first. He smiled warmly at her. 'I've just finished putting those desks together.' He turned his eyes to her grey pyjamas. 'Oh, were you about to get changed?'

'I was about to try.'

'Try? Are you struggling with getting dressed?'

Tessie raised her brow slightly. 'Let's just say, it's tricky.'

Nate closed the door. 'I can help you. I can do it with my eyes closed.' He grinned mischievously. 'I promise not to peek.'

He's actually being serious. Oh well, I don't suppose it's a big deal if his eyes are closed.

She smiled and stood. 'Okay. Well, I can remove the sling and unbutton my shirt. It's a lot easier to slide it off myself, but it's the putting on of the pyjama shirt. I'm going to be wearing a lot of shirts until my arm improves. I can't lift anything over my head. You should have seen the pickle I got into this morning with my bra.' She snorted as she laughed.

Nate was still holding his cheeky grin. 'That would have been an experience.'

Oh my goodness, why did I say that?

She went to remove the sling, but he stepped forward and took over.

'Here, let me.'

'Thank you.'

'You're welcome. Now, when should I close my eyes?'

'When I'm ready to slip off my shirt.'

'Okay, let me lock the door.'

Tessie took her time undoing each button with one hand. Nate's hand kept coming up as if to help, then lowering again. She held her shirt closed and nodded at him.

He moved behind her and closed his eyes. He gently lowered the shirt down, taking extra care with the sleeve on her bad arm.

Oh, everything hurts.

She watched the garment drop to the floor in front of her where he tossed it.

'Okay, now what?' he asked.

My bra. Oh, I didn't think this through properly.

She swallowed hard. 'If you help turn my bra around to the front, I can undo it.' She hoped she did a good job of hiding the nerves in her voice.

'Or I could just undo it.'

There was a couple of seconds of silence.

Tessie felt a shiver run the full length of her spine.

'I still have my eyes closed. I promise,' he said softly.

She was glad he couldn't see her, as she was blushing. 'Okay.'

'Let me just make sure my hands are warm. The last thing you need while in pain is a chill.'

She listened to him blowing into his hands and rubbing his palms. She wanted to glance over her shoulder, but her neck hurt too much. She exhaled quietly as he placed his hands on her back.

As his fingertips slowly slid down to rest upon her bra, she felt her stomach flip and hoped he couldn't pick up on the tension in her body.

He unfastened her bra and then gently removed the straps from her shoulders. His hands slowly trailed the length of her arms.

His touch. It feels as though he's making love to me. He's so gentle. I'm being silly. He's helping me. He's being careful. He feels so good though. I could just turn around right now and propel myself into his arms. If only he knew how much I want to do that. If only he knew how much I'm enjoying his touch.

She watched the white bra fall to her feet. She could hear that he wasn't moving, and she could feel the warmth from his body on her bare back. Goosebumps covered her skin.

Oh my God, Tess. Don't act weird about it. He's got his eyes closed. He can't see anything. Why do I want him to look. What if he did look? What would I do? Why am I feeling nervous? Might have something to do with standing in his bedroom in front of him half naked. Say something.

'Okay, now pick up the pyjama top and help me put my arms into it. Perhaps do the bad arm first.'

She heard him clear his throat and felt him move to pick up the already unbuttoned top.

She winced as he carefully inserted her bad arm into the sleeve.

He stopped. 'You okay?'

'Yeah. It's just painful.'

'How about if I hold it and you move yourself into the sleeve?'

'Okay.'

Tessie slowly manoeuvred into the top and felt his hands run over her shoulders and adjust the collar once it was on. Before she had a chance to move, he spoke.

'Let me do the buttons up.'

She found herself slowly turning to face him before she had a chance to talk herself out of it. She glanced up at his gentle face to see that his eyes were closed, as promised. She stared for a moment, completely lost in him, unsure if time had stopped altogether or whether it was passing by at the speed of light. She dropped her gaze to check she wasn't revealing her breasts.

'You can open your eyes now, Nate.'

He looked straight at her face before focusing on the top button. He reached down and started to close her top.

'How are you feeling?' he asked, fiddling with the third button.

Well, I'm not telling you I'm feeling goosebumps all over me because your touch feels so wonderful. What would you think?

'It feels worse when I move, but I'm okay. I think it went well.'

She watched his eyes roll down to her jeans.

'They next?' he asked.

She knew he was asking for her permission. She nodded.

He unzipped her and slowly pulled her jeans down to the bottom of her thighs as she held on to the top of her knickers.

'Sit down, Tess.' His voice was low and husky, and it brought a tingling sensation rushing through her.

She sat on the edge of the bed and watched him kneel before her and carefully slide her jeans all the way off.

He stood and folded them and placed them on an old paint-stained chair in the corner that had so many paint sploshes on it, it was hard to tell the original colour.

Tessie stood up. 'I won't put the pyjama bottoms on. It's a bit warm in here tonight.'

Nate turned to face her. 'Yep, it's definitely warmer in here tonight.'

She pulled back the bed covers and was about to speak but lost her words when she saw him quickly pull his top over his head. It was hard not to stare at his strong physique. She'd seen it many times before, but tonight, something felt different about his body. She turned back to awkwardly propping up a pillow as he glanced her way.

'If you wouldn't mind closing your eyes for a second, I can get my pyjama bottoms on.' A hint of mischief filled his voice.

Tessie grinned, sat on the bed, and closed her eyes. She could hear him rummaging around.

'Don't know what you're grinning about, Tessie Sparrow.'

'It's a funny night.'

'Yeah, you can say that again. You can open your eyes now.'

She looked over to see him standing there wearing nothing but dark-blue pyjama bottoms.

God, you look so good, Nate. Don't say anything. It's not appropriate, and stop staring at him.

'Do you need help with your teeth or anything else?' He looked towards the bedroom door.

'I already brushed my teeth and washed my face.'

'Me too.'

'I'll have a shower in the morning.'

'I can help with that as well.'

She breathed out a laugh that hurt her neck.

'You okay?'

'Yes. Just don't make me laugh.'

He raised his brow in amusement. 'I wasn't joking.'

Tessie smiled and rolled her eyes down submissively.

'So, are you ready for bed now?' he asked softly.

She attempted a slight nod and climbed in.

'Do you have your meds, Tess?'

She pointed towards the bedside cabinet at the bottle of water and two packets of tablets. 'Daisy put them there earlier.'

He got in bed beside her and snuggled down, turning his face towards her. 'You need help snuggling down?'

She wriggled her way under the quilt, smiling to herself whilst trying with all her might to ignore the pain she was in. 'No. I can manage, thanks.'

'You comfy?'

'As good as it gets at the moment.'

She leaned slightly towards him, and after a minute of silence, she realised that they were just staring at each other. She could sense something in the air between them. Something that was trying hard to pull them closer and closer together until they couldn't get any closer.

Say something. Change this heated atmosphere, because it's not like you can do anything about it. Even if you did have the guts. I really want to kiss him right now. At least run my fingers through his hair.

'I have some news.'

His intense expression didn't change. 'What news?'

'Anna told me today that she's pregnant.'

Nate smiled. 'That's good news.'

'They're not telling anyone yet. Only Joey and Josh know. She wasn't supposed to tell me, but she slipped up. She said I could tell you. Also, she's given me a job running the social media website for her shop.'

'How do you feel about doing that?'

'I like doing the one for this place. I think I'll enjoy it.'

Nate seemed to be studying her eyes. 'As long as you're happy.'

'I am.'

He breathed out a slight laugh. 'At least Jake will get some more playdates soon.'

Tessie tried not to laugh, but a small snort came out anyway. 'Anna will be pleased when his phone starts ringing off the hook.'

Nate nodded into his pillow.

'Did you ever want more kids, Nate?' She watched his taupe eyes gaze into hers.

'I did. I wanted a big family.'

'Me too.'

'We have a family of four. I'm grateful for that.'

Tessie looked to the ceiling as she felt her heart flutter. 'I'm grateful too.'

'Get some sleep, Tess. You need to heal. If you find you need more room during the night, just let me know and I'll leave.'

She turned back to look into his concerned eyes. 'I don't want you to leave.'

He seemed to still for a second. The look in his eyes changed from serious to warm.

'I won't leave, Tess.'

11

Nate

Nate stood at the edge of the shingles down at the bottom end of Pepper Lane, staring out to sea. The sun above shone down brightly, warming him. He adjusted his sunglasses and breathed in the welcomed salty air.

Ever since he was a boy, he loved standing on the small beach in the bay watching the water lap to the shore. He would often wonder what the rest of the world looked like, and if anywhere could be as perfect as Pepper Bay.

He glanced over his shoulder to look uphill at The Ugly Duckling. His family were inside, having just finished their Easter dinner. He loved that pub and Tessie's parents and the homely vibe that they brought to the lane. He loved everything about his home. He didn't want to have to ever move. The thought of losing his farm tore him to shreds inside.

He had just eaten a large turkey dinner with all the trimmings, followed by a chocolate trifle and a piece of white chocolate Easter egg, and yet his stomach felt empty.

Seagulls cried overhead, dipping low to the tips of the calm waves.

Nate watched them for a while, then rolled his eyes back to the shore for a moment. A thought occurred to him out of the blue. He looked towards the clear blue sky.

Erm, hello. I'm Nate Walker. I know I don't talk to you, but if you really do exist, and you do help those in need, please, God, will you help me? I don't need much, and somehow I'll find a way to pay you back, so this is more of a loan, really. I just need some money so I don't lose my farm. Just enough to keep it up and running for another year until I can figure something out.

He looked down at his twiddling fingertips.

I guess you get fed up with people like me only talking to you when they want something.

He sighed deeply.

I'm sorry. I just don't know what to do right now. I feel a bit lost.

He turned his face back to the sky.

Thank you for not taking Tess from me. I do want to say that much to you. No one was badly hurt in the tram, so thanks for that. If you can't help me, can you at least make sure Tess and the girls are okay if I lose the farm, please.

Nate lowered his head and went over to a small wall to sit down.

If you ever see my dad walking around up there, tell him I'm sorry about the farm. I'm trying my best, but we're just not making much money. We haven't for a while. Tess has set up a business page online, so we've been selling our cheese that way. We haven't sold much yet, but it's early days. That's what Tess says. Anyway, I'm sure you've got more important things to do than listen to me talk about cheese, but if you could help at all, I'd be really grateful. Thanks for the chat.

Nate turned sharply, as he felt a presence behind him.

'It's just me,' said Jake. 'Sorry, I didn't mean to make you jump.' He offered him a bottle of cold beer.

Nate took the drink and looked back at the sea as Jake sat down by his side. 'Thanks.'

'It's a beautiful day.' Jake removed his sunglasses from his white polo shirt to cover his azure-blue eyes.

Nate nodded. 'Gran reckons we're in for a mini heatwave.'

Jake laughed to himself. 'Well, I prefer that weather prediction to her snow one.'

Nate remembered saving Anna when she collapsed in the snowstorm during the winter. He rolled his eyes towards the sky.

Thank you for not taking Anna too.

'It'll be a nice day for the Sandly Craft Fayre this year. You can help out on our cheese stall again, Jake.'

Jake smiled widely at him. 'You want me to sell your cheese again?'

Nate shrugged. 'Why not? You did a good job at Christmas. We can have a bigger stall with the both of us working. We can't rely on Gran. She'll just fall asleep, and Joey has her hands full with her cake stall.'

'Josh is going to help her this year. That should be fun to watch. He's never even served anyone a cup of tea before in all the years we've had Gran's tea shop. Well, if he has, I've never seen him.'

Nate smiled. 'Seems funny to own a zillion coffee shops and never serve anyone.'

'I have. Years back, Gramps got me behind the counter of his shops whenever he opened a new one. It was only for half the day, and he served too. He thought it was fun and educational. I didn't do it in many shops, but Josh never did it once. I helped Gran back here from time to time when I was young. I prefer Edith's Tearoom to the Café Diths we have.'

'Your grandmother made the place homely, that's why. No offence to your coffee shop chain, but they're all the same. Edith's has character.'

Jake nodded. 'Yes, it does.'

Nate shifted on the wall so that he was facing Jake. 'Thanks for selling Joey's lollipops in your shops. That was pretty decent of you and Josh. It means so much to her.'

'They're great lollipops. They sell really well. I wasn't sure people would want to eat something with a flower inside, but everyone thinks they're cute. Plus, they taste nice. Gramps picked a really good team to work for him, and they just seem to know when something will work well or not. Mike, he's the one in charge at Café Diths, said yes straight away, and then he sent Regina here to check it out. I'll have to introduce you to our team. See what they make of your cheese. We already have the Pepper Pot Farm logo on the lollipops. We could make the farm name a familiar brand in the shops. You could even get your own farm shop.'

Nate watched Jake look back at the shops in Pepper Lane.

'One here would be great,' he added. 'The Pepper Pot Farm Shop, or Pepper Pot Shop.' He turned back to Nate. 'Something like that.'

Nate was speechless.

Jake gave a half-shrug. 'Something to think about.'

Where is this coming from? You don't normally talk business.

Nate swallowed hard. 'Did Tess put you up to this?'

Jake looked confused. 'Put me up to what?'

'Selling my cheese.'

'No. I only thought about it two seconds ago because we were talking about Joey's bespoke lollipops.'

There were a few seconds of silence.

'It's not a bad idea though,' said Jake quietly.

'Why would people go into a coffee shop and buy cheese?' asked Nate.

'We sell sandwiches, pastries, cakes, that sort of thing. We have small jars of jam that we sell as well. They come from a small business in Devon. Don't see why we can't sell a brand of cheese too. If you're interested, I'll give Mike a call. See what he thinks.'

Nate wasn't so sure, but as he had just asked God for help, and help was being offered two minutes after, he felt he had little choice but to accept the opportunity.

'Why not,' was all he managed to say, not exactly sounding over the moon about the idea.

Jake pulled his phone out of his pocket and called Mike there and then.

Nate wasn't expecting that. It was Easter Sunday. He thought Jake meant he'd call later in the week. He had no time to change his mind.

Stop stressing. Mike will probably say no anyway.

He put his beer bottle on the wall and stood to make his way across the shingles. He slipped his feet out of his trainers and stepped into the cool water. The sea soothed his soul and calmed his nerves. He gazed down at his dark shorts and smiled to himself as his thoughts turned to the time Tessie had tried to dunk him in the sea in the same spot he was standing. She had jumped on his back but still couldn't get him to fall, so he dipped to his knees on purpose just so she could splash his face and feel like the winner. That was a good day.

Jake called out to him, interrupting his memory, and Nate turned to watch his old friend approaching.

'Mike likes the idea. I'll send him a sample in the morning.'

Nate felt like laughing, from shock not joy. 'Really?'

'Yes, really. Don't sound so surprised. I'll take you to London for a few days. You can meet the team and see what you think. They'll explain everything. They taught me all about Café Diths when I had to take over from Gramps.

You'll get on great with them. They're a friendly bunch. A little eccentric in places but easy to be around. They're not what you would expect to find in a boardroom.'

Nate found that his mouth was slightly gaping. He quickly closed it. 'London?'

Jake nodded. 'We'll fly out on Friday. Make a long weekend of it. You can stay at my apartment.'

Without even thinking, Nate asked if Tessie could come.

Jake smiled widely. 'How about we all go. I'll ask Josh and Joey, and I'll bring Anna. I'll show you some sights, we can see a show, that sort of thing. What do you think? I know you've never been to London before. You'll love it. My apartment overlooks the River Thames. It's a great view.'

Nate found himself nodding. Then he had a sudden thought. 'Do we have to fly?'

'It's the fastest way. Don't worry, it's safe too.'

Nate frowned. 'You and Josh crashed into the sea in your helicopter just a couple of months ago.'

'So, what are the odds of that happening again?'

Nate breathed out a short laugh. 'So, I'm going to London by helicopter on Friday?'

'If you want.'

'Just like that?'

Jake's perfect smile beamed.

Nate rolled his eyes to the sky.

Well, if this is your doing, then I guess we'll be safe.

He turned back to Jake. 'Okay. Thanks, Jake. I appreciate your help.'

Jake smiled warmly. 'That's what friends are for.'

Nate looked out to sea.

I'm not quite sure what's going on right now, but thank you.

12

Tessie

The sleek, colourless, contemporary style of Jake Reynold's London apartment did little to impress Tessie. She walked into the black-and-grey open plan kitchen and looked out of the window at the view of the River Thames below.

Tessie had never been to London before. It wasn't quite living up to her expectations. The water looked dull and dreary, even in the sunshine. There weren't as many boats as she thought there would be, and the crowd of people walking along the riverbank took away all of the romantic visions that sat inside her mind.

She decided there and then that the small shingle beach in Pepper Bay was far prettier, homely, and definitely less occupied.

'It's like a showroom in here.' Nate entered the apartment with Joey trailing behind.

Tessie turned to see him plop down the luggage he was holding. He looked tense but was hiding it well. It wasn't the flight over that had him in knots. She knew his shoulders were heavy with worry.

If only he would let people in. His life could be so much easier.

Her eyebrows raised slightly as she thought what a small miracle it was that Nate was actually allowing Jake to help him.

Josh laughed as he squeezed his way past Nate and the cabin cases on the floor. 'Everyone says that about this place.'

Jake cleared his throat as he closed the door after Anna had entered. 'It's practical.'

Anna smiled up at him and lovingly stroked his arm, then she turned to Tessie whilst holding out a hand and pointing forward. 'Come with me. I'll show you to your rooms.'

Tessie came away from the window and followed Anna and Nate down a long corridor. 'There are a lot of doors along here.'

'It's a big place.' Anna pointed to one side. 'There's a nice big bathroom in there.' She smiled over her shoulder at Nate. 'You'll love the huge bath and shower.'

'Didn't you ever want to live here, Anna?' he asked.

She laughed and pointed up at the ceiling. 'After living on the rooftop up there, I'd be happy in a shed, but given the choice, I much prefer Starlight Cottage to here.'

'Starlight is lovely.' Tessie nodded at Nate. 'Before and after its renovations.'

Anna stopped and opened a door to reveal a bedroom with an extra-large bed. 'I'm not sure if you want to share this room, or there's another one next door if you want separate rooms.'

Tessie held back her smile at Anna's awkward expression and twiddling fingers.

'We'll share this one.' Nate's voice sounded firm as he entered the room.

Tessie locked eyes with Anna to see her smiling with excitement whilst Nate's back was turned.

'I'll leave you to unpack.'

Tessie shook her head as Anna left, then turned to see Nate looking out of the window.

'Hey, Tess, you can see the river from this room. No wonder they called this place River Heights. There's a veranda out here as well. Not sure where the door to it is though. I bet Jake's never sat out there. It's actually not a bad view.'

Tessie found her eyes wandering down to his bum.

Not a bad view at all. Oh good grief, where did that come from? Stop looking at his bum. Look at something else. My God, that bed is huge. No chance of us touching each other in that. Not that it matters. My arm is better now, which raises the question, why am I still sleeping next to him at the farm? I should go home now. Why hasn't he asked me to go back home yet? Why hasn't anyone said anything? It's like I've just moved in. Have I moved in? Are we now expected to just sleep next to each other wherever we go? Does this actually need a conversation?

'You all right, Tess?'

Hmm?

'Oh, yes.' She walked over to the sliding mirrored doors along one wall. 'Shall we hang some clothes up? I know we didn't bring much, but still.' She slid one of the doors open to find the rails and shelves completely empty. 'Oh, doesn't look like anyone's ever used this room.'

Nate's eyes rolled down to the bed. 'I bet Jake used to feel really lonely here.'

'Why do you think that?'

He shrugged and kept his voice low. 'This whole place feels lonely.'

Before she had time to think, she asked, 'Do you feel lonely?'

His eyes darkened as they locked with hers, and Tessie felt her cheeks instantly heat.

Why did I say that? What the hell, Tess.

'No.' His eyes softened, causing a flutter to hit her heart.

Joey's head came around the doorframe. 'I'm just putting the kettle on. Anyone want a cuppa?'

Tessie swallowed the dryness in her throat as she turned sharply towards her. 'I'll help.' Before anyone had a chance to speak, she headed to the kitchen, glad to be away from Nate's eyes for a moment.

Jake gestured over at his shiny black fridge. 'I had the fridge stocked ready for us. I thought we can have some lunch before heading over to meet the Café Diths team.'

Tessie headed for the sink. 'Sounds good. I'll wash my hands and make a start on that while Joey makes the tea.'

Jake smiled warmly as he stepped closer. 'Are you okay, Tess? You look a bit flustered. Was it the helicopter flight?'

'I'm okay, Jake.'

'Does your body still hurt at all?'

She shook her head slightly, testing for any signs of pain. 'My neck and shoulder still twinge a bit, but I'm doing okay now.'

'I'll book us all in for a spa day on Sunday. A deep massage should help.'

'I've never been to a spa before.'

'You'll love it. My friend owns the place. You'll get VIP treatment.' He glanced down the wide corridor. 'Nate could do with a facial.'

'Now that I have to see.'

Joey laughed out loud. 'Me too.' She wiggled a white coffee mug their way. 'Saying that, my brother is quite vain, you know. I think he might take to being pampered.'

'I think I'll take to having a massage.' Tessie was now looking forward to her spa day.

Jake pulled out his phone to send a text. 'I'll have Dwight take care of you, Tess. He's the best.'

'Who's the best?' asked Nate, walking over to the shiny white table that sat opposite the kitchen.

'The man Jake's just hired to massage Tessie.' Joey was trying hard to hide her grin.

Nate's stern expression made an appearance. 'That won't be happening.'

All eyes turned his way, and Tessie watched him swallow hard. Was she the only one who noticed the flicker of embarrassment hit his eyes for a split second?

He cleared his throat. 'She's just getting better from her accident. The last thing she needs is someone prodding and poking her body.'

Joey turned back to the kettle. 'Some prodding and poking will do her body the world of good.'

She did not just say that.

'Dwight's a professional,' said Jake. 'He works with injuries all the time. He'll look after Tess. You don't have to worry.'

There was a moment of silence. Jake went back to his phone, and Joey got on with the tea whilst Nate stood there looking awkward.

Oh, somebody say something. Something that doesn't include prodding and poking me.

'What would you like in your sandwich, Nate?' she asked, trying to clear the atmosphere and relax his glare that was aimed at Jake. As no one else had decided to speak, she added, 'There's a lot of choice. Come and look in the fridge.'

Tessie caught Jake and Joey grinning at each other as Nate stared into the large fridge. She gave them a stern telling off with her eyes and turned back to the food only to catch Nate looking at her. She smiled sweetly at him and was pleased to see his eyes soften.

'I want to go for a walk along the river at some point, Nate.'

He nodded. 'Definitely.'

I love it when he looks at me like that. I wonder what our lives would be like if we lived somewhere like this. I prefer the farm. Nate's right, this place does feel kind of lonely. It definitely needs an Anna. She'll make this place homely for when Jake has to come here for work. I already spotted a dog's bed in the corner. I guess that's her way of making a start.

She looked over her shoulder at Jake. 'So, this is where you fell in love with Anna.'

Jake almost blushed. 'Actually, it was out there, in the lift.' He pointed over at the front door.

Anna laughed as she approached from one of the rooms. 'You did not have feelings for me when we first saw each other. I looked like a right mess, for a start.'

Tessie watched her snuggle under Jake's arm. The love in his eyes towards Anna warmed her heart.

I love how you can just see and feel their love for each other.

'How do you know what I was feeling, Anna Cooper?' he teased her.

'Your grumpy face was busy scowling at my wet dog at the time.'

He laughed. 'You still intrigued me.'

'When did you know you had fallen for Jake, Anna?' asked Tessie.

Anna grinned widely. 'I think it was when he bathed Max. Now, that was intriguing.'

Jake smiled and kissed her head.

Joey laughed at her own memories. 'The first time I kissed Josh, I was sixteen, and I thought he intrigued me as well.'

Josh's voice boomed down the corridor. 'I did more than intrigue you, Joey Walker.'

Joey caught her brother's eyes widen her way. She laughed to herself and went back to making the tea.

Tessie suddenly felt lonely. She wanted to snuggle and have loving memories. All she had was sadness and a friendship with Nate Walker that she couldn't quite work out at times. She gazed down at the shiny white floor as Jake and Anna walked away. The fridge door closing jolted her.

Nate slipped his hands under her arms and lifted her to sit upon the worktop. 'You sit there and watch the river. I'll make the lunch.'

Tessie smiled and gazed down at the water whilst controlling her silent sigh.

I wonder how many other people are looking out of a window right now and feeling sad and lonely.

She turned slightly as Nate's head came to rest close to hers.

'Hey, look at that, Tess.'

She could feel the heat from his cheek brushing against hers. She rolled her eyes over to where he was looking to see a boat passing by that had a large banner embossed with red words: Mr and Mrs Lennington.

'Looks like someone just got married,' he added quietly.

She turned her head at the same time as him and smiled into the taupe eyes shining her way. His mouth was so close to hers, causing butterflies to fill her from top to toe.

Nate's eyes briefly glanced at her lips, then he gently rested his head on hers for a second before pulling away to make the lunch.

Oh flipping heck, Nate Walker. I'm in love with you.

13

Nate

The meeting with the Café Diths team went well. Nate was surprised at how relaxed the experience was. He expected a stuffy boardroom filled with suits, but he met a friendly bunch of men and women and a fun room that had its own bar. He found the whole experience was no different to having a friendly chat in The Ugly Duckling with one of his mates.

He had played pool, had a beer, sat on a beanbag, and spoke about his family, along with the business.

Joey and Josh challenged each other to a Super Mario game, and Anna ate five packets of ready salted crisps at the bar whilst Nate, Tessie, and Jake learnt all they could from Mike, which not only included business but also small snippets of East End information because Mike loved to talk about his home.

Anna was the only one who understood every word of Mike's Cockney accent, and translated each time he forgot to use his phone voice.

Pizza had been delivered at one point, and no one seemed to say no to a slice.

Nate thought that he might have found the one place in the world where Robyn would actually enjoy working. He wondered if he should have a chillout area at the farm. He had his small gym in one of the barns. The twins used it too sometimes, but did he now need to add a dartboard, a TV?

Pepper Pot Farm cheese was about to enter the Café Diths chain. Nate just needed to update his equipment for his farm, hire a few more hands, and look into buying his own shop so that the farm had a focal point for the tourists. All of which Jake had advised and Mike had agreed with.

Nate had no idea how he would get a bank loan to cover costs. He was pretty sure he would get refused once the bank manager took one look at his sorry state of affairs.

Jake had told him not to worry. That he would make the necessary arrangements, which basically meant that he would pay for everything.

Even though the meeting was both educational and fun, Nate was glad to get out of there. He felt overwhelmed by all the ideas, offered help, and enthusiasm coming at him left, right, and centre.

He sighed heavily with the weight of money on his shoulders and felt Tessie slip her hand into his as they walked along the river by themselves, having not long left the meeting.

'It's a good idea, Nate.' Her tone was soft and friendly. 'Jake said you can pay him back once everything is up and running, and you won't have to pay interest like you would at a bank.'

Why doesn't anyone understand?

'I don't want to take his money, Tess. He's my friend.'

'That's why he's doing this for you. Let him.'

He felt himself brought to a halt, as Tessie tugged his arm. 'I want you to do this, Nate.'

He stared at her, trying to read deeper into her mind.

She gave a slight shrug. 'I don't want us to lose the farm. It's our home.'

Nate stilled. In that moment, all he wanted to do was kiss her.

Finally, she's saying it's ours. Our farm. Our home.

She narrowed her eyes. 'What would happen to our family if we had nowhere to be together?'

The thought felt like a punch to the stomach.

That can't happen.

He could see tears in her eyes. It was obvious she was trying desperately hard not to blink.

'You once said you'd do anything to protect our circle, Nate. Well, it needs protecting now, and Jake is giving us an opportunity. All you have to do is say yes. I want you to say yes.'

I don't want to say yes to his money. I want to find my own way. I have enough debt without adding to it. Why can't there be another way? Why can't what I have be enough to get this project started? I know why. Everything is old at the farm. It's falling apart. Plus, I can't expect the twins to take on all the extra work by themselves. I know we'll need more help. Bloody money! It always comes down to money. Look at her. Look at the way she's looking at me. She needs me to make everything right. To make our family stable. I'm hurting her. I'm hurting my family. I'm going to lose it all if I don't do this. I have to give it a try.

'I'll tell him yes.'

He watched the relief fall onto her face. The colour in her cheeks came back, and her smile was filled with happiness.

She wiggled her finger at him. 'Come down here.'

He bent over, and she kissed his cheek. He loved it when she did that. Her soft lips on his skin brought out every ounce of willpower he had to stop himself from just taking her in his arms and kissing her back.

'Thank you, Nate,' she said quietly.

He wasn't happy about being in so much debt to Jake, but he knew he had to put his family before his pride.

Tessie squeezed his hand and pointed over at an ice cream van. 'Hey, how about a 99?'

He forced a smile. 'Sure.'

Her hand slipped out of his, making him feel instantly lonely, but then she held on tightly to his arm instead, and he felt his heart warm.

She pointed up at Tower Bridge. 'We should walk up there too.'

He nodded and ordered the ice creams.

Tessie held the cones as he pulled out his wallet.

'How much!' He gasped at the ridiculously high price for a couple of soft ice creams with flakes in them. 'Bloody hell, it's half the price where I live.'

'Just pay him, Nate.' Tessie had her mouth already wrapped around her cone.

He reluctantly handed over his cash and grumbled to himself as he walked away with Tessie by his side.

She giggled and nudged his arm.

'You know that was a right cheek.' He bit into his flake.

Tessie pulled out her phone and took a selfie of them eating their overpriced ice creams.

'I'm going to frame that.' Nate grinned.

'World's most expensive 99.'

They made their way up the stairs to stand on the bridge, and Tessie gazed down into the murky water below as cars slowly passed by behind her. She looked around and took some more pictures.

Nate found himself smiling and relaxing. Just for a while, the farm disappeared from his mind as Tessie's happy smile took over.

She pointed down at the Tower of London. 'Let's sit down there and take some more pictures.'

He allowed her to take the lead and was happy when her hand slipped into his once again.

They sat on a bench, and Tessie snuggled closer to his side. He smiled inside as the warmth of the sun started to fade and the people around them became less. He felt Tessie shiver as a cool breeze blew by.

'Hey, shall we head back now? I think I know the way. Jake did say we can call his chauffeur if we get lost.' He breathed out a laugh to himself.

Chauffeur! I've heard it all now.

'Can we stay a little longer? I like it here.'

'Sure.' He placed his arm around her and pulled her closer towards him. Her close proximity was every bit as soothing as a hot chocolate on a cold night. He rested his mouth down upon her hair and watched as her arm came up to take a selfie of them both in that position.

Tessie put her phone away in her brown leather bag and started twiddling with the strap. 'Things might be a bit hectic for a while when we go home.'

He sighed slowly. 'Yeah.'

'We might not get much time to hang out like this.'

Nate's cosy hot chocolate moment immediately turned stone cold.

'We'll make time. There will always be family time. It's important. That's why I'm doing this. For our family.'

He felt Tessie breathe heavily. 'I like our time together as well.'

Nate felt at a loss for words. He liked spending time alone with her too, but they didn't really talk about it. He was used to hanging out with her because they had been doing that since they were kids, but not as a couple. They weren't a couple now, but he felt so drawn to her and often the intimacy that was missing from their relationship.

How could he allow himself to fall in love with his best friend's partner? There was so much that felt wrong, but so much that felt right. He never meant for it to happen, and he told himself and Henry that many times over. Was he just feeling responsible for her? Were his lines merely blurred? He had many moments where everything seemed so clear. He knew exactly how he was feeling and what she meant to him, but over and over he questioned his feelings. Over and over the guilt crept in and changed the mood between them.

The one thing he was clear on was that he wasn't about to let her go. She was very much a part of his life, and that thought alone kept him going and kept him holding on to her and the connection they had built. He knew he loved her, he just struggled at times to allow that love to surface.

He felt her arms curl around his waist and tighten.

Don't worry, Tess. I'm not going anywhere. There will be a lot more work, but it won't tear us apart. It had better not. It won't, will it? Will it? No, it won't. It can't. We make it work now. We'll make it work whatever.

'If we don't see much of each other during the day, at least we'll see each other in bed.' He waited for her response, but she was silent.

Please say you're going to stay sleeping in my bed. I don't want you to go home. Wait! You said that the farm was your home. You called it our home. You've moved in, haven't you?

Tessie rolled her face up his top to look into his eyes, and he felt his heart thump.

'Nate.'

'Hmm?'

'I wish we were in bed now.'

Are you actually coming on to me or are you just cold and tired? She's still looking at me. Say something. I don't know what to say to that. What do I say? Think. Think. Why can't I think of something to say?

Tessie lowered her head.

You idiot, Nate. What if she wanted more from you right then. What did I just give her? Nothing, that's what. Oh great, I still don't know what to say. My stomach is in knots here.

Tessie shuffled herself off his chest. Her body was facing him but she was looking down at her bag. 'Come on, we should get back. Jake's taking us out to dinner soon, and I wouldn't mind a shower first.'

He watched her stand and turn away.

14

Tessie

Tessie stood in the bathroom, with a large grey towel wrapped around her, glancing at the walk-in shower. There was room enough for four people in there. She looked up at the big square showerhead, then over at the large, light-grey, ribbed tiles.

'Where are the fixtures and fittings?'

Whilst staring blankly at the wall, her mind drifted.

Why did I say all those things earlier? I'm so stupid. I'm going to spoil what we have if I keep this up. I think I scared the living daylights out of him. Pepper Pot Farm isn't my home. The Ugly Duckling is. I shouldn't have pushed my way in like that. It's his fault. He's always saying we and us and ours. When we get back, I'll have to go home. I'm better now. I don't need looking after anymore. He's too polite to tell me to leave. Robyn won't want to leave. She's already moved more of her stuff in. Oh, what am I doing with this man? What am I doing with this shower? How the hell do you turn it on?

She walked over to the bathroom door, opened it a touch, and peeked outside. 'Hello,' she whispered. 'Hellooo.'

Nate stepped out from their bedroom and frowned over at her. 'You all right?'

Tessie flapped her hand at him, quickly waving him towards her.

He approached, and she pulled him inside and locked the door.

'What's going on, Tess?'

She pointed at the shower. 'Look at it. There's no way to turn it on.'

Nate took a large stride forward to study the cubicle. 'Oh yeah, that's strange.'

Tessie stood by his side and looked up. 'It's got a showerhead. That's about it.'

'Maybe it's not finished being built.'

'Looks finished.'

Nate poked his head inside. 'Jake's like James Bond. It probably only starts when a laser goes over his eye or something.'

Tessie snorted out a laugh. 'I could totally see him playing James Bond.'

Nate flicked his slippers off and stepped inside to have a better look, and Tessie followed him.

He started pressing on tiles. 'One of these has got to be a secret panel.'

Tessie glanced up as something caught her eye. 'Hey, look at that.'

The showerhead lit up with tiny blue lights around its rim. Suddenly, freezing cold water sprayed out, along with powerful jets that shot out from tiny nozzles built into the walls.

'Argh!' They both yelled.

She turned to run out of the shower, but he grabbed her and held her captive inside the cubicle with him.

She screamed whilst wriggling. 'Nate, let me go.'

He was laughing loudly, and she started to laugh too. 'Nate, it's bloody freezing.'

He let her go, and they quickly dashed out of the shower.

'Oh my God, that thing is nuts.' Tessie was catching her breath and chattering her teeth.

Nate turned to a tall black cabinet, opened it, and pulled out a couple of large grey towels. He offered one to her. 'Here, change towels.'

She took the towel and looked at him. His dark trousers and white casual shirt were soaked through.

He quickly whipped off his top and pulled down his bottoms.

Tessie averted her eyes and wondered how she would swap towels without him seeing.

'I'm closing my eyes right now.' His voice held a hint of a smirk.

She waited for his eyes to close, then quickly changed towels. Her long red hair was sprawled out across her shoulders, curls galore. 'I'm done, but I need another towel for my hair. It's dripping everywhere.'

Nate opened his eyes and started to dry himself as he looked in the cabinet for a hair towel. 'That was funny.' He chuckled as he approached her and started to dry the tips of her hair.

'It wasn't funny. It was freezing. Crazy shower. I wonder how you heat it up.'

He was staring into her eyes as she glanced up at him.

'You're so beautiful, Tess,' he said softly, turning his eyes back to her hair.

She felt her head whirl, and she needed to swallow, but her saliva had run off, and her legs were suddenly as weak as the rest of her body. She opened her mouth to speak, but words failed her, so she closed it again. She was watching his face as his hands gently stroked her hair inside the towel.

He cleared his throat and took a step back and sat down on the edge of the large white bath, drying the back of his thick hair.

Tessie stepped closer to him and manoeuvred herself so that she was standing in between his legs. 'I think we should talk.'

A dark look swept into his eyes. 'I think we should kiss.'

Her heart pounded so heavily, she was sure it was visible. 'Kiss?'

He gave a slight nod as he blinked. 'I want to try it.'

'Try it?'

'See what it does for us.'

He's making it sound like a new health kick.

She hesitated. 'What if it spoils things?'

'What if it makes them better?'

'So, this is an experiment?'

Nate hadn't removed his eyes from her the whole time. 'If you like.'

Tessie felt the need to be honest. 'I'm scared, Nate.'

His hand reached her face and tucked her hair behind her ear. 'We don't have to try until you're ready, Tess, but just know that I'm ready.'

'Why aren't you scared, Nate?' She felt her voice crack so swallowed to retrieve some moisture.

His big hand covered the side of her face. 'Right now, I don't feel scared of kissing you. I only feel scared of never kissing you.'

Her heart melted as fast as snow under the sun.

Oh my God, Nate. I love you so much right now.

'Hey,' he said softly. 'There's no pressure. I just needed to tell you. Since you've been sleeping by my side every night, I just feel... Well, everything feels right. There's so much going on in my head lately, but when you're with me, I can breathe a lot easier. I'm happy with our lives, with our family, but things have changed since your accident, since you moved into the farm. All I know is, I just want to wake up with you by my side every day. Will you stay when we go home?'

Tessie nodded without hesitation. She glanced at his full lips, and she knew that he noticed.

If we kiss, everything will change. Everything could go wrong. We're so settled with each other. Should we do this? I want to. I so want to kiss that mouth right now.

He rubbed her arm. 'Hey, why don't we get you dressed before you catch a chill.'

Tessie glanced down at her towel. 'I feel warm.'

'Hmm,' he mumbled, also looking at her towel.

Unable to hold it together any longer, she completely lost her inhibitions and dropped her towel to the floor.

Nate's eyes widened along with his mouth. He quickly dipped down to retrieve the towel and wrapped it around her.

Tessie gasped in horror and slapped one hand over her face. 'Oh my God, I'm so sorry. I don't know what came over me. I'm so sorry, Nate. I never meant to embarrass you. I thought that you wanted me.'

He quickly moved her hand from her face and swiped away a falling tear. 'Hey, hey, it's all right, Tess. Bloody hell. I just wasn't expecting that. Christ, you have no idea how much I want you right now. You're killing me here, but I can't make love to you in Jake's bathroom. My sister's just outside, for a start, and I've got no protection on me.'

She watched him glance over at the shower.

'That freezing cold shower is looking pretty good right about now.' He started shaking his head.

Tessie was staring at him in amazement as she swallowed down the lump in her throat. 'You want to make love to me?'

His eyes fell back to hers. 'Oh yeah.' His voice was low and filled with need.

Her head was in a daze. 'This all started with a kiss.'

He raised his brow in amusement. 'That's normally how it starts.'

'But we haven't even done that yet.'

Nate grinned. 'And yet here we are, with you flashing me.'

Tessie bit in her bottom lip, trying to stop herself from laughing.

Nate looked down at the top of the towel huddled around her slim frame and tugged gently on the rim. 'You have a beautiful body, by the way.'

She felt her cheeks heat. 'There's nothing of me.'

'I saw plenty.'

She laughed to herself at what was happening. 'I think I've lost my mind.'

'Yeah? I think I've lost my heart.'

She stopped smiling and placed one hand gently on his chest. 'I'll never hurt your heart, Nate Walker.'

She watched his brow tighten and his chest rise and fall heavily.

'You ready for that kiss yet, Tess?'

She slowly moved her face nearer to his and waited an inch from his mouth. She could barely stand. Her heartbeat had accelerated, and butterflies were on standby in her stomach.

Nate's soft lips pressed down lightly upon hers, and she tenderly kissed him back, exploring his gentle touch. There were no fireworks. No brass band. It was as though they had kissed many times before. It felt right and much needed. She had been worried for nothing. It wasn't weird. It wasn't ruining anything. It was wonderful. The most natural thing in the world, and she knew in that moment that she could spend the rest of her life in his arms.

His tongue slipped into her mouth, and her need for him jumped a few levels. The butterflies were suddenly all over the place, and her breath was shaking in her throat. Her limbs weakened, causing her body to flop forward onto his.

The kiss picked up pace, and her hand wrapped around the back of his head, holding him, signalling to him to not pull away. Her fingernails were gripping into his hair, tugging him closer.

Nate wasn't pulling away. He was pulling her tightly against him, and she could feel how much he wanted her.

She let out a quiet involuntary moan as his lips left her mouth to trail her neck. She tipped her head up to face the ceiling. His mouth was on her collarbone, then on the top of her chest. She was breathing heavily, trying not to cry out his name.

His hands lowered her head back to his, cupping her face and kissing her lips again.

Tessie gasped into his mouth. She wanted every part of him so much. Jake's bathroom had disappeared altogether. There was only Nate and her desire for him.

'Oh God, Tess,' he mumbled on her lips, sounding breathy and in need.

She stared at him through glossy eyes as he pulled back to look at her. His breath was shaky, and his eyes had darkened.

'Tess, I… I.'

He stood, bent down and kissed her cheek, and then went into the shower.

Tessie placed her hand over her mouth and grinned as the freezing cold water washed over him.

His eyes were closed as he pointed over at the door. 'Go and get dressed for dinner. I need a minute to cool off.'

She bit her bottom lip inwards and laughed to herself as she left the bathroom. Her face was flushed, her lips were still tingling, and her legs were wobbly.

He wants me. He actually wants me.

15

'You ladies look amazing,' said Josh, keeping his eyes firmly fixed on Joey's short brown dress.

Tessie glanced down at her emerald-green skater dress and four-inch black high heels.

Nate was also looking at her shoes. *Where the hell did they come from? I need to stop staring at them. I need to stop staring at her, especially her mouth.*

Tessie glanced his way and smiled, and he was sure his heart skipped a beat. He was glad when she turned her attention to Anna.

Anna was wearing a loose black dress. She placed her hand over her stomach. 'I have a little bump showing now. I'll take amazing while I still can.'

Jake frowned at her. 'You look amazing now, and you'll still look amazing even if you're as big as a house.'

Tessie laughed. 'You do look lovely, Anna.'

Anna smiled warmly. 'Thank you, so do you, and so do you all. We've all scrubbed up very well for our evening out.'

'Yes, well, let's get going then.' Josh gestured towards the door.

Nate watched Josh hold Joey's hand as they left the apartment. Anna was on Jake's arm, and Tessie walked behind them. He reached out and placed his hand on the small of her back as she crossed over the threshold, letting her know that she had someone too.

Tessie looked back at him and smiled, and it was all he could do to stop himself from taking her in his arms and whisking her off to the bedroom.

Steady, Nate. Breathe. Just wait. You can kiss her again later.

He gave her a cheeky wink whilst no one was looking, and it warmed him to see her blush.

* * *

The rooftop garden restaurant that Jake had taken them to was filled with fairy lights and outdoor heating. A tall water feature designed to look like a cascading waterfall was along one high wall, and the other walls were hidden behind exotic leafy plants. Soft jazz music was playing in the background, and the inky sky above was barely noticeable in amongst the tranquil setting. The air was warm and holding a slight lemony fragrance. Only one large round table had been placed in the middle of the paved court, and it was occupied by Jake's guests.

'Wow, this place is beautiful.' Tessie sat down in one of the comfy large chairs around the dressed table.

Anna pointed behind her. 'Oh, it's an ice swan. I love those. I've only ever seen them in pictures before.'

Jake smiled. 'I know you've always wanted to see one.'

Tessie took a picture of the beautiful glistening sculpture with her phone. 'Did you have that made for Anna?'

'We can all enjoy its beauty,' said Jake, clearly avoiding answering.

Anna squeezed his hand. 'I love it. Thanks, Jake.'

Nate sat in between Tessie and Joey, glancing around at his surroundings. 'You wouldn't know we were in the middle of London.'

Tessie gestured to his side. 'We can just imagine that there is a beautiful beach on the other side of that wall, and after dinner, we can go for a stroll and listen to the waves lapping at the shore.'

Josh laughed. 'Are you missing the sea already, Tess?'

'I do love Pepper Bay. It's in my heart.'

'Yeah, that place gets you like that.'

Joey nudged his elbow as she turned to the ice swan. 'Hey, Josh, we could have an ice sculpture at the wedding reception.'

Tessie giggled. 'It could be a cow.'

Nate laughed along with Josh, but Jake didn't look too keen.

'I'm not bothered,' said Anna. 'I just wish the wedding day would hurry up and happen. I want to be married already.'

Jake smiled at her whilst wrapping his hand over hers. 'We can get married tomorrow, if you want.'

'Hey.' Joey smiled warmly. 'We won't feel hurt if you two want to get married before us. Do whatever feels right for you both.' She turned to Josh for confirmation.

Josh nodded. 'Yeah. We were only waiting for my wounds to heal.'

Anna shook her head and flapped her free hand their way. 'Take no notice of me. I'm just being impatient because I can't wait to marry Jake. June will be here soon enough.'

'And there's not much to do.' Tessie looked around the table before focusing on Anna. 'You don't want any fuss at the registry office, so we won't be there long. It's only setting up the barn for a small gathering. I'll make it look magical. I promise.'

'I know you will, Tess.'

116

'And if you do want an ice sculpture, then let me know so that I can get that arranged.'

Nate beamed her way. 'Tess has lots of good ideas.'

'You have great business skills as well, Tess,' said Jake. 'Have you thought about doing any courses in that area? You could train and come and work in London for Café Diths, if that interests you.'

Nate immediately felt annoyed.

What's he talking about? She's not going to work in London. Why would she want to work here? Her home is in Pepper Bay.

'You could do a work placement here or something,' added Jake. 'Stay for a few months. Live at River Heights. It's worth thinking about.'

'I have Robyn to think of. I can't take her out of school and bring her here, and I can't leave her behind.'

Nate smiled inwardly.

Yes, you didn't think about that, Reynolds.

'You could do a summer apprenticeship with us,' said Jake. 'That way, Robyn could come here for the summer. I'll hire childminders for the apartment and office. Robyn would be taken care of whilst you are training. Plus, it will only be part-time, so you and Robyn will still have plenty of time to hang out.'

You've just got it all sorted, haven't you, Jake.

Nate was watching Tessie carefully.

Do you want to do this, Tess? Is this something that interests you?

'I… erm.' Tessie was looking for words. 'I also have Daisy to think about. She needs me too.'

'Daisy will be fine.' Nate realised just how snappy he sounded, and so lowered his head away from all the staring eyes coming his way.

117

'I would spend the summer here with you and the girls, Tess,' said Joey, 'but summer is the busiest time for the tea shop.'

Why is everyone trying to encourage Tessie to leave?

'I could spend the summer here with you, Tess.' Anna looked at Jake. 'I have Scott to mind the shop, and Jake wouldn't mind.'

Jake looked as though he would mind.

Anna smiled warmly at him. 'You'll be with us too, won't you, Jake?'

Nate watched Jake's face melt under the glow of Anna's sweet smile.

'Of course.' He turned to Tessie. 'You have plenty of time to think about the offer. Anna and I will be happy to help.'

Nate looked down at his plate as Tessie's eyes rolled his way.

'Thank you, Jake. I'll think about it. It does sound exciting, and I am interested.'

'You could always do a taster day, or week.' Jake nodded. 'Mike would sort that for you. I tried to arrange one for Josh once, but he's not interested in business at all.'

Josh glanced over the table at his brother. 'Hey, some of us prefer to work with our hands.'

Joey nudged him. 'I work with my hands and my mind. I do all the business accounts for Edith's Tearoom.'

He smiled at her. 'That's because you're brilliant at everything.' He looked at Anna. 'She even knows how to milk a cow.'

'I've always wanted to try that.' Anna beamed over at Jake, and he scrunched his nose up at the thought.

Joey smiled at Anna. 'We use machines nowadays, Anna, but you're always welcome to have a go.'

'And can I help make some cheese too?' she asked.

'Anna, do you really want to?' Jake didn't sound too keen on the idea.

She shrugged. 'It's good to try new things, Jake. How will you ever know what you like if you never try anything. That's the way I look at it.'

'Good attitude,' said Josh.

Nate wasn't listening to them. He felt too agitated and even more agitated about feeling agitated.

Tessie deserves happiness, and if working here for the summer, or forever, suits her, then it's none of my business. Yes, actually, it is my business. I told her I won't let anyone break up our family. Well, that includes Jake Reynolds and his business ideas. Oh, shut up, Nate, and order your food. She can do what she wants. Not everyone wants to work on a farm making cheese. She wouldn't leave forever anyway. She just wouldn't. She loves Pepper Bay too much, and she loves our family. I'm pretty sure she loves me. Why are there so many changes happening lately? I asked for my farm to be saved, not my world to be turned upside down.

A waiter came over to take their order, but Nate felt too fed up to eat. He ordered a steak, anyway.

He wanted to talk to God.

Is this all part of your help-Nate-Walker plan, because if it is, well, I'm not too sure about this part of it. Have you thought this through properly? I don't want Tessie leaving me. There's no point saving my home if she's not going to be in it. I want her there with me. What's with all the small print? You adding clauses? I thought you were on my side. Can't I have the farm and Tess? Is that not doable? Well, just so we're clear, that is exactly what I want. I'm not trying to be selfish though, in case that's what you're thinking now. I want her to be happy, of course. If working or training here

119

makes her happy, then I'll back down, but I'd rather you figured out a way to make us both happy.

He sighed quietly into his dinner when it arrived.

I'm sorry. I'm asking too much, aren't I? You've found a way to save my farm. I can't keep asking for you to save everything for me. Just ignore me. I was just taken by surprise, that's all.

Tessie touched his hand, taking him away from his silent conversation. 'You okay?' she whispered.

He nodded as he placed a piece of steak into his mouth and smiled with his lips closed, slowly chewing his food.

16

Tessie

Tessie sat on the edge of the bed. Nate was already lying down behind her. He had been quiet all night. Their dinner had been lovely, and the company was alive with laughter and happiness, loads more wedding talk, and lots of baby talk too, especially when Joey and Josh announced that they're trying for a baby.

Nate was pleased with the news, but he was the quietest one during the night, and that wasn't like him at all. Anna was usually the quiet one in their group, but she had taken over Nate's bubbly and chatty title.

Tessie climbed into bed and turned on her side so that she was facing him.

I know something's wrong. You didn't even offer to show Anna the cows when she said she was interested in the milking process. That's something you would have normally talked about all night, given the chance.

Nate was staring up at the ceiling.

I just want to snog you senseless, Nate Walker, but right now, you look as though you just lost a tenner and found a pound.

She reached her hand over and stroked his cheek.

Don't be sad, Nate. Everything's going to be all right. I promise. I have to stop touching his face. Why is it so hard for me to keep my hands to myself? I know why. I love him. I wish he would kiss me again.

His face softened a touch.

'Are you okay?' she asked quietly, removing her hand.

He caught it before it slipped away, linking their fingers up by his jawline. He lowered his chin and gently kissed her knuckles.

The sweetness in his light touch moved her in every way.

'I'm okay, Tess.' His voice was just as quiet as hers.

She wasn't buying that for a moment. He obviously wasn't all right at all. She had an idea why he was quiet, but she wasn't totally sure.

I need to bring this up now. Get it out the way. I have to be sure.

'Are you thinking about me staying here in the summer?'

He turned his head to face her. 'I want you to do whatever it is that you want to do. I want you to be happy, Tess.'

She felt his thumb stroke over her hand. 'I am happy, Nate.'

He smiled weakly and looked back at the ceiling.

Are you feeling insecure? I know I would be if the shoe were on the other foot. I need you to feel secure. I need you to know I wouldn't leave you. I'd just be gone for a few weeks. I need you to know I wouldn't break up our family. This would be a good opportunity for me. It would be good for all of us.

She shifted her body and winced as a twinge of pain shot up through her shoulder to enter her neck.

Ow! Bloody hell, that hurt.

Nate quickly turned back to her, leaning up on one elbow. 'What's wrong?'

'It was just a twinge.'

Without a word, he set about adjusting pillows, plumping them up around her with all the skills of a nurse and the passion of an interior designer. He gently rested her head down upon the newly arranged bedding. 'How's that?'

She smiled up at him. 'Better. Thank you.'

His taupe eyes fixed on hers. They smiled her way for a second, then suddenly filled with a need. He blinked the look away and went to lie back down.

You were going to kiss me. Don't turn away. Not now.

She touched his arm, and the feel of his skin on her fingertips made her want that kiss even more. 'Nate, will you kiss me goodnight?'

He leaned back over her. 'I'll kiss you anytime.'

Tessie felt her heartbeat pick up.

Oh, I love you.

'Well, now's good.'

He grinned at her, then lowered himself for the kiss. 'Don't move,' he whispered onto her lips. 'Rest.'

She closed her eyes as the warmth from his mouth filled hers. Finding it hard to stay still, her hands automatically came up to wrap around his neck. Her fingernails dug into the base of his hairline as his kiss became more passionate.

'Tess,' he groaned, still attached to her mouth.

She gazed into his eyes as he pulled back slightly to look at her.

'I'm going to need another cold shower in a minute.'

She tried not to snort, but it came out anyway. 'Or you could just stay nice and warm in here.'

His smile was broad. 'It's getting a bit too warm in here.'

'Can't you make it even warmer?'

He blinked slowly. 'We can't.'

Tessie felt her heart sink.

'Why not?' she whispered.

He kept his voice low. 'Your neck hurts. We're in Jake's apartment. We have no protection. How many reasons do you want?'

'None.'

Josh started singing "Come Rain or Come Shine", by Ray Charles. His smooth voice could be heard from two rooms away.

Nate pointed at the wall. 'And there's another reason.'

Tessie giggled.

Nate grinned. 'He's going to put me off.'

Josh stopped singing and switched his music on instead. Ray Charles' song wafted through the wall into their room, and Josh was no longer an issue.

Nate smiled warmly at her. 'I do want you, Tess, but…'

'Anna said there are condoms in the bedside drawer in case we needed them.'

One of his eyebrows lifted in surprise. 'Oh did she?'

Tessie gave a half-shrug into the mound of pillows propping her up. She could tell he was thinking it over.

'Are you ready for this, Tess? It's a big step for us both, even bigger for you.'

I have no idea what I'm ready for anymore. I'm scared of carrying on with my life with no changes. I'm scared of not being with you. I want you so much. I want this with you. If nothing happens between us ever again, I want to have had this moment with you.

'I feel ready, Nate.'

He lowered his head. 'I feel like we're rushing this.'

She gently stroked over his cheek, unable to stop herself from touching him. 'We've been in a relationship for years, of sorts. I want to move forward with you, with our family. Will you kiss me again so I don't have to stretch up towards you?'

His eyes met hers, causing a thump to her heart and a desire in her body. He gently kissed her, and it filled her with the love she needed.

'I love you, Nate Walker,' she whispered onto his lips.

Nate stilled.

There was a moment of intense silence between them. Neither of them moving.

Oh crap! That was too soon. I shouldn't have said it. Oh flipping heck, what is he thinking?

Nate moved away from her, and Tessie felt like she wanted to cry.

She heard him rummaging around on his side, and then he came back to her with a condom wrapper sitting in between his fingers.

Oh my God!

He swallowed hard and tightened his brow. 'You sure about this, Tess?'

'I'm sure. I just wish I could move.'

'Why don't we wait till you stop getting neck twinges?'

'I've waited long enough for you.'

He held a self-satisfied grin. 'Is that a fact?'

'That's a fact.'

He placed the small silver wrapper on the pillow and lowered his head to kiss her again.

Tessie felt her body weaken beneath him before he had even started. She stroked over his muscular arms, slowly tracing over each bump. She wanted to turn her head and kiss his shoulder, but she was worried something in her neck or shoulder might ping.

Nate's mouth slowly moved down her neck. He stopped, leaned up, and started to undo the buttons on her blue pyjama shirt.

She gasped quietly as his mouth gently manoeuvred down to her belly button.

He sat up and pulled off his tee-shirt, and she watched him take off his bottoms and then carefully do the same to her. One of his large hands wrapped around her back, and the other stroked over her hip. His lips met her skin again, gently kissing along her side. He reached up for the condom, struggled to find it, raised himself to look, kissed her on the cheek when he found the wrapper, and then glanced down at her.

'I love you too, Tess,' he whispered.

Tessie felt her heart do more summersaults than Cirque du Soleil. She smiled lovingly at him, then closed her eyes and allowed herself to melt beneath him as he gently connected their warm bodies. She gripped her fingertips into his bare back, trying with all her might not to cry out his name.

She could tell he was doing the same when he bit into the pillow.

Nate almost collapsed his sweating body down onto hers, but held himself close without putting pressure on her. He carefully manoeuvred himself to her side.

'Oh God, Tess,' he whispered.

She felt the warmth of his breath hit her ear. She slowly moved herself to rest on her side, and he reached over to hold her face and kiss her mouth. His heavy breathing slowing on her lips.

She smiled whilst kissing him and placed her hand over the back of his. 'Let's do it again.'

Nate laughed as he caught his breath.

17

Nate

Waking up with a naked Tessie in his arms brought the biggest smile to Nate's face. He tightened his arms around her as she stirred.

'Morning, beautiful,' he whispered.

Tessie rolled her head up to look at him.

He smiled at her bleary eyes coming to terms with what happened last night. He was relieved to see her smile back.

'You stay in bed, Tess. I'll bring us in a cup of tea.'

She propped herself up on his chest. 'I'm going to pop to the bathroom while you're doing that. Where are my pyjamas?'

Nate laughed quietly. 'On the floor.' He kissed her head and shifted her gently from him to retrieve her nightclothes and his own.

They got dressed and Nate headed for the door. He turned and smiled to himself as he watched her taming her wild hair.

God, I love that hair.

He walked into the kitchen, put the kettle on, and then noticed a note on the table as he was heading to the bathroom.

Tessie was sitting up in bed by the time he brought in the tea.

'Everyone's out,' he told her.

'Out where?'

He nodded behind him at the doorway. 'There was a note in the kitchen from Jake. Joey and Josh are out for the day, and Jake and Anna have gone to a baby scan. He said they'll meet us here at lunch to take us out for something to eat.'

Tessie sipped her tea and put the cup down on the bedside cabinet. 'Oh.'

Nate climbed back in bed and put his own cup down and grinned at her. 'You know what this means, don't you?'

Her eyes widened as she shook her head. 'What?'

'I don't have to bite the pillow.'

Tessie giggled as he pulled her closer towards his body.

* * *

The pub lunch was much more Nate than the fancy restaurant they went to the night before. He felt more relaxed and at home and knew how to pronounce all of the food on the menu.

He spoke to Jake whilst Tessie and Anna were in the toilet.

'I just wanted to let you know that I'll take you up on the loan offer so that I can get this business up and running. I'll start making repayments as soon as possible.'

Jake smiled politely. 'There's no rush. Whenever you're ready. I've already spoken to Dolly, the younger one, and she's agreed to sell me half of her shop. It's the biggest in Pepper Lane, and she doesn't need all that space, so she was happy with the arrangement. I've called a building company that my family have always used, and they will be starting the renovations in a couple of days. You can take that on as your farm shop, and you won't have to pay any rent until you want to.'

Nate was taken aback by Jake's generosity. 'I want to. Thanks, that's… I wasn't expecting everything to be moving this fast.'

Jake picked up his glass of orange juice. 'There's no reason to wait once you know what you want.'

Nate's thoughts turned to Tessie. They had spoken about keeping their relationship a secret for a couple of weeks whilst they got used to it. He had wanted Tessie for a long while but had also wanted to keep things the way they were. He hadn't pushed the subject for years, but then Tori called and something shifted inside of him. Tessie's accident didn't help matters, and as soon as he shared a bed with her for the first time, he knew he couldn't hold back for much longer.

He glanced over at Jake, wishing he could be as confident as him.

'Do you always just go for it when you know what you want, Jake?'

Jake breathed out a laugh. 'Honestly, before I met Anna, I didn't put a lot of thought into anything. I just kind of flowed. Even when I knew I wanted Anna, I can hardly say I went for it full steam ahead. She scared the living daylights out of me. I never knew love could make you feel so nervous. Not in a bad way. I was just scared of that lack of control, I guess. People always look at me and see a confident man who gets what he wants, but I'm only human, and Anna's definitely my Achilles' heel.'

Yeah, I know how that feels. The thought of not having Tessie in my life kills me.

As though he could read his mind, Jake asked, 'How are things with you and Tess?'

Nate realised he was twiddling with his fork. He carefully put it back on the plate as though it were made of glass. 'Yeah, we're good, as always.' He waited for Jake to ask if they were together yet. He knew he would. Everybody asked over and over again.

'Okay. I won't ask if there have been any developments. You never want to talk about it.'

Nate shook his head. 'Nope, I don't.'

Jake stopped smiling as he looked across the room at the bar. 'What's going on there?'

Nate turned to see Tessie and Anna talking to a scruffy man wearing an oversized parka.

'I don't like the look of him.' Jake quickly stood.

Nate wasn't worried. He knew Tessie could handle the biggest and rowdiest men at a bar. He'd seen her kick a few out of her own pub quite a few times over the years. He got up and followed Jake.

'Hello,' said Jake, eyeing the shady-looking character standing far too close to Anna.

Anna smiled warmly. 'Jake, this is Mole. We were in a care home together when we were teenagers.'

Nate tried not to grin at Jake's unimpressed expression. He said what Jake should have. 'Hello, mate. Good to meet a friend of Anna's.'

Mole scratched his stubble as he smiled back at Nate. 'Blimey, mate, you're built like the Hulk. Do all those muscles hurt?'

Nate smiled politely. 'Sometimes.'

'You interested in a watch?' asked Mole, tapping the side of his coat. 'I was just asking Anna. I'm flogging some. Got a nice proper Rolex, if you're interested.'

Nate turned to Jake to see what he thought about buying a knocked-off watch from the not-so-legit seller.

Mole slurped his bottle of Bud. He nodded at Jake. 'You look like a Rolex man.'

'He already has a watch, Mole.' Anna grinned. 'Thanks anyway.'

Mole rolled his twinkling beady blue eyes from Anna back to Jake. 'So, is this the one who knocked you up then?'

Anna let out a short laugh as Jake gave the impression he was highly offended.

'This is Jake, soon to be my husband.'

Mole held out his hand to shake Jake's, and Nate hoped Jake would take it. He knew that Jake had a thing for germs, and Mole's hand looked as though it hadn't seen a bar of soap in a while.

Jake shook his hand for all of a split second.

'You look after our Anna.' Mole glared into his eyes, with a twinkle in his own. 'She's a good girl.'

'Yes, I know.' Jake's teeth seemed somewhat clenched, which amused Nate. 'And I intend to look after her and our baby.'

Mole slapped the side of Jake's arm. 'Good to know, mate.'

Nate could see that Jake was starting to get annoyed, especially with Mole leaning so close to Anna and touching her baby bump. 'Okay, well, it was nice to meet you, but we're off now.' He quickly turned to Jake. 'Let's go settle the bill. The waitress will think we've run off.'

'Easily done.' Mole nodded over his shoulder and winked. 'The back door is only there.'

'I'll pay.' Jake went to take Anna's arm to walk away, but she pulled her arm back and flung it around Mole's neck. She kissed him on the cheek, said goodbye, and then headed off with Jake.

Mole nodded in her direction. 'See ya later, treacle.'

Nate tried not to laugh. He looked at Tessie to see her holding back a grin too.

Mole looked up at Nate. 'Is Polly Pocket with you, mate? If not, do ya mind going away, only I'd like to buy the lady a drink.'

Nate plastered a large smile across his face. 'Sorry, Mole. She's mine.'

Mole showed both his palms. 'No worries. Good choice. I'll see you two around.'

The salesman wandered off to find his next customer, which appeared to be a slightly drunken wiry old man in a red tracksuit.

Tessie poked Nate in the chest. 'I'm yours, am I?'

He flashed her his cheeky smile. 'And I'm yours, Polly Pocket, alright, treacle.'

She burst out laughing at his poor attempt at Mole's strong London accent.

Anna approached, interrupting them. 'Anyone buy a moody watch yet?'

Nate laughed. 'No, but speaking of moody.' He nodded behind her to see Jake heading their way.

Anna giggled. 'He's so funny.' She looked towards the door. 'Come on, I want to show you my old bookshop. It's only a couple of streets away.'

Nate waited for Jake to catch up before following the ladies outside.

Jake had the hump. 'I don't know why Anna felt the need to tell that man she was pregnant. Did you see how he just touched her belly?'

Nate nodded as he stepped outside. 'People tend to do that.'

They followed Tessie and Anna along the street. Nate smiled at the women's linked arms and happy voices and the fact that every so often Tessie looked over her shoulder and smiled his way.

Jake stopped Nate before they turned a corner. 'Oh, I might be in trouble here.'

Nate frowned with confusion. 'What's wrong?'

They both turned as they heard Anna gasp.

Nate walked forward. Concern flashed across his face. 'Anna, what's wrong? Is it the baby?'

Tessie nodded down the street.

He followed her eyes. 'What am I looking at?' All he could see was a row of shops.

'Café Diths.' Tessie was clearly trying to convey some sort of silent message to him using her eyes.

Nate wasn't picking up on her secret code. 'What about it?'

Anna turned sharply to Jake, who seemed to have found a sudden interest in the pavement whilst Nate was still oblivious to what was going on around him.

'I'm missing something.' He looked directly at Anna for help.

Anna huffed. 'The only thing that is missing is my old bookshop. It was right there.' Her index finger shot down the street.

Nate took a second look. 'Where?'

Anna was glaring into the top of Jake's head. 'Right where Café Diths is.'

The penny dropped. 'Oh.' Nate looked at Tessie, who was biting down on her bottom lip.

'Jake, when did you do this?' Anna asked him.

Jake lifted his eyes. 'Anna, I couldn't let that ex of yours get away with the way he treated you.'

Nate's eyes widened. 'So you bought his shop? That doesn't sound like much of a payback. You gave him money.'

'Actually,' said Jake, 'he was just renting the premises. I bought the building, put the rent up, and he was forced out. Now he knows how it feels.'

Nate knew if Rob was Tessie's ex, he would have probably just punched him in the face and had done with it.

'I actually think that's quite sweet,' said Tessie quietly. Nate met her eyes, and then they both turned to see Anna's response.

'I'm sorry, Anna.' Jake reached out for her fingertips. 'I know you told me not to get involved, but I really hate that man. I struggled with your instructions.'

Anna took a deep breath and gave him a hug, releasing the charged atmosphere immediately.

'It's okay, Jake. I understand,' she said softly. 'Can we just get on with concentrating on us now?'

He smiled warmly and kissed her head. 'Yes.'

Nate nodded down the street. 'Shall we grab a coffee then?' Tessie laughed and nudged him.

'Okay.' Anna gave Jake a light squeeze. 'Just not in that shop.'

'Don't worry.' Jake pointed forward. 'There's another one further along.'

Nate watched Anna and Jake walk ahead arm in arm. He turned to Tessie, winked, and offered his arm, which she happily took.

'I'm glad I don't have a horrible ex we have to deal with,' she whispered.

Nate gave a slight nod. 'Yeah, I would've just punched him, then probably got arrested.' Tessie placed her mouth on his arm to muffle her laugh. He smiled back at her, then reached into his pocket, as his phone started to buzz.

She glanced up at him, with a slight look of worry. 'I hope that's not the girls saying something is wrong.'

He was pretty sure the girls were fine with Elaine and Ed. Plus, Anna's dog, Max, was keeping them company, and he knew how much Robyn loved dogs. He glanced at the screen and immediately lost his smile. He ignored the caller and put his phone away, trying to ignore the fact that Tessie looked concerned.

'Who was it?' she asked.

He swallowed down the lump in his throat. 'Tori.'

18

Tessie

Tessie stared glumly at her reflection in the mirrored door of the lift in River Heights as it headed down to the ground floor.

I'm short, thin, with a face full of freckles, and mad hair. Tori's taller, curvy, with a clear complexion and straight blonde hair. If she comes back, it's game over for me. Why is she contacting Nate after all this time? She's already told him about the sale of the flat and the money. The arrangements for the girls have been made. What does she want now?

She glanced down at the slice of chocolate cake that was on the square plate she was holding.

I wonder if he ever misses her. He loved her once. Maybe a part of him always will. I can't compete with her. She's beautiful, and she's Daisy's real mum.

She looked into her own eyes.

I'm going to lose him, aren't I?

She went to nod at herself but the lift stopped and the door opened.

Tessie stepped out into the large, light-grey-and-white lobby. She sighed deeply, inhaling a fresh citrus smell, and made her way over to the long, laminated, dark desk across the room.

A man with a dark, weather-worn face stood to greet her. 'Hello, Tessie. What have you got there?'

She placed the white plate on the counter. 'Choccy cake for you, Stan, from Anna. She would have brought it down herself, but Jake's just taken her up on the roof for some sort of surprise.'

Stan's thickset smile widened. He sat back in his comfy green chair and started to eat his cake. His dark eyes were studying the glum woman leaning on his desktop.

'So, what's on your mind, young lady?' His throat sounded sore.

Tessie twiddled with a blue pen she saw sitting there. 'Oh, nothing.'

'Yeah, I know that tone.' He swallowed a large mouthful of cake. 'You know, me and Anna used to sit down here eating our dinner and having these chats. Me asking what's wrong. She would act just like you.'

Tessie straightened up. She scrunched one shoulder up to her ear. 'I'm a bit fed up, Stan. That's all.'

'Anything to do with the big man?'

Wow, he can just see right through me.

She swished one foot in circles on the marble-looking floor. 'His ex-girlfriend called him earlier.'

'What did she want?'

'I don't know. He ignored the call. What does that mean?'

Stan sat forward. 'It means he didn't want to talk to her.'

Tessie slumped her shoulders. 'Well, that much I gathered, but why? Do you think it was because I was there?'

'Didn't you ask him?'

She wearily shook her head. 'No.'

'Why don't you ask him?'

Tessie scrunched her nose up at that idea.

Stan smiled warmly. 'Look, Tessie, sometimes you just have to ask the question if you want to know the answer.'

'What if I don't like the answer?'

'It's still better than not knowing.'

She watched him enjoying his cake.

'She used to be my best friend, you know. Back when we were teenagers. It seems like a lifetime ago.'

Stan nodded. 'Is this Daisy's birth mum?'

'Yes. Did Anna tell you?'

'She caught me up with all the backstories of Pepper Bay.' He smiled to himself. 'She does love a backstory, does Anna.'

'I'm not sure I'm keen on my backstory.'

'Good thing it's a backstory then, and not your future.'

Tessie's thoughts turned to Henry. Guilt hit her hard. What would he say about her making love to Nate? How would that make him feel? It wasn't something she did whilst he was alive, nor did she think that way about any other man. She loved Henry with all of her heart. He was everything to her, and she expected him to be around forever. She never meant for her feelings towards Nate to grow. It just started happening one day. He was there for her after Henry died, and she was there for him. They had little to do with each other for a while but then started to hang out again when their daughters started nursery. She knew then that her feelings towards him were changing, so she backed away. She couldn't feel that way about Nate Walker. Not him.

'I feel guilty that I've moved on, Stan,' she whispered, barely being able to say the words that hurt her heart.

'Do you think Henry would be angry about that?'

She knew he wouldn't. Not Henry. He was the nicest man she ever met.

'He was so easy-going, Stan. Very laid back for the worrier that he was, but he made life easy. Everything was easy with him. We just worked.' Tessie shook her head. 'I don't know what he would make of any of this. How can I ever know?'

'Because you knew him, Tessie.'

'I think he would be happy it was Nate. I'm not sure what he would make of anyone else. Nate was his best friend. It makes me feel so torn at times. How can I look at Nate the way I do and love him? What does that say about how I loved Henry?'

Stan smiled softly. 'I guess it shows us that we can love more than once in our lifetime.'

'I really did love Henry, you know.'

'You don't have to try to convince me, Tessie, nor anyone else. Loving Nate doesn't make you a bad person. It makes you a lucky person to have found love again.'

Tessie smiled at him. 'When are you packing up work and coming to live with us in the bay? We could do with someone wise around the place. Well, I could.'

'May.' He glanced around the lobby.

'It's almost May now.'

'I'll be there more towards the end of the month. I'll definitely be there for the wedding.'

'That's coming around quickly.' Tessie could feel Anna and Jake's love everywhere around her. 'You were there from the beginning with those two, weren't you, Stan?'

Stan breathed out a husky laugh. He coughed and cleared his throat. 'Yes, it was interesting to watch it unfold.'

'They seem an unlikely pair, but they work.'

'That was the same for me and my wife. You don't have to be two peas in a pod for your relationship to work. You just have to love each other.'

'Nate grew up on a farm. I grew up in a pub. We're from the same place but a million miles from each other in a lot of ways.'

'It's not about places, or what job you have. Those things don't connect us.'

I love Nate. I feel so connected to him. Maybe more than he does to me. I don't know. I do know I'd never give him up, but would he leave me so easily?

Stan sighed deeply as he stared over at the main door. 'I'll miss this place, you know, Tessie.'

'You can come back with me in the summer for a visit if you like. I might be doing some sort of an apprenticeship at Café Diths. I'm undecided at the moment.'

Stan placed his empty plate on the counter and stood to wipe some crumbs from his blue shirt. 'What's stopping you?'

She rolled her eyes over to him to find his waiting. They didn't appear ready to believe any lie she might throw his way.

'Being away from Nate for that long.'

'I admire your honesty. How long is that long?'

'Around four weeks. Yeah, I know, it's not that long, but I've pretty much seen him every day for the past five years.'

Stan chuckled. 'Sounds like you need a break then.'

Tessie's mouth curled.

'Do you really want to do this course, Tessie?'

She nodded. 'I do. It will really help me get to grips with running the farm's social media business, and Anna's too. I'll even be part of the Café Diths social media team as well, and I can work from home. Jake comes to London once a month for meetings, so I would come back here with him from time to time. It's a great opportunity, and I would love that job.'

'Sounds to me like you know what you want.'

She reluctantly nodded.

'Hey, Tessie, if he really loves you, he'll still be there every time you go home.'

'What if he still really loves his ex-girlfriend?'

Stan flopped into his office chair. 'Then you'll have a great job to focus on instead.'

* * *

Tessie could hear music as she stepped out of the lift to walk towards Jake's door. It was coming from the stairs that led to the roof. She wanted a sneaky peek at what Jake had set up for Anna, so she crept up the stairway.

I'll just take one quick look. They won't even know I'm there.

She stared out at the darkness of the rooftop to see a couple of large concrete-looking blocks and some fairy lights twinkling away at the far end. She stood still, listening to the tune to find out what song it was. She smiled to herself as she recognised The Drifters singing the song "Up on the Roof".

Oh, that's appropriate for them.

She went to tiptoe away when she saw them appear from behind one of the blocks.

Jake and Anna were dancing under the fairy lights and laughing as they swayed to the music.

The scene warmed Tessie's heart.

Oh my word, how romantic is that.

She took one more glance across the roof as the happy couple slipped back behind the large block.

To think Anna lived in a tent up here. I don't know how she did it. I could never be that brave. And to think that Jake was sleeping in his bedroom directly below her sleeping bag. The universe works in mysterious ways sometimes. Look at this floor. It's so cold and hard. I'll never complain about an uncomfortable mattress again. Oh, Anna. I'm so happy you and Jake finally found each other. Okay, Tess, stop being nosy now. Leave them alone.

She turned and bounced straight off Nate's big chest.

His hands shot out to steady her.

She looked up at him and put her finger to her lips. 'Shh! Jake and Anna are down the end, dancing. It's so romantic.'

He looked over her head and smiled. 'And what are you doing?'

Tessie put on her best innocent expression. 'Being inquisitive.'

Nate's mouth twitched.

'This is where she lived, Nate. Can you imagine? I'm glad she doesn't live here anymore. It breaks my heart just thinking about it. I hope I'm never homeless.'

'You won't be.'

She went to move around him to go back downstairs, but he grabbed her arms and twirled her around.

'May I have this dance, Miss Sparrow?' he whispered.

Tessie muffled her laugh.

'Shh!' he told her.

He picked her up, and she wrapped her legs around him, peppering little kisses along his jawline as she rested her head on his shoulder.

Nate slow-danced with her to the background music wafting their way.

She lifted her head to look into his smiling eyes. 'I've decided that I'm going to do the apprenticeship thingy this summer.'

He gave a slight nod. 'I'll look after the girls, and we'll come and visit every weekend.'

Tessie felt her heart lift.

Nate lightly kissed her nose. 'We'll make it work, Tess. Whatever comes our way, we'll figure it out together, and we'll always find a way to make it work.'

She happily snuggled back into his hold.

19

Nate

Nate stared glumly at the Adonis-like man that Jake had just introduced to Tessie. The tall man's smile looked like an Invisalign advert, and his body was a worthy contender for a Chippendales calendar. He was wearing loose black bottoms and a black fitted tee-shirt that looked as though it had been painted on him.

So, you're Dwight, with the miracle hands who is going to make Tessie melt beneath your touch. Great! Thanks a lot, Jake.

'I've booked you two in for a massage together,' said Jake.

'Yes.' Dwight flashed a professional smile at Tessie. 'Follow me, please.' He peered over his tanned shoulder at Nate. 'Julia will be with you, Mr Walker. Normally, she partners with Macie, but as Miss Sparrow has been in an accident recently, I'll be attending to her every need.'

Not if I can help it.

Nate looked over at Jake to see him waving him away.

'Go on,' Jake mouthed.

Nate watched Tessie enter the warm room and immediately remove her bathrobe and lie down. His eyes lingered for a moment, and he lost his train of thought. He slowly looked down at his own robe.

Everyone except the staff seemed to wearing white robes, and everywhere he looked there were fluffy white towels and matching slippers. His eyes met with a long row of body oils in tiny bottles and then steam coming from a white diffuser sitting in the corner. He knew the zesty scent filling the room was bergamot.

Nate's vast knowledge of essential oils came from the fact that his grandmother had a major love for them, along with incense and scented candles.

Josephine often had something burning in her bedroom, which would leak into the rest of the house. She seemed to favour frankincense oil, dragon's blood incense, and plain white candles.

Nate came home once to find the whole living room covered in flickering white candles. He wasn't quite sure if his grandmother was having a romantic night in or if she was about to sacrifice someone to the gods. He had stayed up late that night just to make sure every last candle had been put out, as he had been worried about the house burning down.

'You have such beautiful freckles, Miss Sparrow,' said Dwight. 'I've always loved freckles on a woman.'

Nate viewed him from his peripheral vision.

'And your hair is beyond gorgeous, Miss Sparrow,' added Dwight.

Oh, behave yourself, Dwight.

Nate took a slow, calming breath.

'You know, such pale skin should be treated with the most loving care, Miss Sparrow. I can see you look after yourself very well.' Dwight smiled warmly.

'I don't really do much,' mumbled Tessie.

'That means you are a natural beauty, Miss Sparrow.'

Is he for real? You are so wonderful, Miss Sparrow. I love your body, Miss Sparrow. I want to get you into bed and make mad passionate love to you with my gift from the gods, Miss Sparrow. Blah blah blah, Miss Sparrow. What accent is that anyway? Whatever it is, it sounds fake, like his orange tan.

'Hi, Mr Walker, I'm Julia.' A squeaky voice came from behind him.

Nate jolted slightly and turned to see a young blonde woman holding out her neatly manicured fingers towards him.

'Lie down, Nate.' Tessie nodded at him. 'I'm sure Julia has other clients after you.'

Nate reluctantly did as he was told. He wanted to run out of the room, but he didn't want to come across as a weirdo. Plus, he wanted to keep his eye on the love doctor, Dwight. He wasn't in the mood to be touched by a stranger or watch another man's hands manoeuvre all over Tessie's bare back.

Tessie groaned.

Really, Tess!

'I'm hitting all the right spots, am I, Miss Sparrow?'

'You certainly are, Dwight.'

Someone else is going to get hit in the right spot in a minute.

'If you're interested, Miss Sparrow, I can take you to our shop afterwards and show you the products I am using here today. I can also give you a private tour of the spa. See what else you like.'

'Nah, she's all right, mate.' Nate knew he sounded blunt, but he didn't care. 'We've got plans after this with our friends.'

'Ah, such a shame, Miss Sparrow. Another time, perhaps?'

Dream on, sunshine.

Tessie groaned again, then started talking to Dwight about her accident, his work, his hands, and how good everything felt.

146

Everything Dwight said came out smooth and filled with lust, which only wound Nate up. He was sure Julia would see his knots from a mile away.

Nate wanted to complain about something to someone, but then Julia got to work on him and suddenly every part of him caved under her magic touch, and he felt surprisingly relaxed.

Bloody hell. This is so good. I could do with this once a week. I wonder if Tessie would be interested in training here. Second thoughts, not here with him. I swear, if I hear him say Miss Sparrow one more time... Ouch! Ooh, that's good. Yeah, right there.

He closed his eyes and after a moment drifted off to sleep.

* * *

'Oh my God, Nate. That was so embarrassing.' Tessie glanced around the glass-walled restaurant that belonged to the spa, before bringing her eyes back to him.

Everything looked minimalistic, light, and cleaned to within an inch of its life.

There weren't many people around, but the ones who were there all looked as though they were models who featured on the spa's website.

Joey put her glass of lemon-infused water down on the table and laughed. 'That is so typical of Nate.'

Nate shrugged. 'So what, I fell asleep.'

A slow smile built on Tessie's face. 'You were snoring, and then you farted so loudly and still didn't wake up.'

His eyes were filled with humour. 'It's not my fault Julia relaxed me and brought up my wind.'

Josh breathed out a laugh. 'Brought your wind down, you mean.'

'I was asleep.' Nate tried for indifferent. 'I didn't know what I was doing.'

Josh slapped his shoulder as he stood. 'That's hilarious, Walker. Wish I were there.'

Joey joined Josh's side. 'Come on, you. I want to buy some products from the shop.' She glanced down at Tessie. 'I'm so in love with the honey cream my girl used on my feet. The smell made me hungry. I want some massage oils too.'

Tessie laughed.

Josh looked at Joey in surprise. 'When will you use massage oil, Jo?'

She smiled widely at him, revealing her perfect teeth. 'I was hoping you would use it on me, Josh.'

Nate groaned. 'Oh God! I don't need to hear this.'

'No, you don't,' said Josh, 'but I do need to go shopping for oils right now.' Joey giggled as she linked arms with him.

Nate watched them walk away. He scrunched his nose up and shook his head at Tessie.

Tessie swirled her spoon around her half-empty coffee cup. 'You know, we could buy some oils. If you like, that is.'

He fixed his eyes into hers as she glanced over the table at him. He smiled inwardly at the thought of Tessie smothered in oil lying naked across the table. She was giving him a look filled with want and desire.

Stop looking at me like that, Tess. I swear, I won't be able to control myself for much longer. I want you so much right now, oil or no oil. I can't cope with this. We need to get out of here.

'Shall we head to the shop now, Tess?' He watched her eyes crease at the corners as she suppressed a smile.

148

* * *

Tessie was sitting up crossed-legged on the bed, looking through her goody bag that was a gift to her from the spa.

'There are some bits in here the girls will love, and I definitely think they'll love these cute soap bars we got them.' She held one up that had a painted picture of a rabbit on one side. 'I love its fluffy tail.' She put it under her nose. 'Mmm, this one's chamomile. I never thought about it in soap before. I just thought it was tea to help you sleep.'

'Our bathroom will smell like a spa.'

'Which is an improvement on smelling like a farm.'

Nate disagreed. 'The farm doesn't smell like a farm. What does that actually smell like anyway?'

Tessie laughed. 'You're never going to know, are you? You've grown up on a farm. You're used to the smell. The smell of cows anyway. Maybe when we get back, you might notice it because of being away for a few days.'

'My gran makes the house smell of all sorts.' He looked over at the window. 'London has a smell.'

Tessie sniffed the air. 'What did you smell here?'

He shrugged. 'Not sure. Dust?'

'Dust? I didn't smell anything. I did expect the river to stink, but it doesn't, does it? I couldn't pick up on much. The sea always smells nice. Rivers are quite bland, now that I think about it. Yes, I definitely prefer the smell of the sea. This place doesn't have that freshness.'

'It's noisy here as well, don't you think?'

'It's all right. It's a city. I guess they're all noisy.'

'And no one says hello to each other like we do back home.'

Tessie put the gift bag down on the floor beside the bed. 'There are a zillion people here, Nate. You can't expect them to all know each other.'

Nate slid the wardrobe door to a close. 'Suppose.' He looked over to see her smiling at him.

'I've had the best weekend here, Nate.'

He walked towards the bed and sat on the end, facing her.

'Yeah, it's been pretty special.'

Her moss-green eyes twinkled his way. 'A part of me doesn't want to go home.'

Her smile has weakened. What is she worried about?

'It's not going to come to an end just because we're back home, Tess.'

'I'm worried things might change. It's different here. It can all be pretend here. Back home, it's real. It's our life.'

Nate felt an unsettling churn hit his stomach. He didn't want to go back to having a platonic relationship with her. He studied her face for signs of hope, but her eyes had dulled, and she had scrunched her knees up to her chest, as though guarding herself.

She can't backtrack now. I won't let her. She loves me. She told me so. I'm not losing her. Not now. Not ever.

'Tess, I love you.' He moved further into the middle of the bed and latched on to her hands. 'I love you. Nothing's going to change when we get home. I won't let it. I promise.'

20

Tessie

Tessie was unpacking her bag in Nate's bedroom. He had gone to collect the girls from Ed and Elaine. She was deciding whether or not to bring some more of her things from home. A part of her wanted to move into the farm, but something was still niggling at her and holding her back.

Why can't life be simple? It seems such an easy step. I've made it complicated. I know I have. Ooh, I feel tense again. I need another massage now. I think I'll have a relaxing bath tonight with my new scented candle and lavender oil. That should do the trick. I wish we had a big bath here like the one in Jake's apartment. Nate fitted in that with me. I wish we had bathed in it now instead of just sitting in it goofing around. That was a funny moment. So was that time with the crazy shower. I wonder if Nate will be up for finally renovating this place. We could get ourselves a huge bath and a big enough shower for the two of us. That would be nice.

She opened the window and felt the heat of the sun warm her skin. She breathed in the fresh air as she gazed out at the cows mooching around in the green field that was part of Nate's land. From that angle, Pepper Lane wasn't visible, and she really could have been anywhere.

I love this view. All this land, looking as though it goes on forever. I'll never get tired of this place.

Tessie really didn't want to be anywhere else, but she knew that when the day came that Nate found out what she had done behind his back, she might never see that view again.

His phone vibrated on the bedside cabinet, waking her from her thoughts. She walked over to see who was calling and felt her stomach flip when she saw Tori's name.

Why is she ringing again? Should I answer it? What would he say if I did? What will she say? Crap! I don't know what to do. She's getting on my nerves. I'm going to answer it.

'Hello, Tori. It's Tess.' She swallowed hard, hoping the agony in her voice hadn't been noticed.

There was a moment of silence down the phone.

'Hello, Tess. It's been a long while.' There was an edginess to her voice that Tessie picked up on straight away. It wasn't a surprise, seeing how they hadn't spoken to each other in years.

Tessie suddenly felt more composed. She sat up straight on the edge of the bed, ready for her conversation. Whatever it might be. 'Yeah, thirteen years.'

Now what?

'How have you been?'

Tessie held back the sarcasm that was fighting to be released. 'Fine. You?'

Tori's voice was quiet and calm. 'I'm doing okay.'

Are you going to ask after your niece? What about your daughter? That's it, I'm getting to the point.

'Nate told me about the money for the girls. That's all sorted, so why do you keep ringing him?'

She heard Tori breathe deeply.

Yeah, what the bloody hell have you got to say about that?

'I just want to hear his voice, Tess.'

Tessie wasn't quite sure what to make of that statement. It wasn't what she was expecting to hear. Although, a part of her half-expected something along those lines, and now she felt a cocktail of emotions running through her all at once. Aggravated was the most potent.

'You want to hear his voice? What are you trying to say, Tor? You still have feelings for him?'

It appeared Tori was hesitating, which only made Tessie's temper rise a notch.

'I'll always have feelings for him,' said Tori softly.

'Well, he doesn't have feelings for you anymore.' Tessie shocked herself with her outburst.

Calm down, Tess.

'You know, Tori, you can't just walk back into his life after thirteen years of no contact. I'm not sure what you're expecting to gain from this. You left him without telling him you were going, and you left Daisy. Do you honestly think he is just going to welcome you back with open arms after all this time?'

'Of course not. I know what I did, and I know what I lost…'

'You didn't lose anything. You walked away from it. There's a difference.'

'No offence, Tess, but this is between me and Nate. I know you're his friend, but it's actually none of your business.'

None of my business! I'm the one sleeping next to him. I'm the one he says he loves. I'm the one who helps raise your daughter. I'm the one she calls Mum. Don't say it. Don't you bloody well say it, Tess.

'Nate's life is none of your business, Tor. You need to stay away from him. I won't let you mess him up again.'

'I'm not trying to mess him up. I'm trying to make things right. I want him to know how sorry I am. I want him to know that I miss him sometimes.'

153

'Sometimes!'

'He's a big part of my life, Tess. I don't need to tell you that.'

Tessie could feel her heart galloping in her chest. Her face felt hot and her hand strangling the phone was shaking slightly.

'He was a big part of your life, Tor, but he isn't anymore. You just need to accept that. He has made a life without you, and he doesn't want you back.'

'He hasn't told me that.'

Tessie was rendered speechless for a moment.

Why hasn't he told her that? Why hasn't he put her straight? What is he playing at?

'I'm sure he doesn't want to hurt your feelings by being blunt with you.'

Yes, that's probably it.

'He has been nothing but sweet to me on the phone, and I think I know him better than you, Tess.'

Maybe you did. Maybe you still do. I'm not sure now.

Tessie tried to create some moisture inside her mouth before speaking. She wanted to sound perfectly normal, and not like the nervous wreck that was starting to make an appearance.

'So, basically, Tori, you're going to keep calling him, hoping to rebuild a connection.'

'It's a start.' Her voice was still calm.

A start for you. An ending for me.

'And what about Daisy?'

'What about her?'

'Are you going to call her and rebuild?'

'I wasn't planning to.'

Are you for real?

'How exactly will your new life with Nate work if you don't involve my…' She paused to correct herself, as she was going to say *daughter*. 'Daisy?'

'Well, of course I'll involve my daughter. Just not yet. I have to smooth things over with Nate first.'

'Smooth things over with Nate! You haven't just had a row, Tor.'

'I know, Tess. I'm not expecting overnight miracles.'

'No, but you are expecting a bloody miracle.'

Tessie sat in bewilderment whilst another moment of silence filled the air between her and her once best friend.

'I do have an excuse, you know,' said Tori, raising her voice slightly. 'My twin brother had just died. I was a mess.'

Resentment started to bubble in Tessie's chest. She was silently seething and could feel the potential of an explosion.

'You were a mess! You were a mess! How did you think I felt? I'd just lost the love of my life. I was pregnant with his child. Did you see me leaving her behind and running off to the other side of the world? No, you didn't.'

'Tess, I'm sorry. I know you were upset too.'

'Upset! Upset! Are you purposely trying to wind me up, Tor? Your whole family left Robyn behind. Henry's own daughter. I don't want to hear about how bad you were feeling, if it's all the same.'

'You know, I didn't call to upset you. I didn't actually call you. I called Nate. Why are you answering his phone anyway?'

Anger surged through. 'Because it was sitting next to me in our bedroom.'

Tension loomed.

'Your bedroom? Yours and Nate's bedroom?'

Tessie could hear the tremble in Tori's voice, and then she couldn't help the smugness in her own.

155

'That's right. Our bedroom. The one we share together.'

'Since when?' snapped Tori.

'Since, none of your business.'

'Would you jump in my grave that quickly, Tess?'

'Are you having a laugh, Tor? That grave's been cold for thirteen years.'

'It's still a stab in the back for our friendship.'

'Our so-called friendship ended the day you left me and your niece behind. Where was your arm to comfort me when I was breaking down over Henry? Where was this wonderful friendship then, eh?'

She's got a bloody cheek!

'Nate's always been mine,' shouted Tori, making Tessie jump.

She removed the phone from her ear. 'Well, he's mine now.'

Tori lowered her voice. 'I can't believe you did this to me, Tess. Of all people. Well, enjoy your time with my man while you can, because when I show up, he'll drop you like a hot potato.'

Show up? You can't come here. You'll hurt Daisy. I swear to God, I'm going to smack you straight in the face if you show up here. I need to calm down. Think, Tess. Be rational.

She took a silent, calming breath. 'Look, Tori, you need to stop making this about what you want. There is Daisy to consider.'

'I'm sure she'll be happy to see me. I'm her mother, after all. She'll warm to me eventually. She'll want me in her life.'

For God's sake!

'Daisy is settled. She is doing really well at school. She is happy at home. She doesn't need you rocking the boat.'

'I wouldn't be rocking the boat, Tess. She would be happy to see me and her dad back together. She will want that happy family.'

This woman is seriously deluded. What is she playing at?

'She has a happy family now.'

'I'm sure she is very happy and well cared for, but I'll complete her life.'

'Her life is complete. You have no idea what our life is like here.'

'And you have no idea how much better it could be if I was there.'

Tessie felt something snap inside her. 'No one wants you here.'

'No, Tess, you just don't want me there. You know that as soon as Nate sees me, he'll want me again. I was the love of his life, and I'm the mother of his child, not you.' Her tone spat bitterness in its purest form.

Tessie felt the impact of the spite hit her straight in the gut. She immediately reacted with her own strike. 'I'm the mother of his child actually. Daisy calls me Mum, and when me and Nate are ready, we'll have some more kids and make our happy family even bigger, and there will never be room for you, so stay away from my family, Victoria Evans, or I'll…' She froze, with her mouth gaping.

Nate, Daisy, and Robyn were standing in the bedroom doorway, looking just as shocked as she was.

Nate stepped forward and slowly removed the phone from Tessie's tight grip and hung up the call.

21

Nate

Nate turned to their daughters, his jaw tense with frustration. 'Go and unpack your things.'

Neither of the girls said a word. They just left for their bedrooms.

He turned back to Tessie, knowing full well his face was filled with thunder, but he could see she was mortified that the girls had overheard some of her conversation with Tori, so he tried hard to simmer his bubbling temper.

I don't bloody believe this. What the hell am I going to say?

He calmly sat by her side, knowing he needed to find some balance in his frazzled brain. The last thing he wanted to do was to shout at her, but another part of him really wanted to show her just how angry he was.

Relax. Take a moment. This can be sorted.

He steadied his breathing. 'What was that?'

Tessie was scrunching her hands in her lap. She didn't even attempt to fight back the disappointment in herself. 'I'm so sorry, Nate.'

'What happened?' He heard his words catch in his throat. He swallowed hard and waited patiently for her to reply.

Tessie was avoiding eye contact. She was fidgeting her feet and clearly hesitating. 'She said she was going to show up here. She said she wants you back.'

Oh, she did, did she? We'll see about that.

He watched Tessie's head jolt as though something had just sprung to mind.

'I understand you haven't exactly been discouraging her. She said you've been quite sweet. Why haven't you put her straight, Nate?'

Great! This is all Tess needs. I'm finally winning back her trust and her heart. The last thing either of us need is for her to think that I'm going to turn my back on her again.

'Because, unlike you, I've been trying to keep her sweet so that she didn't just show up and disrupt Daisy's life.'

That came out wrong. I need to soften my tone. None of this is Tessie's fault. I should have dealt with this from the start. I've been too soft.

Tessie shifted on the bed so that she was facing him. 'Sometimes, you have to just tell someone bluntly so that the message is loud and clear.'

Nate creased his brow in agitation. 'I think it's pretty clear now, Tess.'

Her eyes dropped to her lap. 'I didn't mean for Daisy to hear. Now she knows it was her mum on the phone. Oh God, I need to talk to her.'

He tugged her back down as she quickly stood. 'No. Leave her a while. We'll talk to her later. Together. As her parents. And stop calling Tori her mum. Say bio-mum or Tori or something else.'

She didn't respond.

Why now, Tori? Why the bloody hell are you coming into our lives now?

A bird's whistle came through the window, disturbing the silence that had suddenly occurred in the bedroom.

Nate stared over at the sunlight bouncing off the windowsill. He wished he was outside flying free with the birds or just going for a walk in the fields. He always felt free walking across the green fields on his own. He had once seen his mother doing exactly that. He hardly had any memories of her. She had left when Joey was a baby. He had always hated his mum for leaving. He couldn't believe it when his daughter suffered the same fate.

How would I feel if my mum turned up one day? Joey would be pleased, I think. I'm not sure I would. I've never missed having a mum. How can you miss what you've never had. I'm sure Daisy doesn't miss having Tori around. She doesn't know her. She's always had Tess, anyway. She doesn't go without a mother's love, because she has Tess. Joey and I had Gran. I don't need anyone extra in my life. Not my mum, not Tori, not anyone. I've got exactly what I need. I just hope Daisy feels the same way. I just hope she tells me if she doesn't. I'm going to have to talk to her at some point. I need her to be honest and open about this.

Tessie started to absentmindedly scratch her index finger on his jeans.

He stared down at her finger and then held her hand.

What are you thinking, Tess? How are you feeling? I need you to be open with me.

'Is Tori right, Nate? Would I lose you if she came back? She said as soon as you see her, you'd…'

He quickly grabbed her face and cupped it in his hands. He noticed the misty water sitting in her sad eyes, and his heart sank a little.

Oh no, Tess. Don't you think that.

'No one, no one, is breaking up our family. No one is coming between us either. I love you, Tessie Sparrow. You need to hear that, feel that, and believe that. I. Love. You.'

He leaned over and kissed her trembling lips, hoping to God she would feel secure with him.

Please believe me. Just believe me.

160

'I love you so much,' he whispered onto her lips.

Tessie propelled herself into his arms, hanging on to his neck for dear life.

'I'm scared, Nate.'

He held her tightly. 'Don't be. We'll figure this out. It's going to be okay.'

'I know you're angry.'

He pulled her away from him so that he could look at her. Her face was worn and flushed and in need of some happiness. He quickly swiped away a falling tear from her cheek.

She smiled weakly at him. 'You are, aren't you?'

'I am. I didn't want Daisy to hear any of that. I don't want Tori in our lives, and I certainly don't want her thinking she can get back with me. I'm angry because the only way to save our farm is by taking handouts from Jake Reynolds, and I'm angry because sometimes I think your heart is so beyond repair, there's nothing I can do to help you, and I'm fed up with having the thought of not waking up to you every morning because you've moved back home. I'm pissed off with the whole lot.'

Okay, Nate, breathe. Just breathe.

She kissed him gently on the cheek, and he felt the wetness of her eyes dampen his skin.

You break my heart when you cry. Please don't cry, Tess. I'll fix it. You can rely on me. I promise you, I'll fix this whole mess.

She closed her eyes and rested her head on his. 'I love you, Nate.'

He went to speak but felt another presence in the room. He looked up to see Daisy hovering in the doorway.

Tessie looked over and waved her towards them.

Daisy snuggled underneath her dad's free arm. 'So, that was Tori on the phone.'

'Yes,' he replied.

Daisy chewed her lip for a moment. 'What did she want?'

I have no idea how to answer this. How can I tell you that she hasn't actually asked me about you? Christ! What do I say?

'Her family still owned the flat above Dolly's shop. They just sold it to Dolly's niece, who is also called Dolly. They want to put the money from the sale away for you and Robyn for when you're older.' He paused. Words were a struggle.

Daisy started to pick at the ends of her hair.

'She was also thinking about rebuilding relationships with you and me. You know, just getting to know me again, and getting to know you,' he added.

At least that's what I think she's doing. God, I don't know what this woman really wants from us after all this time.

Nate glanced over to see Robyn in the doorway, leaning against the frame.

'What do you think about that, Dad?' asked Daisy quietly.

Before he had a chance to answer, Daisy looked over at Tessie. 'You're not happy about it, are you, Mum?'

He could tell that Tessie was lost for words. He had to say something to fill in the gap. 'We just want to do what's best for you.'

Daisy looked over at Robyn. 'What do you think, Robs?'

Robyn shrugged. 'I don't know. It's up to you if you want to get to know her. I don't want her breaking up our family though.'

'She won't do that.' Nate held a hint of authority in his tone.

'I wouldn't let that happen either,' said Daisy. 'I love my family, and I'm happy with the way things are. I'd like to tell her that, if that's okay.'

'It is.' Nate held back a sigh. 'But that's not something you have to do. That's my job. Unless you actually want to speak to her, I'll tell her for you.'

Daisy snuggled closer to him, and he tightened his grip on both her and Tessie.

'I don't really want to speak to her, Dad. But she has to know that I'm not being mean. I just don't want her upsetting my mum or taking you away.'

'Hey.' Nate gently lifted her face. 'No one will ever take me away from you.' He looked over at Robyn. 'Or you.' He turned to Tessie. 'Or you. We're a team here, right? We stick together, no matter what.'

A hint of a smile hit Robyn's mouth. 'Does this mean that you and Mum are finally together? Properly together?'

He smiled at Tessie and saw in her eyes that he could tell the girls the truth. 'Yes, we are.' He felt proudness fill him. 'I love your mum very much and she loves me.'

Robyn sprinted forward to land on his lap. 'Group hug,' she mumbled into his chest.

All arms gathered around each other.

'Family hug,' said Daisy.

Nate kissed each one of them on their head. 'You lot are my world, you know that?'

'We love you too, Dad.' Daisy snuggled further into his hold.

Thank you for my family. These are the best moments. There is nowhere else I'd rather be than huddled with my girls. Thank you for my blessings. I'm not going to cry.

Scruff hobbled in and licked the bottom of Nate's jeans before curling up to sleep on his feet.

Nate felt his heart warm for the love surrounding him. There was no way in a million years he was going to let Tori in the door. He knew he had to call her back at some point. Things had to be said. He just wasn't looking forward to the conversation or what might happen afterwards.

22

Tessie

Tessie stood on Pepper Lane staring up at the newly painted sign above the shop that was now named Pepper Pot Farm Shop. The outside had been given a pastel-blue-washed colour, and Scott Harper, a local artist, had designed the sign to match. Inside had light-wood flooring, cream and duck-egg-blue Welsh dressers lined with an assortment of jam and chutney, and Joey's flower-infused lollipops sat upon the cold counter that was home to the farm's tasty cheese. A large ornamental chicken, carved from dark wood, took up one corner. It sat upon a basket filled with straw and was surrounded by organic eggs. It had a big friendly smile and brought a cheer to all who saw it sitting there.

The lights were on, and Nate was inside talking to Jake and Dolly.

Tessie focused on Dolly's multicoloured jumper because she didn't want to catch Nate's eyes and have him wave her in. She didn't want to go inside. Nate's farm business was coming together nicely, and he was starting to look relaxed and almost happy. The last thing she wanted was to tell him the truth and watch it all come tumbling down.

When he finds out that it's my money paying for everything, he's going to hit the roof. All the while he thinks it's simply a loan from Jake, he's settled enough knowing that he can pay him back in instalments. With me, oh, it's going to be a whole different story. Why does he have to be so pig-headed? He's a stubborn old fool with too much pride. If it was me who needed his money, he would give me the lot. So, fair's fair. We're supposed to be a team. Oh, this isn't going to end well. I should just walk in there now and tell him. Rip the plaster off in one go. Get it over and done with.

Dolly flicked her mousey hair and rolled her chestnut eyes over towards the window. The movement caused Tessie to stir. She quickly smiled back at the bubbly woman who was waving at her.

Nate looked through the shop, smiled warmly, and gave Tessie a slight wave through the window before being distracted again by Jake.

I'll do it another day. Yeah, I know, I'm a coward.

She glanced down to the sea to her left, then glanced uphill at The Ugly Duckling. She decided to go to the pub to speak to her mum.

The familiar smell of beer-infused wood hit her nose as soon as she opened the large dark door. There weren't many people inside, as the weather was sunny and warm, so most of the customers were sitting in the beer garden out the back.

She frowned up at Freddy, who was standing at the top of a step-ladder pinning floral bunting over the top of the dark-wood bar. 'What's with the bunting, Fred? You're supposed to be the chef not the decorator.'

He glanced down over his broad shoulder and flicked his apricot curls out of his eyes.

'I said I'd do it. I don't mind. Annie Lennox wants to try it out this year for the Sandly Craft Fayre tomorrow.'

Tessie laughed to herself at what he had called her mum. Everyone who looked at Elaine saw the resemblance. Everyone except Elaine.

Freddy stretched over the high beam. His white tee-shirt lifted, revealing his flat, toned stomach.

'Oi, Tessie Sparrow.' Molly walked through a doorway that was behind the bar. 'You've got your own man to gawp at. Keep your eyes off mine.'

Tessie grinned at her.

Molly flashed her a smile whilst tightening the elastic band holding back her long dark hair. 'If the rumours are true, that is.'

Freddy stopped pinning the bunting and looked down. 'What rumours?'

Molly leaned over the bar, grinning dreamily into Tessie's eyes. 'That Tessie and Nate are finally a couple.'

Freddy's thick lips curled up. 'Is that true, Tess?'

Tessie couldn't help smiling at the fact. She had no control over her expression. 'Yes, Fred, it's true.'

'About bloody time,' was all he had to say upon the matter.

Tessie felt the smile inside of her fading.

Might not be for much longer when I tell him the truth about the business, or rather, the finances. Oh what a tangled web we weave, or rather, I weave, and all by myself too. I don't even have anyone to blame.

She looked across the bar at Molly. 'You working here properly now, Molls?'

'Just a few shifts here and there in between me working in Edith's Tearoom. I don't mind. I get to see Freddy more.'

Freddy looked down at her and winked.

Tessie felt her heart warm for the love between them.

'Do you know where my mum is?' she asked them both.

Freddy stuck his arm out towards the back door. 'Outside.'

She quickly made her way out to the beer garden, happy to avoid Molly stroking Freddy's leg across the bar.

The heat from the sun burned into her pale skin immediately, and she quickly lowered her head whilst squinting.

Bloody hell, Josephine was right about a heatwave coming around. It's certainly getting hotter. Something else to burn me. I need to stop feeling sorry for myself. There's nothing I can do about it now anyway. The damage is well and truly done. Not that it actually is damage. Not in my opinion. I think I've done a good deed. It's not my fault how other people receive acts of kindness.

She raised a hand to her brow to shade her eyes as she peered over the wooden tables and benches scattered around, looking for her mum.

Elaine was sitting alone at the furthest table, next to the decking area at the back. A large beige parasol was shielding her from the strong sunlight.

Tessie walked along the winding pathway that was lined with tulips and daffodils and sat opposite her mum.

Elaine looked up from her notepad. 'Oh, hello, babe. I'm just checking my to-do list for the fayre tomorrow. Molly's going to help me in the beer tent, so you're free to help out Nate, if you want.'

'He's got Jake helping on his stall.'

Elaine grinned. 'Cheeky bugger. That's because of how many gift baskets Jake sold at Sandly Christmas Market. He knows Jake's good looks pulls in the punters.'

Tessie cleared her throat dramatically. 'Erm, I think you'll find that Nate is also highly attractive. He always gets loads of attention.'

Elaine lowered her pen and raised her eyebrows. 'Yes, well, let's hope he keeps his attention solely on you from now on.'

Tessie frowned with confusion. 'What's that supposed to mean? You make it sound as though he's cheated on me.'

Elaine gave a half-shrug.

Tessie rested her hands on the table. 'Mum, he didn't cheat on me. We were only friends when he started dating. It wasn't any of my business.'

Elaine tutted and made a puffing sound. 'Oh, he knew back then how much you liked him. Any fool could see that. He chose to ignore you and go elsewhere. Now, don't get me wrong, I like Nate, and I love seeing you two together, but I'm just not sure how invested he is in you. That's all I'm saying. I worry you'll get hurt again.'

'Mum, I wasn't into Nate back then. He was just my friend.'

'Some friend. He didn't even believe you about Dana.'

'Are you ever going to let that go?'

Elaine nodded unconvincingly. 'Look, Tess, Nate's lovely. I know it. You know it. Everyone knows it, but I'm your mum, so I'm allowed to worry about what happens to your heart. Technically, it's my heart too. I made it.'

Tessie rolled her eyes.

'It's not just you involved, Tess, it's our Robyn too. Plus, we've got Daisy calling us her grandparents now. I don't want that girl upset either.'

Oh please, don't remind me. I don't know what I'm going to do if Nate ends our relationship over money. The girls will be devastated, and Mum will want to smack him one. I have to tell him. I have to tell her. Oh God, what's she going to say about this? Oh, why have I done this to myself? I know why, and everyone is going to have to just deal with it. Including me.

'Mum, I need to tell you something.' She glanced over her shoulder to see if they were out of earshot.

The customers were chatting happily amongst themselves, and the table closest to them was empty.

'Are you going to tell me you're pregnant?'

'What? No. Mum, just listen. I've done something, and I'm not sure if it's a good thing anymore.'

Elaine leaned across the table. 'Whatever it is, love, we'll sort it. Your dad's very good at covering things up. He'll know what to do. Will the police be paying us a visit?'

Tessie frowned to herself, wondering what exactly her dad had covered up in the past to make him the expert. She knew he looked like a pirate, but she was pretty sure that was where the similarity ended.

'Erm, no. It's nothing like that. I…' She decided not to ask the mass of questions accumulating in her head about her dad. 'I want to tell you something about Pepper Pot Farm.'

Elaine looked intrigued and slightly relieved. 'What about the place?'

'Well, erm, it's…'

Elaine huffed. 'Spit it out, Tess. You don't have to faff around with me.'

Tessie took a deep breath. 'The farmhouse is falling apart, and the business had started to go downhill. I created an online account to advertise the cheese, and the shop is finished and ready to open in the morning. Dolly, next door to the shop, younger Dolly, is over in the bay at the moment sorting out her flat and shop ready for when she moves in and opens up, so she said she'll man the farm shop tomorrow while we're all at the fayre, as she's not ready to sell her own bits yet. I said I'll work in the shop. I can run the Instagram businesses from there as well, and Molly appears to have taken over my shifts here, and Nate will be busy with all the new dairy equipment being installed. Jake's hired people he knows to build everything. He seems to know a lot of people,

170

and the twins are really putting in the extra hours now, and Jake's sending me on a course, and well…'

'You still haven't got to your point.'

'I paid for it all, Mum.'

There was a moment of intense silence, which was rattling Tessie's insides.

'He thinks Jake has loaned him the money,' she added. 'I told Jake to tell him that. I knew I had more chance of saving the farm if Nate thought the money was Jake's.'

Elaine seemed to be mulling over her response. Her exhale sounded exhausted. 'Well, Tess, it's your money. You can do what you like with it.'

Tessie's shoulders slumped. 'It's your money really, Mum. She should have left it to you, not me and her local cats' home.'

Elaine smiled softly. 'You know I would never touch my mother's money. She disowned me for marrying your dad. I haven't lived off that money for years. I would've only given it to charity if she did leave it to me. I didn't want anything from her. She never gave me the love that I needed as a child, and that's all I ever really wanted from her. I found my home and my love with your dad. That money she left you was put in a trust so that you could make your own mind up about it when you were old enough. You've had it sitting there doing nothing for years. I guessed you would have had to make a decision about it one day.'

'I don't know if I've made the right one.'

'What's the main problem here, Tess?'

Tessie knew exactly what it was. 'Pride.'

Elaine nodded. 'Men can be funny about women paying the bills, love. I've always pulled my weight around here, but when I left home, your dad and a few personal items were all I had. He made sure I ate and kept warm. We weren't exactly equal back then, but I pulled my sleeves up, figured out what to do, and joined in with his family. I didn't want to be someone he had to look after. I wanted to be his teammate.'

Tessie warmed inside at the relationship her parents had. She loved the way they were together. The way they still looked at each other after all the years they had spent together. She loved how calm and happy her childhood had been thanks to their love.

Elaine reached over and held her hand. 'If Nate wants you in his life as his partner, then he has to take as well as give. He can't make you afraid to chip in. You shouldn't be afraid to say anything to your partner. You're team players. You work together. It's as simple as that.'

So, why doesn't it feel that way? Why am I so scared to tell him the truth? I know he'll leave me, that's why. He's going to go mad. He won't accept it. He just won't. I can't tell him yet. I'll have to wait till everything is up and running and he can see the turnaround. Maybe he'll be a bit more forgiving when it all works and the farm is back in business. I haven't even figured out how to renovate the farmhouse yet. There's no way he'd let Jake pay for that. The business is one thing, his home another. Oh, Tessie Sparrow, you and your big bloody ideas.

23

Nate

With Nate and Jake serving behind Pepper Pot Farm's stall at the Sandly Craft Fayre, many of the gift baskets had been sold by lunchtime, and mostly to young, eyelash-fluttering ladies who unashamedly offered their phone numbers along with their money.

The springtime fayre was awash with white wooden huts that had vintage bunting draped in zigzags hanging from rooftop to rooftop across wide walkways.

Sellers were offering everything from handmade shopping bags to blown glass ornaments. Arts and crafts filled every nook, with lessons available in many areas such as needlework, photography, and candle making.

There was a flower arranging contest in one large marquee, and local vet Brook Brown was helping with educational talks to children over in the petting area. The Donkey Sanctuary had brought along three of their donkeys to help raise awareness for their charity. All three donkeys wore a straw hat that had a fake flower in its rim and seemed quite happy to allow visitors to stand next to them and have their picture taken.

Face painting and pasta necklace making were side by side with the sweet stall and candy floss machine.

Joey Walker's bespoke lollipops were for sale at the Pepper Pot Farm hut, along with the farm's cheese, eggs, and Josephine's homemade conserves.

Anna had a hut where she was selling local artwork that was normally found in her bookshop and art gallery in Pepper Lane. Her assistant, Scott, was working back at the shop, selling to the visitors who liked to travel from Sandly over to Pepper Bay on the tram. Her hut was directly opposite Nate's, as requested by Jake so that he could keep an eye on her, as her pregnancy rendered her tired quite often.

Joey was in the hut next to Anna's. Her homemade baked goods filled the area with a sweet and chocolatey aroma.

Josh was on duty to help sell the cakes for one hour and then help sell the paintings with Anna for the next hour throughout the day.

Josephine was sitting at the back of the farm's hut, half asleep in a deckchair, enjoying the gentle waft of air from the fan that blew her way every few seconds. Nate didn't even bother asking his grandmother to help serve. Although, she did cut up some cheese samples at the start of the day and offered to read the palms of all the testers who stepped forward.

Nate was missing Tessie. He knew she was helping Elaine in the beer tent, but he also knew that Molly was over there, so he did wonder why she hadn't been to see him.

Dolly was running his new shop for the day, and the twins were helping to install all the new equipment up at the farm. Ruby was in Edith's Tearoom, with Molly's little sister Kerri as her helper for the day. Robyn and Daisy were pottering around the fayre with Scruff and Max, and Ed and Freddy were busy in The Ugly Duckling. Even Freddy's dad, Wes, was giving boat rides around the bay.

Everyone was organised and busy for the day, but Nate was sure that Tessie would have popped over at one point. It was lunchtime already, and he hadn't seen her or their daughters all day. Every time he looked over at his sister she was either serving a customer or wrapped up in Josh's arms, and their closeness made him miss Tessie even more.

He picked up his bottle of water and took a large gulp. The heatwave had fully kicked in, and the sun was scorching. He was glad of the shade of the hut and the coolness coming from the cold counter housing the cheese, but the hot air was still surrounding him. He wiped his brow and checked that his grandmother didn't look overheated.

'Hello, Nate.'

Before he had even turned around, he knew who it was. His shoulders slumped, his heart rate accelerated, and his eyes lost all trace of a shine.

'Dana.' His tone was flat. He wasn't greeting her.

Dana Blake flashed her smirk of a smile his way. Her tall lean figure stood straight with confidence.

Nate was glad his grandmother was asleep behind him. He knew that Josephine would hit the roof if she saw the woman who had tried to sell their farm from under them. She'd probably throw another hex Dana's way too.

Jake glared sideways before turning his eyes towards his brother across the walkway.

Josh was laughing about something with Joey, and both Jake and Nate knew it was only a matter of seconds before Joey caught sight of Dana.

'How's business?' asked Dana, almost sounding as though she actually cared.

Nate took a calming breath. 'Go away, Dana.' He made sure he kept his voice low. He didn't want a scene.

Jake had finally made eye contact with Josh, and Josh immediately tried his best to keep Joey facing away from the aisle.

Dana raised her perfectly drawn eyebrows in amusement. 'Surely I can still say the odd hello to you, Nate.'

'I'd rather you didn't say anything to me, Dana.'

She gave a slight huff. 'We had a tiny misunderstanding five years ago. I've let it go. Don't you think it's about time you did the same?'

Are you kidding? A tiny misunderstanding! I was going to marry you. You were just plotting to sell my home. You have no idea how much I actually hate you. Joey's going to see her in a minute. Go away.

He tightened his lips and clenched his jaw. 'Just go away, Dana.'

She leaned a little closer to the counter dividing them. 'I was thinking, maybe we could grab a coffee and talk things through.' She added a softer smile. One that used to tug at his heart strings once upon a time. 'We used to be friends, after all. I'm sure we can rebuild.'

Rebuild? What is it with everyone wanting to rebuild lately?

'All I want is for you to stop talking to me, stay out of my life for good, and never come near me again.'

Nate felt quite pleased with his calm attitude towards her. He was pretty sure she had now received the message loud and clear. He could see Jake standing over the other side of the hut, trying hard not to interfere, and he knew that Josh was keeping Joey occupied.

Everyone, relax. I've got this. She's about to leave any moment.

Dana pouted at him. 'I'd like to make amends, Nate. Surely you would allow me that much. I know how to make you smile. You know I do. Don't you miss that about me at least?'

The memory of her in his bed turned his stomach. It was something he had chosen to forget a long time ago. He had taken the bed they had shared and set fire to it out the back of the house. He knew at the time he was being a tad dramatic, but it felt good to watch it burn. He had no idea back then that years later he would be sharing a bed with Tessie Sparrow. He was so glad he had bought a new one. He was so glad Tessie was the only woman to have slept in that bed.

'He doesn't miss anything about you, Dana,' said Tessie.

All eyes looked down the walkway to see her standing there with her arms tightly folded across her chest. Nate swallowed hard. He was sure Tessie would lunge at Dana at any moment. Tessie didn't move. Her expression wasn't readable to anyone.

'Ah, the trouble maker.' Dana glared over at her.

Tessie didn't respond.

Jake did. 'You're the trouble maker.'

Dana rolled her eyes his way. Her face alive with sarcasm and bitterness. 'Jealous, Jake, because you're the only man here I haven't kissed?'

Joey spun around. She stared straight at Dana, then tried to leap over the counter, but Josh quickly wrapped his arms around her tightly, and he wasn't about to let go anytime soon. 'Let me go, Josh.'

Nate started to feel his temper bubble. 'Why don't you just go away, Dana. No one wants you here.'

Dana gave an uncaring shrug of the shoulders. 'All I did was say hello to you, Nate. I was trying to make amends. I asked after your business, one that I hear Jake is paying for.' She paused, glanced at Tessie, and then looked back at Nate. 'Or is he?' She blinked slowly whilst smirking.

What does that mean?

177

Nate saw Tessie take a step forward. His face turned ashen and panic-stricken all of a sudden.

Anna had finished reading her book. She noticed the standoff between the huts. She quickly stood to catch Jake's attention and then passed out.

'Anna!' shouted Jake, vaulting the counter.

All eyes were on him. Dana instantly became invisible, as Nate, Tessie, Joey, and Josh quickly surrounded Anna's stall.

Jake was on the floor with her, holding her in his arms.

Anna groaned. 'Ooh, everything went black, and I felt sick.'

Nate quickly went back to his own stall, grabbed a fresh bottle of cold water from beneath the counter, and handed it over to Jake.

'Just small sips,' said Joey, sitting by her side.

'I'm going to fetch the doctor.' Josh looked down the walkway. 'He's in the first aid tent.'

Anna slowly sat up. 'I'm okay. I probably just need some lunch.'

Joey pointed at Nate. 'Grab a cookie from my hut.'

Nate did as he was told, and Anna soon found a giant chocolate chip cookie shoved towards her mouth.

'Nibble on that until we get you some lunch.' Joey smiled warmly at her.

Nate looked down at Jake to see that he was as white as a ghost. 'She's all right, mate. It's this heat and the pregnancy, but Anna's right, lunch would be good right about now.'

'Spiky Rick's got a stall here, serving cold pasta and salad dishes,' said Tessie, pointing down the walkway. 'All freshly made this morning in his restaurant.'

'Ooh, that sounds nice.' Anna licked her dry lips. 'I like his food.'

Jake held the water to her lips. 'Take some more, Anna, and I'll get you some lunch.'

'I'll go,' said Tessie, shooting off.

Nate felt in awc of the way Jake and Anna were looking into each other's eyes. He knew that look. He openly shared that with Tessie now. Joey leaned back and twisted the fan so that it was wafting over Anna.

'I think it's time we went home, Anna,' said Jake quietly. His voice clearly broken.

Anna smiled at him. 'Help me up to the chair, Jake. I feel much better now. I probably shouldn't have got up so fast in this heat.'

Jake slowly lifted her into her seat and knelt by her side.

'Nice cookie, Jo.' Anna nibbled away.

Joey smiled. 'I'll get you some fresh orange juice from the juice stall.'

'Yes, good idea.' Jake nodded.

Joey stepped outside the hut and then leaned over the counter. 'Josh is coming with the doc.'

Nate opened the hut door for the old doctor to enter. 'We think it's because she's pregnant, Doc.'

Doctor Tully opened his black bag and politely asked Jake to take a step back so that he could do some checks on Anna.

Nate waved Jake over to him and placed his hand on his shoulder from across the counter. 'It's all right, Jake. Everything's okay now.' He watched some colour come back into Jake's cheeks.

Tessie was soon at his side, holding the food, and Joey was at his other side with the juice by the time the doctor had given Anna a clean bill of health.

Nate watched everyone relax as Anna happily tucked into tomato and basil penne pasta and salad. For the first time since she had fainted, he glanced around to see if Dana was still about.

Thank God she's gone.

He looked down at Tessie as he felt her snuggle under his arm. He kissed her head of curls and smiled inwardly.

'Right.' Joey looked around at everyone. 'I think I'll get us all some pasta and juice, and then we can pack up early and head up to Starlight and watch a film together, and Anna can put her feet up.'

Nate smiled at his sister taking charge. 'In that case, I'm going to find the girls. They're around here somewhere, probably getting Scruff's face painted. Probably your dog too, Anna.'

'Oh, poor Max,' she mumbled through a mouthful of food.

Tessie looked up at Nate. 'You help Joey with the food. I'll find the girls and bring them back here. You'd better get them something to eat as well.'

His heart warmed as she pulled him down so that she could kiss his cheek.

'I love you, Nate Walker,' she whispered in his ear.

For the first time in a long while, Nate felt that everything was finally going right with his life.

24

Tessie

Tessie sat up in bed watching Nate get changed into his pyjamas. Her shoulders were slumped and her face matched. She hadn't enjoyed the fayre at all this year. She had too much on her mind. She was worried about talking to Nate so much, she had started to avoid him. She knew that he had an idea that something was wrong because she wasn't usually the quiet type. When she had finally decided to go and see how he was getting on, Dana Blake had made an appearance. Seeing her flirting with Nate and trying to tempt him back into her life only made the day worse.

I still don't know how I didn't just smack her one straight in her smug face. Maybe I do know. Maybe I'm just like her. Plotting and scheming behind Nate's back. I now have secrets and lies. Did Dana know? She looked at me strangely as though she knew my secret. She can't know. Only Jake and I know, and Anna, of course. I'm so glad Anna is okay. I remember feeling faint a couple of times when I was carrying Robyn.

'It was nice tonight, all of us up at Starlight.' Nate climbed into bed. 'I'm going to have to sort out the old barn tomorrow. Get it ready for the wedding. Anna can't wait. She's really excited. I'm glad she's okay. She scared the living daylights out of me.'

Tessie forced a smile. 'Yeah, she scared us all, but she bounced back pretty quickly, so that was good.' She watched Nate faffing about with his pillows.

I know he's going to mention Dana in a minute. He'll say something. I know he will. I'll be surprised if he doesn't.
She looked at the back cover of the book Anna had given her to read.
Tess of the D'Urbervilles. Hope you have a better story than mine, Tess. A happy ending, at least. I wonder what someone would write about me? Woman uses inheritance to save her man but doesn't tell him. Ever! How about, barmaid thinks she's an expert dairy farmer after eating a piece of cheese. The secrets and lies of a farmer's wife. Now, that sounds like an interesting read. How about, Tess, the prize idiot. Sounds more like me. Tess of Pepper Pot Farm. The story of how one lone woman destroys a family, a farm, and a man. Oh my God, I'm the villain. That's not right. I was only trying to help.

Nate's fidgeting was starting to get on her nerves. She put her book down on the side and turned to face him.

His gentle eyes slowly rolled her way. 'Tess, about Dana today…'

'There's nothing to say, Nate. She lives in Sandly. We're bound to bump into her from time to time. It can't be helped. At least now she knows you don't want her talking to you. At least, I think she got the message.'

'I made it loud and clear. I think she just wanted to cause trouble. She gets off on things like that. She probably thinks I've suddenly got a load of money. I don't know what I ever saw in her. Biggest regret of my life.'

Tessie sighed. 'Well, at least she's no longer in your life. I dread to think what kind of impact she would have had on our Daisy growing up.'

'Please don't say that. I hate that I brought her into Daisy's life.'

I hate that you did that too. Of all the people you could have picked, you chose her. Everyone knows how vile she is, but not you. You must have been the only person on the Isle of Wight who didn't see what she was made of. I'll never get my head around it. You'll never know how worried I was for Daisy back then with her around. Do you know what, I'm going to tell you something I've not told you before.

'Daisy used to phone me every day back then, you know. She always wanted to come over and spend time with us at the pub. I couldn't give her everything she needed back then. It killed me. I knew she was sad, but I didn't have the authority to involve myself. I'm glad those days are behind us, but that's the main reason that woman winds me up.'

Nate lowered his eyes. 'I didn't know that about Daisy. I wish I did. She never told me she was unhappy. She never said she was calling you so much. I hate those days, and I hate Dana too. I was so proud of you today. You know, not fighting with her. You don't normally hold your temper around her.'

'She's not worth my energy. Besides, we had Anna to worry about when she fainted.'

He breathed out a laugh. 'I thought Jake was going to pass out at one point.'

'He does worry about her so much.'

Nate snuggled back into his plump pillow. 'I don't know why. Anna's pretty tough. She's been through a lot on her own. I think she'd survive anything. Remember when she was trapped in the snowstorm last year?'

'Yes, it was a good thing you found her and got her warm quickly.'

'She scared the living daylights out of me then. I'm starting to think that woman will be the death of me.'

Tessie smiled. 'Poor Anna.'

183

'She bounced back quickly from that ordeal as well. If it were down to Jake, he'd keep her wrapped in cotton wool.'

'I think he just loves her so much, and he doesn't want her to feel as though she's fighting alone anymore. She's never going to be alone again. She definitely has a teammate now.'

She watched Nate turn his head and smile warmly at her.

'It is nice to have a teammate.'

Oh God, you're going to hate me when I tell you the truth about the money. You won't look at me like that then. You won't see a teammate. You'll just see another liar. I have to tell you. I can't let this go on any longer. It's not like you'll strip the farm of all the new equipment and leave it on the drive for me to take away. You'll be angry, but I think you'll still carry on using it all. I hope. How do I approach this? How shall I start? I don't want to start. Mum's right. I shouldn't be afraid to speak to my partner about stuff. I shouldn't be afraid to help him out of a mess. Oh, but this is Nate, and he can be a right grumpy old sod when he wants to be. Plus, he has far too much pride for his own good. Take a breath, Tess. You've got this. Tell him now. He can just swallow it. Don't let him fight you. We're a team. I'm going to hit him with that.

Nate leaned over and kissed her lips, setting off a flurry of butterflies.

Tessie found herself rendered useless for a moment.

Wake up, Tess. It's time to talk.

'Nate,' she mumbled against his kiss.

'Shh!' he mumbled back. 'I don't want to talk. I want to make love to you. Every single part of you. I love you, Tess.'

Tessie felt her body weaken as he pulled her closer towards his warmth.

Oh God, Nate. I love you so much. Don't let me go. Please, don't ever let me go.

His kiss heated as his hands slid down her body. His lips moved to her neck, and Tessie wrapped her arms around his shoulders, reaching up and running her fingers through his hair.

She couldn't allow herself to think. All she could do was feel. She was feeling him. His love. His need for her. She blocked the guilt that tried to surface.

He's making love to me because he doesn't know I've betrayed him. If he knew, I wouldn't be in his bed.

His mouth was working its way over her body, and she couldn't fight off the rush of excitement and tingling sensation that his loving touch was creating.

She placed her hands on his head and arched her back. Her breath let out his name as he kissed inside her thigh.

Oh, Nate. I need to stop you, but I can't. I can't move away from your touch. I want you so much. This isn't fair. What I'm doing with you is wrong. False pretences. I'm lying to you even more. God, I love you so much. Don't stop. I need you. I need to feel you. Please don't hate me. I love you. Don't cry. Don't you dare cry, Tess.

It was the first time that Tessie had felt there was something wrong with their lovemaking. It was because of her secret. The traitor in her was stopping her from fully relaxing into his hold, but he had a hold of her, and he wasn't stopping, and she didn't want him to. She surrendered to her need for him.

Nate kissed along her body, making his way back up to her neck. He carefully lowered himself over her and told her how much he loved her.

Tessie's thoughts disappeared as she melted beneath the man she loved with every fibre of her being.

My beautiful Nate. I have waited for you for so long. Loving you in silence from a distance. Always keeping you close to my heart. I often dreamed of times like this, wrapped around your naked body, your hands in mine. You loving me back. I don't want this to ever end. Nate stilled. He looked deeply into her eyes. *Please don't look at me that way. I don't deserve the love in your eyes. I don't deserve this affection. Not while I'm keeping things from you. I want you so much, Nate. Stay with me forever. Please understand. I can't lose you. Not now.*

She wanted to cry, but he kissed her, and the only thing she could concentrate on was loving him. All that mattered in that moment was they were together.

If this is the last time you touch me, I want to remember every second.

She tightened her grip around his body.

25

Nate

Nate stood in the middle of the old barn, looking around him. He smiled to himself at the memory of his dad working there. There wasn't much life left in the old place. It housed bales of straw and hay and a few farming tools that didn't get much use. Everything had been shifted to another area of the farm. The once main building had little purpose, only memories.

Daniel Walker was a tall burly farmer who loved two things in life. Pepper Pot Farm and his family. Although, he dedicated most of his time to his farm. He worked long hours and spoke more to his cows than his mother, wife, and two kids who lived with him.

Myrtle was his favourite cow. She had adopted him from the moment he had helped bring her into the world. Myrtle followed him everywhere whenever she could. She was often found in the barn standing by his side whilst he worked.

Dan had been raised by his father not to pet the cattle. They were stock and were to be treated as such. When they were no longer of use to the farm, they were slaughtered, so attachments were not good for anyone.

Once Dan's father passed away and the farm was handed down to his only son, Dan never saw any of his cows slaughtered again. He found his peace in his work. He loved his family, but he never quite felt he fitted in with them as much as he did with the cows. He always found Myrtle, with her human-like ways, a good listener in times of need. Even as a child, he preferred animals to people.

Everything changed for him the day his wife suddenly left home. She gave no warning and left him the saddest letter he had ever read. His heart broke into a million pieces. He knew she wasn't well. She had changed soon after their youngest was born. He didn't know how to help her, so he stayed away, thinking that space would give her what she needed to heal. It always worked for him.

Being a single parent who worked long hours wasn't something he thought he would be able to cope with, but he somehow managed to juggle the two. His mum was a huge help, and he was always grateful for her. He found Nate to be the easy child. He would be at his side more than Myrtle, wanting to learn everything about dairy farming.

His daughter, Joey, was a worry for him. He wished so hard that her mother would return just for her sake. He tried to give her everything he thought a young girl would need, and he poured extra love her way. He knew she wasn't interested in cows and chickens. She loved the cat, but that was about it. He was pleased when she took an interest in baking and started hanging around Edith Reynolds down in the tea shop. The sparkle in Joey's eyes helped him breathe. Both his children had found their passion.

Nate laughed to himself at the memory of his dad catching Joey and Josh kissing in the barn. They were only sixteen, and Dan wasn't best pleased at first.

Josh Reynolds came to Pepper Bay every summer, and every summer he seemed to grow closer to Joey, so Dan started to get used to seeing him hanging around the farm.

Dan had a soft spot for Josh because he knew that the lad had lost both his parents in a car accident back when the boy was ten. He knew that Joey related to Josh because of that.

188

Neither of them had a mother. Josh Reynolds had a completely different life to his Joey. He was the grandson of a millionaire. She was a farmer's daughter. It often amazed Dan how they seemed to effortlessly connect. It would make him wish he'd had more of a connection with his wife.

Nate glanced up at the top level of the barn. His thoughts turned to Tori. They would sit up there and talk about their future. All the things that they would do. She always wanted to marry him, and he agreed they would one day. He could hear her voice.

'When we're older, Nate, we can have a hundred kids and a million more cows. We'll have the biggest wedding Pepper Bay has ever seen, and we'll have the biggest farm in England. Everyone will wish they were us. That would make me happy.'

'I'm happy with just you and me and this piece of straw we're sitting on. I don't need anything else, Tor.'

'We can have more than a piece of straw, Nate. We can have the world.'

'You are my world. I love you, Victoria Evans. You're all I'll ever need.'

'I'm not going anywhere without you, Nate Walker. We're going to be together for life.'

He had curled his little finger around hers, and they had shaken on their deal to be together forever.

Nate shook his head slightly as he stared at the straw. He sighed deeply at how innocent and easy life seemed back when he was a teenager. He had no idea that by the time he was twenty-two his dad would be dead and his girlfriend would be pregnant.

Every responsibility had dropped so heavily upon his shoulders at once. He was barely breathing back then.

One day, his best friend Henry had taken him for a walk along the beach to help clear his head. The stretch between Sandly and Pepper Bay was often used when the tide was out. The rocks that fell from the cliff gave no warning. Nate could do nothing to save Henry.

Nate lowered his eyes from the upper level of the barn to stare down at his hands. He could see Henry's blood. Thirteen years later, and he could still see it smeared into his skin.

I'm sorry, Henry. It's my fault you were on the beach. You must hate me so much, especially now I'm with Tess, and Robyn is calling me Dad. I don't know what to say to you. If you can somehow hear my thoughts, just know how sorry I am for how life turned out for us. I didn't want it to be this way. Never in my wildest dreams did I think that my life would be this way. I never looked at Tess in that way when we were growing up. She was just my friend. Tori's best friend. Your girl. I wish I knew what you had to say about this. Just know that I love Tess and Robyn so much, and I promise to keep them safe. As strange as this might sound, I do wish you were here, Henry. I wish you were here too, Dad.

He took a calming breath to ease his weary soul. He glanced over his shoulder at the empty doorway and visualised Myrtle's big head poking in. The thought made him smile.

He walked across the barn and climbed the wooden ladder. He sat upon a clump of straw and swung his legs over the side and watched one of the chickens wandering down below. He knew it was Polly. Daisy had named them all. Daisy loved the animals like family. She would have adored Myrtle. He had told her all the old stories and bought her a cuddly toy that resembled the black-and-white cow.

He flopped back and rolled away from the edge and closed his eyes. He reached out his fingers and picked up a piece of straw to twiddle with. He felt peaceful, content. He didn't spend a lot of time surrounded by silence. There was always some form of background noise in his life. He liked the quiet moments when he could let go and not think too much. Something came to mind. There was someone he wanted to talk to. He opened his eyes and glanced up at the roof.

It's me again. Nate Walker from Pepper Bay. I want to say thank you for everything that's happened to help save my farm. That's if you had a hand in it. I did ask for help. I've now got help. I wasn't expecting anything, if I'm honest. I still feel a bit weird about it all. I have a shop, new equipment, new buildings. I'm flashing my body on Instagram, along with the twins. Although, they're happy about it. Our cheese will be sold in every Café Diths around the world. I'm about to hire more staff. I can't keep up. It doesn't feel real. I want to say thanks for Tessie Sparrow as well. I thought I knew true love, but I didn't. Not till she became a part of my life. I really am grateful.

His thoughts were interrupted by the Hart twins talking outside the barn.

Most people couldn't tell the difference between Liam and Lee Hart, but Nate could. He even knew which one was talking.

'How did you find that out?' asked Lee.

'One of the contractors knew. I think he saw something he shouldn't have,' said Liam.

Nate frowned in amusement.

What have they found out?

'If that's true, Liam, wait till Nate finds out. He's going to hit the roof.'

Nate was no longer amused.

Find out what?

'I think it's lovely what she did,' said Liam. 'I like Tess. She's good for him. He should thank her.'

'He won't.'

'This farm is on the up and up now, thanks to her. Our jobs are safe and a lot easier now we have up-to-date equipment to work with. Even the cows look happier.'

'I know, Liam, but you know how proud Nate is. When he finds out Tess paid for all this, well, let's just say I wouldn't want to be in her shoes.'

Nate felt his blood boil.

Tess paid for all this? She's been lying to me? No. They've got this wrong. One of the contractors misread something or heard wrong. Tess wouldn't do this. Jake wouldn't do this to me. Why would she use her grandmother's money on the farm anyway? Tess knows I wouldn't accept her money. She knows... Wait, she knows exactly how I would react. She's cooked this whole thing up with Jake so that I would use her money. She bought everything. Did she make Jake sell my cheese in his shops too? Did she make me out to be some sort of charity case? What has she done? How did she think this would make me feel? They all knew. They were all plotting and laughing behind my back, just like Dana. Thinking I'm pathetic, just like Dana thought. How could she do this to me? I thought she loved me. She's made me a laughing stock. Everyone on the Isle of Wight will be talking about me. There goes the poor loser Nate, who can't afford to keep his own business or family. I need to speak to her. Now.

26

Tessie

Tessie could hear Nate yelling her name through the house. He didn't sound too happy. She walked to the top of the stairs and peered down. 'I'm up here.'

He stopped at the bottom and glared up at her.

What's the matter with him?

'Is it true that you paid for the farm shop and the new buildings for the cows and cheese and bloody well everything?'

Oh my God, he knows. How does he know?

'Who told you?'

His nostrils flared. 'So, it is true.'

Keep calm, Tess. You knew this day would come. Just talk to him. Explain. It's not like you can attempt to pull off some sort of spectacular lie right now. He knows.

She took one step down. 'Nate, I was going to tell you.'

'Oh yeah, when?' He didn't wait for an answer. 'Have you seen what's going on out there? I don't feel as though I even know how to make cheese anymore with all that fancy-schmancy, shiny equipment. Everywhere I look there's stainless steel, conveyor belts, and wires. I need to bring in extra milk from Jason's farm to cover demand, which means having a proper driveway if I'm going to have tankers rolling up and down every day. I haven't even started to interview anyone to work here, and I haven't got enough cheese to see us through to the next batch. Do you even know how long it takes to make cheese? Do you know how much extra work you have given me? I didn't need your help. All you've done is put extra weight on my shoulders and make me look like a useless idiot to everyone. Well, thanks a bunch, Tess.'

Tessie swallowed down the hurt and rolled back the tears forming. She could feel her body trembling with agitation.

He had better stop shouting at me.

Nate wasn't finished ranting. 'Did you tell Jake to sell my cheese in his shops?'

She went to speak, but he cut her off.

'I thought he was my friend. I thought you were my friend. Well, I don't need pity from the likes of either of you. You both stood there and lied to my face. Thought it was funny, did you? Stupid Nate won't find out.'

Tessie could feel her temper rising.

He'd better zip it before I lose it.

'Now, you listen here, Nate Walker. No one felt sorry for you. We were just trying to help save Pepper Pot Farm. I knew you wouldn't take my money, so I asked Jake to pretend it was his because I had more chance of you agreeing to his loan terms.'

'What loan terms?' he snapped. 'He didn't give me any terms. He just told me to pay him back whenever I felt like it. Now I know why.'

'It's my money, and you're my partner, so I can spend it on our family business if I want to.'

Tessie realised she was shouting louder than him. She took a breath, not wanting to be angry. She needed to remain in control of herself. She knew how fiery she could be if she let loose.

Look at his face. He hates me. I've never seen him look at me like that. Wait, yes I have. The day I told him that Dana Blake planned to sell his farm without him knowing. He hated me that day as well.

194

'It's not your business. It's mine.' His shout made her jump.

Tessie felt a punch to the gut. For the past five years he had always used words like *ours* and *us*. He had included her in his life.

'So much for us being a team, Nate.'

He let out a sarcastic laugh. 'Ha! Team. Don't make me laugh. After the stunt you've just pulled. Where was the teamwork in that? You did everything behind my back.'

Tessie could feel her body heat. 'Well, I wouldn't have to if you weren't so stubborn.'

'I have a right to refuse your money. That doesn't make me stubborn.'

You are stubborn. And a big fat pain in the backside when it comes to money.

'Well, Nate, you can stick the money and *your* business where the sun doesn't shine. I'm going home, and I'll leave you to it. Sorry I gave you work.'

She watched his foot move to the first step. His breathing was heavy, his face flushed, and lips tightly pursed. She wasn't quite sure what he was going to do or say next, but she wasn't about to give him the chance.

I've had enough of this. He can get stuffed.

She quickly made her way down towards him, slipped on one of Robyn's shoes that was on a step, twisted her ankle, and fell down the stairs.

'Tess,' shouted Nate, catching her at the bottom.

Ow! That bloody hurt.

'Tess, are you all right?'

She pushed his hands away from fussing over her body and tried to stand. Her adrenaline was pumping, and her hip hurt so much.

'I'm fine. Get off me. I don't need your help.'

Nate didn't move. 'Tess, have you hurt yourself?'
She stood, winced, and held her hip. 'I'm fine. Get off. Stop touching me.'
How many times have I told Robyn about leaving her flipping shoes everywhere!
'You're not fine. You've hurt yourself,' he said softly.
Tessie slapped his hand away and proceeded to put on her shoes.
'Where are you going?' His voice went back to snappy and cold.
Away from you.
'Home.'
'You're hurt.'
'I'm fine.'
She stormed out the door, and the strong sunlight hit her face, causing her to squint and lower her head.
'At least let me drive you.'
She didn't look back. 'I don't need your help, just like you don't need mine. So, get lost, Walker.' She tried her hardest not to limp her way down the long driveway towards Pepper Lane. She wanted to pretend that her hip was perfectly fine, so she tightened her lips and continued with her powerwalk.
What a cheek! His business. Extra work. Most people would be grateful to have their business take off. To make more money. I saved that farm. His farm. That's right, Nate Walker, your farm. Yours. All yours. Ouch! My hip is killing me. Oh my God, it is so hot. I should have brought a hat, and a bottle of water. Why did I have to fall down the stairs? Talk about embarrassing. Who does he think he is talking to me like that? I'm not taking that. I didn't take that. I left. Yeah, good for you, Tess.

She reached Pepper Lane and had a quick look to see if he had followed her.

He hadn't.

She slowed and placed her hand on her bruised hip and started to hobble along the road, heading downhill to the pub. *I don't know who he thinks he is sometimes. Shouting at me. I'm not allowing that sort of behaviour. Henry never shouted at me. Henry wasn't like that at all. Oh, Henry, will you walk with me? Hold my hand. I know you're there. I want to lean on your shoulder. I want you to hold me. Tell me everything will be all right. Everything was perfect with you. Why did Nate have to shout at me? He really hates me now. I just wanted to help him. Do you think I did the wrong thing? Maybe I went about it the wrong way. He has serious trust issues after Dana Blake, which is fair enough after what she did. He trusted me though. He didn't when I tried to tell him what Dana was up to. Oh no. He was on her side back then.*

She stopped at a stile and sat for a minute, leaning slightly away from the pain.

It's not like Nate doesn't know what to do with those new contraptions. The twins know how to use everything, and they're the ones doing the interviews and the training. They take a lot of the weight from him. He overreacted, in my opinion. I guess it was a bit of a shock, but still. He had no right to talk to me like that. He can shove it. I know I don't know anything about making cheese, but the twins do, and they told Jake everything that was needed. Unlike Nate, they don't live in the dark ages. Jake arranged everything. I just signed the cheques. Oh, Henry, what have I done?

She pulled out her phone from the pocket of her dress and sent a text to Mike over in London.

'I'm going to ask him if I can have that taster day now. Well, actually it's more of a taster week for my course. I was going to do it after the wedding, but if I go now, I'll have some breathing space from all this farm business. When I get back, I'll have the wedding to keep me busy. The girls will be okay for a week. They're at school mostly anyway, and I'll get them to help Dolly and Josh down in the shop on the two Saturdays I'll be away. That's if Mike agrees. What do you think, Henry? Good idea?'

Tessie looked glumly down at her phone, as Mike had immediately replied with a thumbs-up and *ready when you are* text.

Oh, well, that's that then. Looks like I'm going to London. Let's see if I can leave in the morning. I'll have to call Jake.

'Hello, Jake. I've just arranged with Mike to do my taster week. I'll be leaving in the morning. Thought I'd let you know.'

'Sure, Tess. I'll have the helicopter ready.'

He makes it sound as though we're in the FBI or something.

'No need. I can get the ferry and train.'

'Don't be daft, Tess. Frank will fly you there tomorrow, and I'll have a car waiting for you at the other end. I'll see you in the morning, and I'll give you my key to the apartment.'

'Thanks, Jake.'

You make everything so simple.

She got up, groaned, and started to limp her way down the picturesque setting of Pepper Lane, passing the pale-yellow thatched home called Lemon Drop Cottage.

'Tess, is everything all right?'

'Not really. Nate found out I paid for everything. It didn't go down well. I need a break, and this week away will do me the world of good.'

198

She could hear Jake breathing down the phone. It was obvious he didn't know what to say next.

'Tess, are you sure this is the right time for you to be away?'

She nodded, even though she knew he couldn't see her. 'Trust me, Jake. It's the perfect time.'

27

Nate

Robyn and Daisy were eating their breakfast before school. Neither of them had said much all morning or the night before.

Tessie didn't come home yesterday. She didn't call. The girls didn't ask where she was last night. They haven't said a word all morning, neither did Gran when she was in here earlier. Something doesn't feel right.

Nate was clock-watching. 'You'll be late for school if your mother doesn't hurry up and get here.'

'Doesn't matter.' Robyn shrugged. 'It's Friday.'

'Every day matters.' Nate shook his head at her.

'She's not taking us anyway.' Daisy glanced towards the kitchen door. 'Josh is. He'll be here in a minute.'

Nate could feel his nerves rattle. 'Why is Josh taking you to school?'

Daisy looked over at him sheepishly. 'Because Mum went to London about an hour ago.'

Robyn quietly left the table, put her empty cereal bowl in the sink, and made her way to the front door.

Nate steadied his breathing, as he could feel his heart pumping. He kept his voice low. 'Why has your mum gone to London?'

Daisy gave an unconvincing shrug as she stood. 'She has that taster week for her course.'

'That's not till after the wedding.'

Daisy put her bowl in the sink on top of Robyn's. 'She moved it.'

He kept his eyes on his daughter. 'She didn't tell me.'

'She probably thought you would shout at her again.'

Nate's mouth gaped as Daisy quietly walked out of the kitchen.

'Josh is here,' called out Robyn.

Nate went to speak but the front door slammed shut. He closed his mouth.

Josephine entered the kitchen and started to clear up the breakfast things.

Nate sat in a chair and silently watched her, waiting for her to have her say on the matter.

Josephine kept quiet, which was unusual for her.

'Say something, Gran. You know you want to.'

She shrugged and started to wash up.

Nate huffed. 'I don't know why everyone's got the hump with me. I'm the victim here. I was the one who was lied to. They tricked me. I have a right to be angry.'

Josephine scoffed. 'Victim, son? Little dramatic, don't you think?'

Nate unravelled his clenched fists and started to fidget his feet under the table. 'I can't believe she just took off.'

'I can.'

Nate sighed loudly.

Yeah, well, I don't need her. She can keep her secrets and lies. It's only a week. It's not like I'll miss her in that time. I need a break from her anyway. She doesn't realise how much she has hurt me. This is a good thing. I'll be okay.

'Best thing that's ever happened to you, that girl,' said Josephine, still leaning over the sink.

Nate slumped on the inside.

'Young Dolly and Josh are going to look after the shop till Tessie gets back, and the girls are doing shifts on Saturday, thanks to Tessie. You can just worry about yourself.' Josephine dried her hands on a green tea towel.

Nate watched his grandmother leave.

Well, maybe I will.

He flopped his chin down into his hand and just stared at the emptiness of the doorway.

The front door opened and Joey walked in. She kicked off her shoes, slid her feet into a pair of cream slippers, and made her way into the kitchen. She placed down a basket of homemade cinnamon swirls.

'Eat one of these. It'll cheer you up.'

He rolled his taupe eyes to meet her matching pair. 'How do you know I need cheering up?'

'Tessie left for London first thing. So, I know.'

'Bloody hell, did everyone know but me?'

Joey went to the sink to wash her hands. 'You would have known too if you didn't shout at her. Actually, she'd still be here if you didn't overreact.'

Nate turned sharply to her. 'Did you know about her paying for everything?'

Joey shook her head as she joined him at the old, large, pine table. 'Nope.'

He picked up a pastry and stared at it.

'I thought it was a lovely thing she did, Nate.'

His flat expression faced her way. 'You didn't think it was lovely when Josh paid for everything at Honeybee Cottage. You wanted to use your money. You even had the hump about him giving you the place.'

'That's different.'

'No, it's not. Plus, look how much Tess has paid out on this place. It's way more than Josh gave you. Flashing your money around doesn't solve problems.'

Joey giggled. 'It kind of did solve yours.'

'It has given me a ton of work.'

'It's given you a wonderful opportunity to make this small family business into something big and amazing.'

'Do you know how much cheese we are going to make now?'

Joey smiled and bit into a cinnamon swirl. 'A lot.'

Nate put his pastry down and got up to make a cup of tea. 'I don't think the girls are talking to me. Well, not properly.'

'You know, you could ring Tess and apologise.'

He glanced over his shoulder as he slammed the kettle down. 'Why do I have to apologise? Why is no one allowing me the right to be angry about this?'

Joey swallowed her mouthful of food. 'You have every right to be angry about being lied to, but it wasn't a bad lie. Tessie just knew you wouldn't accept help from her. I'm still surprised you took it from Jake.'

'I only did that because I asked for help and the next minute he showed up with help on offer. I felt obligated.'

Joey frowned in amusement. 'Who did you ask to help you?'

Nate rolled his eyes to the ceiling.

She followed his stare. 'Really?'

He turned back to the kettle. 'Worked, didn't it.'

'Well, in that case, it really doesn't matter who the help came from. If you really didn't want any, you shouldn't have asked.'

'I didn't know it would come with a clause.'

Joey laughed. 'You always have to read the small print, Nate.'

He sat by her side and gently nudged her arm with his own. 'I feel rotten for shouting at Tess. You should have seen her face. She gave it back to me though. She was shouting louder than me in the end. Then she slipped and fell down the stairs. My heart flipped. I know she hurt herself, but she wouldn't let me near her. She stormed out.'

'You're not the only one who can get angry, Nate. You know what she's like when she gets fired up. You have to get a grip on your temper too. You don't realise how intimidating you look when you're mad. People don't know that your bark's worse than your bite.'

'Tessie does. She knows every part of me. She also knew that what she did would anger me, that's why she kept quiet, but that's no way to have a relationship, Jo.'

'Oh, I know that. Things will calm down for you both. This week away will do you both good. Help clear the air.'

Nate slowly shook his head. 'I'm not so sure it will, Jo. You don't know what I said to her.'

Joey narrowed her eyes and clenched her teeth. 'What did you say?'

'She said she was helping our business. I told her it was my business, not hers. I made her feel like an outsider. I made her feel unwelcome. That's why she left. She told me she was going home. This was her home, and I took it away from her. I'm surprised Robyn's still here.'

'Robyn loves you, and she made this place her second home a long time ago. I can see why Tessie stormed off though. It would tear me apart if Josh said something like that to me.'

Nate twiddled with a piece of wicker sticking out of the side of the basket in front of him. 'I don't think I can make it right again, Jo. Not now. She'll always think that every time we row she'll have to leave. I took away all of the security and stability I've been building with her for the last five years.'

Joey reached out and held his arm. 'Oh, Nate. You and your big mouth.'

* * *

Nate tossed and turned in bed. He was wide awake, uncomfortable, and missing Tessie like crazy. He rolled his head on the pillow to stare over at the empty space by his side.

I should just call her again. No, I'm not going to. I've sent her messages. She hasn't replied to any of them. Clearly, she doesn't want to speak to me. Flipping heck, Tess. Why won't you just call me back? You're driving me nuts. I wouldn't mind, but you've got the cheek to call me stubborn. Now who's being stubborn! I'm going to sleep. I'm not thinking about this anymore.

He closed his eyes, as if that would help.

A creaky floorboard made him shoot upwards.

Tess?

Daisy poked her head around the bedroom door.

Nate sighed to himself and swallowed down the wave of disappointment he felt.

'What's wrong, Daisy?'

She stayed in the doorway. 'I can't sleep.'

He propped himself up against his pillows and waved her over.

She quickly climbed into bed on Tessie's side and snuggled under his arm. 'I'm worried, Dad.'

He kissed the top of her head. 'Now, what have you got to be worried about, hmm?'

'I don't want another mum to leave me.'

Nate felt a kick to his heart. He still hadn't spoken to Tori about not turning up in their lives, and now he had messed things up with Tessie, and Daisy was going to suffer for all of it. He tightened his grip on her.

'Tessie is just on her course. She would never leave you. She told you all about it, didn't she?'

He felt Daisy's head nodding against his chest.

'You mean everything to her. She'll be back next week, and I bet she's been texting you.'

'She has, and she called after school.'

Well, at least I know she's still alive.

'See. She'll always be there for you.'

'But will she be there for you?' asked Robyn, standing by the door.

How do I answer that?

Nate waved Robyn over, and she climbed into bed to sit beside Daisy. He watched the two girls link arms and comfort each other.

'Hey, everything's going to be all right. Your mum is just on a course for a week. That time will fly by. She'll be back before you know it, and I understand that she's lined up some work for you both on Saturday in the shop.'

Robyn groaned.

'I'm looking forward to it,' said Daisy, sounding more cheerful.

Robyn started to play with Daisy's long hair. 'Has Mum spoken to you today, Dad?'

Nope.

'Sure. She's settled in nicely into Jake's apartment, and Anna's friend, Stan, works there, so she has him to chat with if she gets bored when she's not in the office.'

'You could go there and keep her company,' said Robyn.

'Ah, she doesn't need me there. She's working.'

'I think she'd like to see you.' Robyn let go of Daisy's hair and snuggled further down under the covers.

Nate watched as Daisy did the same. He knew he was in for a restless night with those two taking up all the bed space. He sat in silence and waited for them to drift off to sleep. It didn't take long.

Scruff sleepily trotted in and fell asleep at the foot of the bed.

Nate could sense that even the dog was missing Tessie.

Seriously, Tess, you've been gone five minutes and everyone's miserable.

He reached out to the bedside cabinet to pick up his phone. He sent two texts. One to Tessie saying that he loved her, and another to Jake.

28

Tessie

Tessie yawned and stretched, enjoying the large comfy bed in Jake's spare room. The last time she slept in that bed, Nate had made love to her for the first time. She glanced up at the ceiling, remembering how wonderful she felt that night. *Oh, Tess, don't even think about it. Get up, get washed, and have some breakfast. It's Saturday, you have the weekend to yourself. What should I do? Go for a walk along the river. Have lunch with Stan downstairs. I'll call the girls after they've finished their shifts at the shop. Okay, now I have a plan. What should I do about Nate's calls and texts though? Should I carry on ignoring him? Oh, I don't want to deal with this now. I need a cuppa.*

She sat up and flipped back the bed covers and tried for a spring in her step as she stood. She looked at her phone, but it was dead, so she plugged it into the charger and stretched her arms up into the air.

Today is going to be a good day. I'm happy. I'm focused. I'm in London. The sun is shining. I'm on my own. That's okay. It's all okay. Everything will be okay.

She made her way into the bathroom, took one look at Jake's unusual shower, and opted for a washdown in the bath.

She got dressed, wearing a lemon sundress, and tied her curls up into a ponytail. She brushed her teeth and smiled widely at herself in the mirror.

Tessie hardly wore makeup, so decided against it for the day. Her face held its own natural glow, which she had received many compliments for over the years.

She placed her fingers beneath her eyes and stretched down the bottom, studying the whites for signs of her ugly-crying, miserable, late night.

Not too bad, considering I was up most of the night thinking about Nate. I bet he slept well. I bet he wasn't lying awake worrying about me. I bet he didn't imagine himself holding my hand. I wonder if he did send any more messages last night. I haven't checked my phone yet. I'll give it ten more minutes to charge, and then I'll have a look.

She headed for the kitchen to check out what Stan had put in the fridge for her.

Eggs. Milk. Fruit cocktail. Banana smoothie. Juice.

There was bread on the side, so she decided to make scrambled eggs on toast and have that with a glass of orange juice. She knew full well that making scrambled eggs reminded her of Nate, as that was his favourite breakfast.

I wonder what the girls had for breakfast this morning? Probably cereal, if Robyn had anything to do with it. Josephine might have cooked them a huge fry-up to fill them up for work. Wish I could see Robyn's face on her first day. That would be funny. Hopefully, she might actually enjoy doing something. At least Dolly will be helpful. It would be funny to see Josh working too. Rich kid Josh Reynolds going to work. Ha! He has come a long way. Joey's been good for him.

The sleek digital radio on the side looked easy to operate. It had a shiny black on-off button, so she pressed that and hoped it was less complicated than the shower.

The music came on. It was tuned in to an oldies station, and Otis Redding started singing "I've Been Loving You Too Long".

Tessie swayed to the music as she set about making her breakfast. She cracked an egg in a bowl and then looked over at the door, as someone knocked. She turned the music down low.

That must be Stan.

She opened the door, and her mouth gaped, barely registering what she was seeing.

Nate was standing there.

Their eyes lingered on each other's faces for a moment. Neither of them appearing to be able to move.

Oh my God.

He held up a bunch of pink tulips that still had the supermarket price sticker on the wrapper. A half-hopeful smile traced his lips. 'I'm sorry, Tess.'

Tessie's heart jumped into her throat. It was all she could do to stop herself from falling into his arms, but she casually stepped back, allowing him to enter.

He placed the flowers on the table and turned to face her as she closed the door.

'Nate, what are you doing here?'

'I had to come, Tess. I couldn't leave that row between us any longer. I never should have reacted that badly. I never should have said what I said. It is our business. We are partners. We are a family. We're in this together, and I was being an idiot. I hate what I said to you. I hate that I made you leave. I hate myself. I had to see you. I need to tell you how sorry I am, and how much I love you. I don't want to lose you, Tess. It feels so wrong you not being at home.'

Tessie swallowed hard, as all of his words hit her heart one by one. 'I'm just on a course for a week.'

Oh, shut up, Tess. We both know why I'm really here.
Nate dropped his gaze. 'I know, but when you come home, I hope you come home, not back to the pub. I want to put the business in your name too, so that you always know you're a part of it.'

Wow! I wasn't expecting that. I wasn't expecting any of this. I still can't believe you're actually here. I want to touch you so much. I need to just put one hand on your face. If I just stroke your hair or touch your neck. Don't you do it, Tess. Don't move.

She placed her hands behind her back. 'You don't have to do that, Nate. That's your family's business.'

'You are my family, Tess.'

She stared dreamily into his hazy, faraway look, and time slowed.

Stop looking at him like that. Wake up. You need to talk.

Tessie made her way over to the table and sat down, offering him a chair.

'Nate, I love you with all of my heart, but I don't want to spend my life with someone I'm afraid to talk to about big things like money. I know it's hard for you to accept help, especially from me, and I know I hid everything from you, which is something you hate. I'm sorry for the way I went about things, but I'm not sorry for spending my grandmother's money on something good.'

He reached his hand over to hold her arm. Just that simple innocent touch had more of an impact than a kiss.

Tessie placed her free hand on his. She breathed deeply, trying hard to concentrate on not allowing her hand to stray.

Talk, Tess. Just talk to the man.

'Her money has been sitting there for years, Nate, doing nothing for anyone. Mum won't touch it, even though it should be her inheritance. Her mum wasn't a nice lady, and so I thought it would help balance things out if I used the money to do some good. I wanted to save the farm because I love the place. I didn't mean for it to get so out of hand, but the twins were so excited to talk to Jake about all the updates needed, and the next thing, we were this major player in the cheese world, and I was in over my head, and I started to get a bit confused, but I kept it to myself like I'm some sort of queen cheese expert person, but I'm not. I don't know what I'm doing, and I wanted to talk to you about it so much. I wanted your help, but I knew I couldn't speak to you because you would hit the roof, and, well, it all went belly-up for me.'

She watched the corners of his mouth curl up and his taupe eyes brighten.

She tried to suppress her own smile but failed miserably. 'I don't know what I'm doing, Nate.'

He scraped back his chair and beckoned her closer. 'Come here.'

Tessie's mind didn't have time to respond. Her body had taken over. She got up and sat down on his lap, curling up into a small ball against his chest. She smiled as his strong arms wrapped around her, and she effortlessly softened into them.

I love being in your arms so much. This is my favourite place in the whole world. I could stay here forever. That's what I'll do. I'll stay like this for a ridiculous amount of time and pretend that none of this happened.

'The business is going in both our names, Tess. This isn't happening ever again. I'll teach you everything you want to know and don't want to know about how to make cheese, and that along with all your business sense will make our family business a success. We'll be all right. I don't want you treading on eggshells around me. We have to be straight with each other.'

Tessie hung on to his every word. Falling in love with him over and over again.

I love you so much, Nate Walker. More than it's ever possible to tell you or show you.

She looked up at him, her eyes wide with love, and kissed his mouth. The tingling sensation on her lips filled her heart. She gently stroked his hair and then rested her hand on his shoulder. She could see his sad smile.

'You look tired, Nate.'

'I didn't get much sleep.'

'Crying over me?' she teased.

He brightened. 'No. The girls got in our bed and stayed there all night. I hardly had any room.'

Something's wrong.

She stopped smiling and shot him an enquiring look. 'That's not like them. Were they all right?'

'They are now, but Daisy was worried you'd left her, and I don't know what Robyn was thinking. You know what she's like. She keeps it all inside, but for her to come in last night with me and Daisy told me that she wasn't feeling too good either.'

Tessie sat up. 'I would never leave either of them. I told them I was going on a course. I think Josephine might have told them a little bit more about what happened between us. She heard us shouting.'

'It's all my fault. I never should have put my family in that position. Everyone hates me. I've been told off left, right, and centre.'

'Nobody hates you, Nate. It's our first row as a couple. We both made mistakes, and now we've learned lessons. The girls are new in this with us too. They never worried before, because we weren't together then. Now, they have so much to lose. We all do, which is why we have to work harder.

213

Work as a team. There'll be no more secrets from me. I'll do everything I can to make those girls feel stable and to make our family strong.'

'Well, with you at the helm, we're definitely strong. You weren't gone five minutes and we all fell apart. You're the rock here, Tess. You're our glue. I don't want to ever be without you.'

'I'll admit, when I walked out of the farmhouse, I did feel as though our family had been torn apart. It destroyed me.'

Nate lowered his head submissively. 'I'm so sorry, Tess. I'll never make you feel that way again, and I want you to know that as soon as I go back later on, I'm going to call Tori and sort things out with her once and for all. Hopefully, then, she won't make any surprise visits.'

Tessie raised her brow in surprise. 'You're going home later today?'

He nodded. 'Jake's downstairs talking to Stan about the new cottage he's had built for him up by Starlight, and then he's going to see some jeweller to pick up all the wedding rings, and then we're heading back. I knew you'd be busy all week with the Café Diths team, and you have Stan for company, so I asked Jake to bring me out here today so that I could talk to you. I had to clear the air. I was scared you would think I didn't love you anymore.'

She smiled warmly at him. 'I know you love me, Nate. I'll always love you and our family. I'm not having any more insecurities going around. You're loved. I'm loved. Our girls are loved. Our home will be filled with love. I'm going to call the girls later on. I'll reassure Daisy.'

'Everything's fine now. I told Daisy you'd never leave her. She soon settled down and went straight to sleep. They both did. I'm the only one who didn't get any sleep.'

Tessie lightly stroked his cheek. 'Would you like to go to bed now?'

'I could do with a nap… Oh, wait, you mean…'

She kissed him. 'Yep, or are you too tired?'

'I'm never too tired for you, Tessie Walker.'

Tessie giggled into his chest. 'Oh, is that my new name now?'

She could feel his smile on the top of her head.

'It will be one day, hopefully,' he said softly.

Her eyes twinkled up at him. 'Oh, it definitely will be.'

Nate tenderly kissed her cheek, leaving his lips lightly pressed against her skin for a few seconds, and then smirked like he knew exactly what he was doing to her.

Tessie gave up trying to calm the butterflies fluttering. She closed her eyes for a moment after he slowly pulled away from her face.

'You know, Tess, what we're about to do is called make-up sex,' he whispered, as though speaking any louder would break the magic between them.

Tessie grinned, opened her eyes, and moved her leg so that she was straddling him. 'Ooh, I wonder if it's any good.'

He stood, taking her with him, and carried her towards the bedroom. 'Oh, it will be. You have my word.'

29

Nate

Nate sat down in his old barn and stared down at the phone in his hand. He knew he had to call Tori. He just didn't want to.

Why me? Why can't these people just leave me alone? My life is finally getting sorted. I really don't need her coming back into it. Perhaps if I ignore her, she'll go away. I can't do that. I promised Tess I'd sort this out once and for all. I have to do this for Daisy's sake. I can't have Tori just turning up whenever she feels like it. Come on, Nate. You've checked the time. It's a good time to call Australia. God knows how much this will cost. Just breathe. Take a breath and get on with it.

He felt his stomach churn as soon as Tori said hello. Her voice was filled with delight. He caught his breath, feeling as if he were treading water.

'We need to talk properly. I know what you said to Tess. We have things to discuss.' He felt his conversational skills leave him. He wished he had compiled a list or something to fall back on.

'Is it true what she said? That you two are together?' Tori's voice was soft and calm.

'Yes, that's true. It's none of your business though, and I don't want to talk about Tess. I want to talk about Daisy. Do you have plans to come here to see her?'

There was a moment of silence down the phone. He couldn't even hear her breathing.

'Hello? Tor?'

'Yes, I'm still here. Look, Nate. I want to explain something. I've been going through a tough time lately. I'm going through a divorce…'

'You're married?'

She hesitated. 'Yes.'

He huffed quietly to himself. 'You kept that quiet. Got any more kids?'

'I haven't seen you in thirteen years, Nate. I didn't realise I had to let you know my every move.'

He opened his mouth to speak but then closed it again. He had no words.

Tori continued, 'No, I don't have any more children. I didn't want any.'

Sounds about right.

'So, what has any of this got to do with me and Daisy? Are you bored now or something? Your life's not going too well, so you thought you'd come along and mess up ours?'

'That's not why I contacted you.'

'I want to know what you want, and I want you to be honest about it.'

'I called you because of the money for Daisy and Robyn, but then I realised that I missed your voice. Sometimes, I miss you, Nate.'

Nate swallowed down the anger he felt. 'If you really missed me, Victoria, you would have called sooner. It seems like you're only calling now because you're lonely because of your divorce.'

There was silence.

'Do you even want to get to know Daisy?' he asked. He had to know.

He heard her clear her throat. 'I wanted to talk to you.'

'Just me?'

'I… well, I… I missed you, Nate.'

Nate raised his brow in astonishment. 'You don't miss Daisy at all?'

He heard her quietly huff. 'I don't know her, Nate.'

No, you don't.

'Do you want to get to know her?'

'Honestly, I think she's better off without me in her life.'

His mouth gaped for a moment. 'So, you thought you could just have some sort of phone relationship with me that never crossed over to us being together again because, you know, that would actually mean involving Daisy.'

He shook his head whilst waiting for her response. He was waiting a while.

'Are you going to speak, Tori?'

'I'm not coming over, if that's what you're worried about, Nate.'

'Well, yeah, I was a bit worried about you turning up out of the blue and messing with Daisy's head, especially after what you said to Tess.'

'Oh, she just annoyed me, that's all.' She paused. 'Does Daisy really call Tessie her mum?'

Tell the truth.

'Yes.'

'Well, I'm not going to say that doesn't hurt, because it does.'

'Daisy is her own person. She loves Tess, and it was her own choice to view her as a mother. You don't have any right to express how you feel about it. You left Daisy before she was even on solids. She doesn't know you, and she doesn't want to know you. I did ask her. She doesn't want you to come here. I'm sorry to say that, but you have to know. I can't leave this hanging in the air any longer. Everyone deserves to know exactly where they stand in this situation.'

'Yes, I think I get the message.'

'Look, Tor, I'm not trying to be nasty to you. I don't want us to talk like this to each other. We used to share so much, and I know that Henry's death hit you hard. He was your twin. He was your best friend. I don't want bad blood between us. Sure, when you left, I hated you for a long time, but it's been thirteen years. I'm past all that now. I moved on. I rebuilt my life. I'm happy. Daisy is happy. I want you to be happy, but your happiness will never include me. I'm not what you really want. I'm definitely not what you need. I don't love you anymore. I haven't loved you for years. I've got good memories with you and the most beautiful daughter in the world thanks to you, but that's all we have together.'

'I'm sorry for what I did to you, Nate.'

He could tell she was being genuine. Her voice was quiet and broken.

'It's in the past, and that's where I want it to stay.'

Tori gave a slight laugh that crackled the phone. 'I can't believe you ended up with Tessie. Did you always like her?'

'No, Tor. It was only you back then. Tess was just my friend. We've shared a lot over the years. I guess we just grew on each other.'

'It seems strange.'

Yeah, I never saw it coming either, but here we are.

'Do you really love her, Nate?'

You have no idea.

'Yes, I do.'

'Well, I guess that's that then.'

'I want you to know that Robyn calls me her dad. I never asked her to. She came to me with that. I would never try to take Henry's place. We all just came together as a family, and we're happy with what we've created. I just thought you should know that too.'

'Henry was a good person. The best. He would be happy knowing that Tess and Robyn are loved and in safe hands. You know what he was like. If he's watching you, he'll probably think it's a bit strange seeing you and Tessie together, I know I do, but he would give you his blessing. We both know that he would. Henry loved her more than anything. He was so excited to become a dad. He loved you too, Nate. I don't think he'd want anyone else raising his kid but you.'

Nate's brow furrowed. He swallowed the lump that had appeared in his throat. His heart ached for his old friend. The memories they had shared. He stared down at his free hand. Henry's blood wasn't there like it usually was. He remembered holding him in his arms and screaming out for help. He would give anything to have Henry back, even though he knew it meant losing his family.

'Thanks, Tori.' He knew she heard the crack in his voice, but he didn't care.

'A part of me will always love you, Nate Walker. I promise I'll leave you alone now. Maybe I'll think about contacting Daisy when she's a grown woman, but in the meantime, if she ever did want to contact me, tell her my door's open.'

'Is there anything else you want me to tell Daisy?'

'No.'

Seriously? Not even, I'm sorry I left you, or I love you, Daisy.

'Okay, Tor, well, I'm glad we cleared the air anyway.'

'Goodbye, Nate Walker.'

Nate sighed inwardly. 'Bye, Tori.'

The phone went silent, and he ended the call and placed his mobile down on a bale of straw and took a deep breath, filling his lungs with some much-needed fresh air. He flopped backwards and stared up at the roof.

30

Tessie

Tessie walked in the living room of the farmhouse to see a giant handmade banner draped over the old, grey-stone, open fireplace. *Welcome Home Mum* caused her eyes to tear, her heart to warm, and her smile to widen.

'I've only been gone a week.'

Daisy gave her a tight hug, and Scruff approached and licked the top of her slipper.

Tessie bent over and removed the sticky pink ribbon from the top of Scruff's head, even though he didn't seem to mind it being there.

'I missed you.' Daisy snuggled deeper into Tessie's body.

Tessie kissed her head. 'I missed you too, but we did speak every day.'

Daisy smiled her way. 'I know, but it's not the same. I'm glad you're back now.'

'Yeah.' Robyn giggled. 'Because Dad's been useless without you here.'

Nate frowned. 'Erm, I've been coping quite well, thank you very much.'

Daisy stepped away and shook her head. 'I've done all the organising. Gran's done all the cooking, and Robs even tidied her room. Dad's hardly slept, hasn't eaten much, and has been walking around blind. He tripped straight over Liam.'

Tessie wasn't sure whether to laugh or be concerned.

Nate huffed and flapped his arms to his sides. 'He was on all fours on the floor. I didn't know he was there.'

Daisy laughed. 'It was so funny.'

Nate shook his head. 'It wasn't. I could've flattened him.'

'Ooh, we've got cake in the kitchen,' said Robyn. 'I helped Auntie Joey make it.'

Tessie widened her eyes.

Daisy nodded. 'I know. Shocking isn't it?'

Everyone laughed but Robyn.

'It's chocolate.' Robyn left for the kitchen.

Tessie looked at Nate. 'I guess we'd better have some then.' He winked at her, and she felt her heart flutter.

The Hart twins were in the kitchen. Lee was finishing off a cheese-and-ham sandwich, and Liam was sipping tea.

'Welcome home, Tess,' said Lee. 'We're waiting on a bit of that cake.'

'I'll cut it.' Robyn took charge before Daisy could.

'I've got some photos to show you, Tess.' Liam waved his phone in the air. 'We've been taking selfies of us hanging out with the new equipment.'

'And the cows.' Lee laughed at his brother.

'Oh, what have you two been up to?' Tessie took Liam's phone to have a look. She laughed to herself whilst admiring their toned, light-brown bodies. 'Well, these will certainly go down well on Instagram.'

Nate peered over her shoulder and frowned. 'What are you even doing, Lee? Don't say working. I'm talking about that stupid look on your face.'

Lee grinned widely, revealing his gorgeous smile. He ran his hand through his dark hair. 'It's not stupid. It's my smouldering look.'

Nate raised his brow and smiled. 'Is that right?'

'He gets a lot of compliments on Instagram.' Tessie smooshed the side of her face into Nate's chest and smiled to herself when his arm instantly wrapped around her.

'I would prefer the compliments to be on the cheese.' Nate put one hand over the phone to hide the screen.

Daisy placed some plates on the table, and Robyn brought over a bread knife and proceeded to slice the cake into rather large crumbling chunks. Nate picked at a piece and popped it into Tessie's mouth.

'Mmm.' Tessie was nodding at Robyn whilst smiling.

Lee scrunched his nose up at Nate. 'I'm not sitting here watching you feed Tess. I'll take mine outside with me.'

Nate laughed.

Liam carried on eating his. His dark eyes flashed upwards. 'I'm not bothered.'

Tessie turned around and looked up at Nate. His eyes were smiling down into hers. She warmed as he gave her a slight wink.

'Good to be home?'

She nodded. 'Yes.'

* * *

Tessie was standing in the old barn, with only one chicken for company. She looked down at Polly mooching around her feet.

'What do you think, Polly? Will we get this place looking magical in time for the wedding? The new flooring is getting installed in a couple of days. I don't think you'll like it in here anymore.'

Polly made a rustling noise.

'You still have the whole farm. We'll get all this hay and straw out of here, but leave behind some bales as seats and decoration.'

She looked up at the top level.

'Do you know, I've never been up there.'

Tessie climbed the old ladder, feeling her legs wobble, as she wasn't that confident in its structure. She glanced around the platform.

'It's quite roomy up here,' she mumbled, staring over at the back wall. 'It's actually really cosy.'

I can see why Joey and Josh used to come up here.

She laughed to herself at the thought.

'Not sure how comfortable having sex up here would be though.'

'There's only one way to find out.' Nate peered over the top of the ladder.

Tessie jumped. 'Oh my God, Nate. Did you tiptoe?'

He stepped up onto the platform and wrapped his arms around her. She snuggled into him, and he effortlessly lifted her up.

'What do you say we try this out, Tess?'

Tessie had her legs tightly wrapped around him. She peered over his shoulder to look down below. 'Someone might come along.'

He dropped to his knees and lowered her gently to the straw-filled ground. 'We'll be quiet.'

'No, I'm not doing it during the day. The girls might come in.'

Nate kissed her neck and grinned. 'We'll come back tonight then, but for now, we can just fool around.'

Tessie giggled as he put some straw in her hair.

'Christ, Tess, that's one hell of a sexy look,' he whispered.

225

She raised her hand to touch the straw. 'Farmers!'

Nate bit his lip. 'Not sure I can wait till tonight.'

She grabbed his face and pulled him closer to her mouth and kissed him hard.

He laughed on her lips. 'You're not making this easy for me.'

It's not easy for me either.

She closed her eyes as his hand slid under her dress to stroke her thigh.

'Tess, these clothes are coming off in a minute.'

Oh, I don't think I want to stop this. I can't move away from his touch. How can each touch from him have that much of an effect on me? I wish it was night-time now. Oh, sod it!

She wrapped one leg over his and waited whilst he unbuttoned his shorts. His hot breath was all over her neck. His need for her obvious.

She grabbed his face, and he cupped hers. They locked eyes, revealing their love, then she pulled him towards her and started to kiss him passionately, no longer caring about where they were or what hour of the day it was.

God, I love this man.

Nate lifted her dress up to her waist and fumbled with the front of his shorts.

Their breathing was heavy but hushed.

Tessie tried to pull her knickers down, but Nate was in the way.

'Oh God, Nate, I really want you. Hurry.'

He quickly tugged at her knickers whilst kissing her collarbone. 'I want you too.'

'Mum,' called out Robyn.

Tessie and Nate froze.

'Mum,' Robyn called louder. 'What are you doing up there? Your shoe is down here.'

Tessie glanced down at her feet to see she had lost a sandal at some point. 'Yes, one sec.'

Nate rolled off her, and she quickly stood, holding on to the side of her dress tightly so that her knickers didn't fall past her knees.

Robyn looked up at her. 'I need your help in the kitchen. Freddy's given me a recipe to make for your special welcome home dinner tonight, and Gran's staying over at Joey's. Will you come and help me with the preparations? I have to make a pastry and put it in the fridge.'

'Sure, I'll be right down.'

'What are you doing up there anyway?'

'Seeing what needs to be cleared out ready for the wedding.'

Robyn frowned. 'Why have you got straw all over your hair.'

'Your dad thought it would be funny to throw some at me.'

Oh crap, I shouldn't have said that.

'Is Dad up there too?'

Nate was making sure his shorts were fastened. He popped his head up. 'Yep, just helping out.'

Robyn headed for the doorway, mumbling that they were like a couple of kids.

Nate turned to Tessie and grinned at her flushed face. He pulled her back down onto the straw and kissed her smiling mouth.

She slid her fingers into the back of his hair, showing him her desire was still very much there.

'Tess,' he groaned.

'I think we've got five minutes,' she whispered.

He kissed her hard, and Tessie felt her heart flip.

'Mum,' shouted Robyn. 'Come on.'

Tessie shot up so quickly the blood rushed to her head. 'Yes, coming.'

Nate flopped onto his back and sprawled his arms out.

Tessie giggled and quickly straddled him. She bent over to kiss him again.

His hands shot into her curls, holding her tightly against his face.

'Mum!'

Tessie stood up. 'Yep, I'm here.'

Nate's laugh lines were clear as she secured her knickers back in place, tidied her creased dress, and pulled some straw from her hair.

Tessie poked her tongue at him and made her way down the ladder.

Lee raised his eyebrows at her as she passed him by outside the barn.

She tried not to blush as she pulled some more straw from her hair.

'It's all right, Tess, you're with a farmer now. We've all been there.'

Tessie narrowed her eyes at him. 'Haven't you got work to do, Lee?'

He laughed to himself. 'Yes, boss.'

She turned to see Nate walking out of the barn. He had a big soppy grin on his face, which only made Lee's smile widen.

'A little hot today, eh, boss?' he called out.

Nate grinned over at Tessie, and she felt her heart warm with love for him. She laughed to herself as she gave him a cheeky wink.

31

Nate

Nate stared across the kitchen table at Tessie eating Robyn's homemade mushroom, bacon, and leek pie. He loved his family and was happy to be able to sit down with them and enjoy a meal. His father had made sure he was always at the table at dinnertime, so Nate made sure he was too. He worked long days and had delegated a lot of family time to his gran over the years. It wasn't something that he liked doing. He wanted to be there for sports days and school assemblies, but he didn't have the time. He was grateful for his grandmother, and his sister whenever she had stepped in, but he was even more grateful for Tessie. She seemed to be able to make everything work. Sometimes he wondered if she shared the same number of hours in the day as him, as she seemed to fit more in.

Tessie was chatting with the girls about helping with the wedding plans during half term, and the girls seemed happy to get involved.

Nate was concentrating more on getting into bed with Tessie come night-time. The day had dragged for him. From the moment she came home it was all he could do to stop himself from carrying her straight upstairs. The thought kept making a slow smile creep across his face all day, and the twins didn't even bother asking what he was thinking about, as they seemed to be able to read his mind.

He caught her eye as she glanced over at him.

Can you read my mind, Tess? Do you know what I want?

He saw her face warm, and he knew it wasn't from the steam wafting off the creamy mashed potatoes.

It was hurting his cheeks fighting back the smug look of satisfaction he felt knowing the effect he was having on her.

Tessie went back to her food, and Nate thought that it would be the safest option for him too. He tried to clear his mind so that he could have some sort of normal dinnertime conversation without his voice cracking under the strain of his hidden need for his partner's affectionate touch.

'So, girls, how do you like your bridesmaid dresses, any good?'

Daisy's whole face lit up with excitement. 'I don't want to spoil the surprise for you, Dad, but we look like princesses.'

Robyn gave a slight shrug. She wasn't as enthusiastic about parading around in a ballgown but was still willing to take part.

Nate smiled proudly at them both. 'To me, you already are princesses.'

Tessie swallowed her mouthful of food and raised her fork over at him. 'Oh, and you need to go up to Starlight tomorrow for your final fitting.'

Nate grinned. 'Don't want to spoil the surprise, but just so you all know, I look like a Disney prince in my suit.'

They all laughed at him, and he frowned with amusement. 'What a cheek! What's with the laughter? I'll have you know, I can pull off the Disney prince look when I want to.'

Tessie cast him a significant look whilst holding her fork close to her heart without getting dinner on her top. 'You're my prince, Nate Walker.'

The girls giggled, and Nate felt honoured to hold that title for her, even if they were just being silly about the matter.

Daisy rolled her eyes. 'Princes don't normally wear wellies and milk cows, Dad.'

'Princes come in all shapes and sizes.' Tessie smiled Nate's way to see him give her a quick wink whilst the girls weren't looking, and then he went back to finishing off his green beans. She smiled across the table. 'Well, that was a lovely dinner. Thanks, Robyn.'

Robyn picked at her veg with her fork, swirling the greens around the edge of her plate. 'Next time, I'm having sweetcorn with mine.'

Tessie looked over at the mess Robyn was making with her leftover food, that was definitely not about to be eaten anytime soon. 'You don't have to eat the green beans if you don't like them.'

Robyn instantly dropped her fork.

Daisy was still happily eating. 'I like mine.'

Tessie glanced over at the warm oven housing an apple strudel that was filling the kitchen with an inviting sweet aroma. 'I say we take our afters into the living room and eat in front of the telly.'

'We can watch a Disney film,' said Daisy through a mouthful of mash.

Nate groaned and scrunched his nose. 'As long as it's not that snow one again. Even I know the song lyrics off by heart now.'

'Frozen.' Robyn grinned. 'I love it.'

'I don't mind which one.' Tessie shrugged over at Nate. 'I like them all.'

Nate smiled broadly whilst placing his hand dramatically over his heart, pretending to swoon. 'Oh, to live in a fairy tale world.' He laughed at Tessie rolling her eyes at him, then turned to his daughters. 'I like the one where the girl in it looks like your mother when she was young. That has a good story.'

'Brave,' said Robyn, as Daisy giggled.

Nate got up from the table. 'Right, I'll switch the TV on so it's ready. Don't touch the washing up. I'll do that too.'

Tessie looked at the girls and smiled. 'Well, we can't argue with that.'

'We can.' Daisy scraped her chair back. 'We're doing everything tonight. You can rest as well, Dad. I'll put the telly on, and Robyn can wash up.'

Robyn grimaced. 'Thanks!'

Daisy left the kitchen, laughing to herself, and Tessie turned to a distraught Robyn. 'Just give them a quick rinse under the tap and leave them in the sink. I'll do it later on.'

Robyn sighed deeply and dramatically. 'Why can't we have a modern kitchen like the one at the pub? We could have a dishwasher.'

Nate saw Tessie's eyes flash his way.

'It would be nice to renovate this place, Nate.'

You want to spend more of your money.

He covered up the shadow of disappointment that had just enveloped his heart. He wanted to be the one who paid for everything that his family needed. 'Once the business has taken off, we'll sort this place out.'

Tessie was about to smile warmly at him but stopped halfway through when a loud crashing noise coming from the living room shook the house.

What the hell was that?

Nate was at the living room door before anyone had a chance to speak. His face paled, his heart stopped beating, and the strength in his legs weakened.

Half of the living room ceiling had caved in, completely covering the area around the sofas in plaster, rotten wooden splinters, and a huge cloud of thick dust. The glass ceiling light was shattered all over what could be seen of the coffee table, and the top part of the stone fireplace had crumbled down to the no longer recognisable rug.

Nate only felt his body jolt back to life when Tessie screamed and ran into the room. She started throwing pieces of debris left, right, and centre whilst crying out Daisy's name. He waved the dust from in front of him and quickly fell to his knees by her side as Daisy's lifeless body came into view.

Robyn was crying in the doorway, and Tessie told her to call an ambulance.

Nate felt his arms automatically reach out to pull his daughter into his chest, but Tessie stopped him.

'Careful, Nate. Don't move her. You might do more damage.'

He watched as Tessie brushed the dirt from Daisy's face, checked her pulse and airway, and quietly spoke to her, reassuring her that everything will be all right. He wasn't sure if it would be. He had no words to add. He could hear Robyn in the background talking on the phone and hear Tessie constantly talking to Daisy, but their voices seemed muffled and slow.

Daisy groaned, and something jolted in Nate, bringing all of his senses rushing back at the same time.

'Try not to move, Daisy. You're going to be okay,' said Tessie. 'Just don't move your back or neck, okay. I'm right here. We all are. We're just going to sit here till the ambulance arrives. It's all right.'

Come on, Nate, get yourself together. Breathe. Focus. You've got this. Daisy needs you. Just breathe.

He leant over and stroked her hair.

Daisy was lying on her front. Her eyes opened and she coughed.

'Don't move, Daisy,' he whispered close to her ear.

'Can you tell me if anything hurts?' asked Tessie.

Daisy started to whimper.

Tessie kept her hand lightly on Daisy's shoulder, and Nate watched her lean forward and kiss her cheek, telling her it will be okay.

He looked into Tessie's worried eyes, unsure of how to help. She met his stare and gave a slight nod down at Daisy, and he knew that she was silently asking him to join in with the reassurance. He gently wiped some more dust from Daisy's face. 'It's all right. You're all right.' He glanced up at the gaping big hole in the ceiling and couldn't even begin to process what had happened. He looked back down. 'Tell us what hurts, Daisy, so we can see if we can move you.'

'My back.'

Nate and Tessie shared a concerned look.

'Okay. Stay still for a bit longer.' He rested down on his side so that he was face to face with his daughter. 'We'll just lie here for a while.' He felt as though time had stopped altogether as he numbly waited for the paramedics to arrive. He wasn't sure how long they had been waiting. He held on to Daisy's hand that was close to her face. Wrapping the warmth from his palm over her small fingertips.

Tessie stood and stumbled over debris to get to the other side of the room to fetch a clean blanket from an old floral chair in the corner by a vintage table lamp. She came back and gently placed it over Daisy to keep her comfortable.

'Mum.' Daisy's voice sounded croaky as though dry and sore. Her small body was trembling and looked so frail.

Tessie stroked her dusty blonde hair away from her forehead. 'I'm right here, baby.'

'I'm scared, Mum.' Daisy started to cry.

Nate could see that Tessie was silently crying behind Daisy's back. He used every ounce of his willpower to make sure that his daughter could see the positivity in his face.

'Hey, there's nothing to be afraid of. The ceiling fell down on you because it's old and rotten, but I'm going to fix this whole house so that nothing like that ever happens to you or any of us again. You're going to be just fine in a minute, but first we just need the doctor to look at your back, okay.'

Daisy was staring right at him. Her deep blue eyes were filled with water, and her face was ashen and covered in dust.

'Am I going to die?' she asked softly.

Nate felt his heart thump, and Tessie looked ready to break down.

'Of course not,' he whispered. 'You've just hurt your back, that's all.'

Robyn ran to the door. 'They're here.'

Nate felt parts of his body leave him. He was so relieved to see two paramedics enter his house, he could have jumped for joy. Just their presence alone was a comfort.

He moved out of their way as Tessie explained everything they needed to know, including Daisy's date of birth, allergies, fears, and her last tetanus vaccination.

Nate sat back against a wall and watched as the medical team got to work on his daughter. He turned his head slightly as Robyn slid down to his side and placed her head on his arm. He reached out and held her hand.

'It's all right, Robs. She'll be fine.'

'Are you sure?' she whispered.

He swallowed hard and shifted so that he was sitting more upright. He didn't want to appear slouchy and deflated. His girls needed him to be strong. He had to pretend he was, for their sake. He couldn't fall apart now.

His eyes widened as the paramedics sat Daisy up. That was a good sign.

Tessie was still talking to them when her dad arrived in the doorway.

'What the bloody hell has happened here?' Ed was keeping his voice low. He squatted to Robyn's side and looked directly at Nate.

'I called Pops. I was scared.'

Nate kissed the top of her head. 'It's all right.' He turned his eyes to Ed. 'She's hurt her back.'

Tessie approached. 'They think it's just bruising, but we're going to hospital now to check her over.' She smiled weakly at her dad. 'Dad, will you stay here and watch Robyn, or take her back to the pub with you. Scruff's upstairs, I think. Find him, and take him back with you as well. Josephine's at Joey's for the night, and can you turn the oven off, please, there's dessert inside.'

'Don't you worry about a thing, love. Your dad will fix it.'

Nate released Robyn into Ed's arms and stood to hold Tessie. 'Hold on, Tess.' He kept his voice soft in her ear. 'It's almost over.' He watched the exhausted emotion in her eyes swiftly strengthen.

She gave him a slight nod. 'I'll just fetch my bag and Miss Myrtle.'

Nate turned back to the paramedics as Tessie went off to get Daisy's lucky toy cow that slept by her side every night.

236

32

Tessie

Joey had the front door to Honeybee Cottage wide open for Nate to carry Daisy through to the hallway. She guided him upstairs to one of the spare bedrooms whilst Tessie stayed downstairs with Josh.

'I'll put the kettle on, shall I?' he offered, nodding over at the kitchen.

Tessie shook her head. 'I'm going back up to the farm to get a few overnight things for us.'

Josh grabbed his car keys from a glass bowl near the door. 'I'll drive you.'

Tessie felt so exhausted in every way, she couldn't be bothered to argue her case that she could walk. She allowed herself to be escorted to his car.

As she fastened her seatbelt, Robyn came to mind. 'I'll have to pick up Robyn on the way back.'

'That's fine.' Josh started the engine. 'But Elaine called an hour ago to say that Robyn had fallen asleep.'

'Oh, okay.'

At least she's settled. I'll get her first thing.

Josh was pulling onto Pepper Lane. 'Jake's already been up the farm with a builder. I don't think Nate's going to be able to stop my brother from fixing the ceiling. Jake's on a mission to make sure the house is secure, whether Nate likes it or not.'

I don't think Nate will be arguing with anyone right now.

'That's okay, Josh. I'm going to use the rest of my grandmother's money to renovate the farmhouse. Jake can get his builders on site as soon as possible. Oh, I don't know what the steps are. We'll need plans first, won't we? An architect, a structural engineer or someone.'

Josh gave a slight nod as he pulled onto the long driveway that led up to the farmhouse. 'You can speak to Jake about it in the morning. He'll know who to hire. I have a friend who is an interior designer. She did Honeybee for us. I can get her involved with the farm if you like.'

Tessie felt her heart coming back to life. 'You and Jake are good friends.'

He grinned cheekily at her. 'So are you and Nate. Besides, as far as we're concerned, we're family. We've been part of each other's lives since childhood. We'll always be there for each other.'

She got out of the car and stared over at the house. A feeling of dread surged through her body.

At least the rest of it is still standing.

She jumped as Josh's arm rested on her shoulder.

'It's all right,' he said softly. 'It's been cleaned up.'

She rolled back her tears. 'You did that?'

He removed his arm and raised his shoulder to his cheek. 'We all helped.'

Tessie took a breath and headed inside.

The living room was practically empty. Everything had been removed barring the bookcase, side table, and chair in the corner. They were over by a long glass door that led out to a small garden patch where Josephine liked to grow herbs.

Tessie glanced up at the gaping hole in the ceiling.

'The builder said you were lucky there wasn't anything much going on in the room above. Any heavy furniture would have fallen through and landed on…' His voice faded.

She touched his arm. 'It's all right, Josh. Yes, the builder is right. We're definitely lucky.'

'We weren't sure what you wanted to do with the sofas. There wasn't any damage except dirt. We cleaned them up as best we could and then covered them in dust sheets and put them in the big barn.' He smiled to himself. 'I don't know why we still call it that. It's hardly the biggest building anymore.'

Tessie sighed. 'I reckon we'll be having a big bonfire at one point. A lot of stuff can go. This place is going to get the attention it needs once and for all.'

She thought about how much care and attention Nate would be needing from her right now. He was settling Daisy down for the night, and Joey was at his side, so she had time.

The doctor at the hospital had been extremely thorough with her tests on Daisy and confirmed that Daisy had been very lucky indeed. Her back was badly bruised, and they were warned that the bruising would look worse than it currently was and were told not to worry about it. Daisy's head scan got the all clear, but she was monitored for a while because of a mild concussion, which was down to her head connecting with the coffee table when she was pushed to the floor.

Nate's hand had gripped Tessie's so tightly at one point in the hospital, she lost all circulation in her fingertips and had to wriggle free.

'I won't be a minute,' she told Josh.

'Take your time. I'll wait in the kitchen.'

Tessie made her way up to Daisy's bedroom to make up an overnight bag. She made her way over to the window and opened it to feel some warm night-time air. She backed away and sat on the bed. She pinched the bridge of her nose, sighed deeply, and then rubbed her hands down her tired face.

Bit by bit, the blur of the evening started to clear.

A thin film of sweat lined the back of her neck, and she swallowed hard to create some moisture in her dry mouth, which still felt clogged with dust. The image of Daisy lying crushed on the floor flittered through her mind. Playing over and over.

Tessie's heart was galloping, and her temples felt bruised. She wanted to protest at the memory coming at her, but she was too exhausted to fight back.

No one was around her. She didn't have to be in control. She could just fall apart if she wanted to, and a part of her really wanted to.

She could hear a flurry of whispers and was sure her mind had completely taken over. Could she hear the paramedics? Was it Robyn's voice as well?

Why are they still all talking? I need this image to leave me alone. I can't keep seeing it. It's done. It's gone. It's over. Leave me alone. Daisy is fine. I don't need to relive this. Come on, Tess. Wake up. Keep busy. Get Daisy's things. Get everyone's things. Nate will be wondering what's keeping you.

She slapped the tops of her thighs. 'Right, let's get this show on the road.'

She stood and idly wandered around the bed.

Don't go over the what ifs. Don't punish yourself, but what if I had put my foot down with Nate ages ago. We could have had this place sorted by now. This wouldn't have happened. No. Stop. Just stop.

She grabbed a pink sports bag from the top of Daisy's oak wardrobe and filled it with everything Daisy would need for her stay at Joey's.

She didn't have to worry about Robyn, because Robyn still had lots of her stuff back in her old room at the pub, and

Elaine and Ed had catered for both the girls needs for anytime they stayed over.

She closed the window and left the room to collect some bits from the bathroom before entering her own bedroom.

The bed looked inviting.

I could sleep.

She sat down on Nate's side, grabbed his top pillow, hugged it to her chest, inhaling his oaky scent, and stared blankly at the wall.

Nate walked in and stopped dead in his tracks.

Tessie gazed over at him. His face lacked emotion, and his eyes looked lost and alone.

He went to speak but no words came out, and then his legs suddenly caved beneath him.

She watched as he sank to his knees, cupping his face in his hands.

He was gasping for air as he broke down and cried on the bedroom carpet.

Tessie tossed the pillow to one side and fell to her knees before him. Her arms flopped over his back, holding him tightly as he let the wave of tears pour from him.

Let it all out, Nate. Just let it all out.

His arms reached around her and pulled her onto his lap. He held on tightly as his sobs continued, muffled by her shoulder.

There was no way that she was going to let go first. He needed her, and she was staying put until he was ready to face the world again.

Nate's cry started to quieten down. He was catching his breath and trying to steady his racing heart.

She could feel the tension in him relaxing.

'Sorry, Tess,' he managed.

The agony in his tone made her heart break. She swallowed and held back her own tears and kissed his head whilst stroking the back of his hair.

'Shh, now, Nate.'

His arms tightened around her again, and she hung on to him.

Tessie could feel the dampness coming through her clothes from his sweat and tears. Her shoulder was cold and numb, but she didn't move. She couldn't move. He needed her. He was treading water, and if she let go first, he could easily slip away.

Nobody's drowning. Not today. Not on my watch.

She tenderly kissed his head again. 'It's all right, Nate. Everything's all right now.'

His hand came up to her cheek, followed by his head rising from her shoulder. His face looked worn through, and tears were still visible in his taupe eyes.

She gently kissed the tip of his nose.

'I love you, Tess,' he whispered, sounding as exhausted as he looked.

'I love you too, Nate.'

He rested his head on hers, dropping his tired gaze to her lap.

'I don't know what to do,' he said softly. His voice was filled with cracks.

Tessie stroked over his arm. 'We're going to collect our overnight things, go back to Joey's, have a good sleep, and then get busy tomorrow fixing this place.'

He sighed slowly. 'It sounds like a plan.'

'It's a start.'

He moved his head and looked her in the eyes. 'I promise I won't fight you on your gran's money for this place. You can do what you want. I just want this home to be safe for all of us.'

Tessie kissed away a falling tear from his cheek. 'It will be, Nate. It's all going to be fine.' She offered a warm smile. 'Jake Reynolds is on the case already. You know what he's like. We'll probably come back tomorrow to find that he's airlifted a whole new house here.'

Nate breathed out a laugh. 'We have good friends.'

Tessie remembered what Josh had said to her earlier. 'And so do they.'

Nate's sad smile lifted a touch. 'I'm so lucky to have you in my life, Tess. I don't know what I'd do without...'

'That's not something you have to think about, Nate Walker. I'm always going to be here with you.'

He leaned forward and placed the lightest of kisses upon her lips.

Tessie glanced up at the ceiling for a second. 'We're not having the best time of it lately, are we?'

Nate slowly shook his head.

She nudged his arm and waited until his eyes met hers. 'At least we're all still together. We can get through anything as long as we stick together.'

'I think we've been through too much throughout our lives.'

Tessie wrinkled her nose. 'Everyone has stuff to go through. We'll probably have more stuff come our way over the years too, but we'll manage. Whatever it is, we'll cope.'

His eyes softened. 'You will. You're much better in a crisis than me.'

'I'm only strong because you've always held me up.'

Nate shook his head a touch. 'Not true. I let you down in the early years.'

243

'I remember when Henry died. You came and sat in my room with me every night for two weeks and just held my hand. You would watch telly with me or play cards.'

Nate smiled at the memory. 'I didn't know what to do.'

'Nobody ever really does. Not in any situation. I think we're all winging it.' She took a steady breath. 'I know we've had our moments, but we've had more good moments, and we've always held each other's hand, mostly.' She snorted out a short laugh, which made him smile.

'It's funny what life can do to you,' he said quietly. 'You might plan to go one way, thinking you know where you're heading, but you end up in a completely different place, and you're better off for it.'

'Yeah, I never thought I'd be living here.'

He cupped her face with one hand. 'I'm glad our roads met, Tessie Sparrow. I'll always get down on my knees and kiss that road.'

Tessie felt her heart warm. She loved him so much. She suddenly frowned down at his lap.

'Speaking of knees. Let's get you up. Your legs must be hurting.'

She stood and offered her hand to help him, which he took.

He groaned as his legs straightened. 'Come on then, let's get back. I've left Joey sitting with Daisy.'

'How is she?'

'Daisy went straight to sleep as soon as her head hit the pillow.'

'Yeah, well, it is late. Josh is downstairs. He probably wants his bed too.'

They both stared over at their bed, longing to fall asleep.

Tessie nudged him. 'Get a bag and put our PJs and undies in it. I've got everything else. I'll meet you downstairs.'

She stopped in the doorway, peering back at him as he set about his task.

I'm glad our roads met too, Nate Walker.

33

Nate

Nate put his coffee cup in the kitchen sink and leant towards the back door so that he could see Tessie down the hallway, who was about to answer the front door.

'I'm going back to work, Tess.'

He heard her mumble something, and then she called back to him.

'Nate, wait. Monty is here.'

Montgomery James? What's he doing up here?

Nate was filled with curiosity as he made his way towards the front door. He stopped at Tessie's side and automatically placed his arm around her waist.

'Hello, Monty. What can I do for you?'

Monty furrowed his light eyebrows and seemed to smile apologetically as he offered his hand for Nate to shake. He was a tad red-faced, and his voice held a hint of empathy.

'Hello, Nate. I'm actually here on official business. Would it be okay if I came in?'

Nate and Tessie moved to one side.

'Yeah, sure.' Nate frowned. 'I'm curious now, Monty. What does a solicitor want with me?'

Tessie guided them down the hallway. 'We'll have to sit in the kitchen, Monty. As you can see, the other half of the house is under construction.'

'That's all right.' Monty entered the kitchen. He plonked his black briefcase on the table and flicked open the locks.

Tessie reached out for the kettle. 'Do you want a cuppa?'

Monty shook his head, making his blonde curls bounce, which looked way more cheerful than his rueful face.

'No, thanks, Tess.' He glanced over at Nate. 'Sit down for a sec. Let's get this sorted as quickly as possible.'

Nate and Tessie sat opposite him, wondering what was going on.

He doesn't look very happy, and he certainly doesn't look as though he wants to speak. His Adam's apple is bobbing so much, it might just pop right out of his mouth.

'What's this all about?' asked Nate.

'My client has given me instructions to speak to you so that you have a chance to settle before this is taken any further.'

Nate could feel the agitation in him rising. His palms had started to sweat, and his heart was pounding. 'Settle what?'

'Who's your client?' asked Tessie.

Monty's protruding throat gave away his swallow, yet again. 'Dana Blake.'

Nate almost choked on the laugh that remained stuck at the back of his mouth.

Tessie turned to him, then back to Monty. 'I think you had better get to the point.'

Monty nodded, swallowed hard, and cleared his throat. 'Yes. Miss Blake would like you to pay her back the money you took from her when you were a couple. If you refuse, she's not only going to take you to court, she's going to inform the police that you stole that money.'

Nate's jaw hung loosely, and his eyelids stopped blinking. He turned slowly to face Tessie to see that he wasn't the only one who was gobsmacked.

An almost hypnotic silence filled the air.

Nate had been caught completely off guard. Seething resentment slowly started to creep its way to the forefront of his mind. His mouth twitched as his eyes narrowed towards the man in the blue suit sitting awkwardly at his kitchen table.

Monty lowered his gaze. 'I'm sorry, Nate.'

Tessie appeared to come back to life. 'What money does he owe her?'

Monty pulled a file from his briefcase and scanned it. 'It was originally two thousand pounds, but she wants interest paid, so she wants six back.'

Nate watched Tessie's eyebrows raise so high they could have touched the moon.

'Six grand!' she yelled.

Nate saw her waiting for an explanation from him, but before he could say anything, she was facing Monty again.

'Were there any written agreements between them about this loan?'

Monty cleared his throat. 'According to Dana, it wasn't a loan. She claims Nate used her money to buy his gym equipment without her permission and that the money was from the forced sale of her grandmother's necklace.'

Nate could hear the words that he wanted to say whirling around in his head, but for some reason they weren't entering his mouth. He had to practically force himself to breathe and hoped that would help.

'She gave me that money,' he managed.

Tessie was glancing between him and Monty as though watching a tennis match.

Monty cleared his throat. 'She said she let it go back then because she loved you. She also said that you agreed to pay her the money back when you broke up, or as she has put in her statement... When he broke my heart and forced me out of my beloved home knowing I had nowhere to go.'

Nate's head bobbed slightly as a small laugh escaped his tight lips.

Tessie was amazed. 'You don't actually believe that Nate forced her into selling her grandmother's necklace and then secretly took that money and bought his gym equipment, do you, Monty?'

'It doesn't matter what I think, Tess. It won't look good in court.'

Nate found his voice. 'I didn't know about the necklace. This is the first I'm hearing about that. As for the gym, she offered to pay for that because she never paid for anything all the time she was living here. She said it would be her way of chipping in. In fact, she didn't pay for sod all here. She didn't pull her weight or help out with Daisy. All she did was go shopping all day, for herself. I didn't want her money, but she persuaded me in the end. I did tell her when we broke up that I would give her that money back. I just haven't had a spare two grand sitting around in the last five years, but I never forgot about it. I still had every intention of paying off my debt to her as soon as I got my business up and running properly. She was top of my list.'

Tessie's hand came across and rested gently on his arm.

He glanced into her worried eyes. 'I didn't steal her money, Tess.'

'I know you didn't,' she replied swiftly. 'You would never do anything like that. You don't have to convince me, Nate. I know what a good person you are. I also know how evil she is.'

Monty smiled with sympathy. 'I'm sorry, Nate. We all know what she's like, but my hands are tied. If it wasn't me she hired, someone else would be here right now, and they wouldn't care about your side of the story.'

Tessie scoffed. 'She's heard about what's going on with the farm, and she thinks Nate has won the lottery or something and that's why she's rocked up now asking for over the odds. The greedy…'

'How long have I got to give her back the money before she starts spouting her lies?' asked Nate.

'One week.'

Nate's shoulders felt lead-heavy. He nodded slowly. 'Okay. I'll find the six grand.' His voice was as deflated as he felt.

'No, we won't,' snapped Tessie, slamming her fist down on the table. 'She can get stuffed. Tell her she'll get her two grand back tomorrow, but not a penny more, and if she wants to go to the police and pretend that Nate stole her grandmother's necklace or forced her into selling it or whatever, well, you tell her we'll see her in court, and we'll have Jake Reynolds' solicitors with us, and they'll eat you for breakfast, Montgomery James.'

Monty and Nate jumped as Tessie's chair crashed backwards across the floor as she jolted out of her seat.

Nate stood and placed his hand over her pointing index finger and calmly lowered it from Monty's face.

Monty's eyes were wide and on full alert. 'Don't shoot the messenger, Tess.'

Nate pulled Tessie into his side to comfort her and simmer her temper. He could feel the heat coming from her trembling body.

The last thing we need right now, Tess, is you flying off the handle and storming over to Sandly to punch Dana in the face. I know that's what is going through your mind.

Monty tossed his paperwork into his case and quickly closed it up. 'I'll go and let her know your terms right now.' He stood and looked directly at Nate. 'I don't want this dragging out either, mate. This is your reputation she's trying to destroy, but you know what she's capable of if there's a few quid in it for her.'

Yeah, I know. She tried to sell my farm from under me. She upped the selling price on The Book Gallery when she found out Jake wanted to buy it. That was her mum's business. Betty Blake's money, but she took most of it and put her mother in a home. Tess is right. Dana's only doing this because she thinks I'm loaded.

'I'll see you out, Monty.' Nate walked him to the front door.

'I am sorry, Nate,' said Monty, crossing the threshold.

Nate gave him a smile that didn't reach the eyes. 'You're just doing your job.'

'I'll call later to let you know how I got on. I'll be advising her to take the two grand and drop the accusations, but even I can't make an educated guess on how she'll respond.'

'Okay. I'll speak to you soon.' Nate watched his old school friend climb into a shiny dark-blue convertible and drive off.

'Well, that was an unexpected conversation,' he mumbled to himself.

Tessie's hand rested gently on his back, and he turned into her embrace.

'I suppose I could sell my truck.'

Her head moved deeper into his jumper. 'No, Nate. I'll give her the money.'

'Isn't that what they call robbing Peter to pay Paul?'

'Not in our case. You don't have any debt with me. I'm not like her. I would never do anything like that to you. Everything I paid for was for us. Our future. Our family.

251

Once the house is finished, we won't have any of my grandmother's money left. We're using the interest now.'

There was a moment of silence between them.

Nate reached one arm out and closed the front door, making sure he still held Tessie close to him. He wasn't ready to move away from her loving hold.

Her head rolled up his jumper to stare softly into his eyes. *God, I love your eyes, Tess. Everything feels a lot easier with you on my side.*

She took a breath that vibrated through his chest.

'At least I know now why you're so against taking people's money,' she said quietly.

'I was always going to pay her back, Tess. I just didn't have it. I should have offered instalments back then. Why didn't I think of that?'

Tessie picked at the fluff on his brown jumper and then gently caressed his chest, loosening his tension.

He picked her up and carried her over to the stairs and sat down on the second step with her on his lap.

'I really have no idea why that woman hates me so much.' He sounded just as baffled as he felt. 'I never did anything to her.'

Tessie scowled. 'She's pure evil. I hate her guts.'

'Yeah, well, you leave her alone if you see her. I don't need you getting arrested for assault.' He breathed out a laugh and shook his weary head. 'I thought you were going to smack poor Monty at one point.'

She sat upright on his knee. 'I was fuming, Nate. How is someone allowed to just make up lies about someone. She should be arrested just for that. She could destroy your name and our business with that kind of slander. In fact, if she keeps that up, I'll sue her. See how she likes it.'

'I don't think we'll need Jake's solicitors with you on the case.'

Tessie huffed. 'Well, she winds me up.'

Nate rested his head against hers. 'Oh, Tess, why are we having such a bad run lately? What else can go wrong? Forget I said that. We've got the wedding in two weeks. I'm glad Dana doesn't know about that. Can you imagine. She'd probably try to swindle some money out of Jake to keep quiet.'

Tessie's fingertips started to slowly swirl around the bottom of his hairline. Her delicate touch was soothing his tired soul.

He closed his eyes and allowed a soft smile to creep across his face.

'I texted Jake while you saw Monty out. Told him we might need a solicitor,' she said quietly.

'Joy.'

'I think she'll take the two grand, Nate.'

He opened his eyes. 'I feel like loading up that gym equipment in my truck and dumping it on her doorstep.'

'I feel like wedging a dumbbell right between her teeth. That'll wipe the smug look off her hideous, gold-digging face.'

Nate raised his brow in amusement. 'Remind me never to get on the wrong side of you.'

She snuggled into his shoulder and tenderly kissed his neck, sending a shiver of delight all over him.

'We could sell all that gym stuff if you want and buy new equipment.'

'That's okay, Tess. It's all been sterilised from her evil aura. Gran even burned sage in there.'

Tessie giggled. 'Is that true?'

'Well, the saging part is. Gran was smudging the whole farm after Dana was gone. The cows weren't best pleased with the odour.'

He smiled widely as she moved her face to look at him.

'Give me a kiss,' she whispered.

Nate met her soft lips and rested there for a while.

34

Tessie

The inky sky above the glass roof of the swimming pool at Starlight Cottage was all Tessie could see as she floated on her back in the middle of the pool, with the main lights for the room switched off. Lots of bright twinkling stars sparkled down at her, helping to relax the tension in her body that Monty's visit had caused that morning. All she could think of all day was how many different ways she could punch Dana Blake in the mouth. She knew she had to calm down. She couldn't afford to do anything stupid. Her family was relying on her to stick around, not get locked up for criminal damage to Dana's smarmy face.

Just relax. Breathe and look at the stars. Life is good, and it's going to get even better. Oh, I love this place. Hello, stars.

The chlorine in the water was all Tessie could taste and smell. She did prefer swimming in the sea because she loved the feeling of the openness, the movement, and the scent of salty air, but the quietness of the pool was relaxing.

Oh my goodness, I had no idea how much I really needed this. I might just stay here all night. Float away my worries. Float away my fears. Float away my nightmares. Float away my tears. I've not said that in a while.

Ever since she was a girl, Tessie had loved to swim. Edith Reynolds had given her a spare key to Starlight's swimming pool and told her she could swim there whenever she liked.

The swimming pool was a decent size. It was warm and had a cosy changing area and a power shower to its side. There was also a small room used as a storage cupboard for inflatables and water aids and all of the cleaning equipment. Tessie had been taught by Edith how to maintain the pool.

The summer was her favourite time for sea swimming. First thing in the morning was the best time. She would put on her wetsuit and join a couple of other locals who also preferred an early morning dip in the cold water of the bay.

She once joined a local freshwater swimming group but got into a spot of bother swimming in the river one time, and that was enough for Elaine and Ed. Tessie was under strict instructions to only swim in the sea or pool from that moment on. Even Nate worried about her sea swimming. He also preferred the safety of Starlight's pool.

Tessie stared at the stars, thinking about how long it had been since she swam. How much it relaxed her. How she loved swimming under the watchful eye of the stars. She had completely forgotten that Starlight Cottage had permanent residents when she let herself in, checked the water quality, got changed, and dived in.

Anna entering the pool house, sipping hot chocolate and saying hello, quickly reminded her.

Tessie's arms splashed down. She quickly straightened up and bobbed. 'Anna. I'm so sorry. I was in such a tizz, I actually forgot myself.'

Anna giggled and sat down on a nearby folded-out chair by a side wall panel that held a soft white light. 'I saw you from the bedroom window when the garden lights suddenly came on. I did wonder if you might be sleepwalking. Perhaps I should say sleep-swimming. I also thought that maybe I was the one who was sleeping, dreaming about the Little Mermaid.'

Tessie swam to the side and rested her arms on the edge and smiled up at Anna.

'Edith gave me a key to the pool house when it was first built. I've always been allowed to swim here whenever I wanted. I cannot believe I forgot that you and Jake live here. Of course I know you live here.' She slapped the side of her head, causing spits of water to flick out. 'I don't know where my brain is at tonight.'

Anna removed her large white mug from her lips. 'I think I do. Jake said that you might need a solicitor to fight some charges that Dana Blake is bringing against Nate.'

Tessie gave a slight nod. 'She's such a bitch, Anna. She's always been that way. It's like she was born evil. What did Jake say about it all?'

'He wasn't surprised. He called Nate earlier to offer his support. Jake's asleep on the sofa at the moment with Max. They've had a busy day watching John Wayne films all day with Josh.'

Tessie giggled along with her.

'I know.' Anna sighed. 'It's a hard life. He says he doesn't get to do it often now that Josh is taking turns with Dolly at the new farm shop until you step in down there full time.'

Tessie glanced back at the pool. 'Yes, I haven't been very well organised, what with everything going on at the moment, but that will all change starting Monday. Dolly's shop is opening in two weeks. She's been great helping out, but I can't rely on her any longer. I need to sort my schedule once and for all. Between Josh, Liam, Lee, and myself, we'll have the farm shop running properly. Also, I'll give you back the key to the pool house when I get out.'

Anna flapped her hand. 'No, don't. Edith gave you that key. You can swim here whenever you like.'

'But it's your home now, Anna.'

'Pepper Bay is my home now, Tess, and you lot in it are my family. This was your pool way before it became mine. I want you to still use it when you want.' She smiled softly as she looked around. 'It doesn't get used much. Jake swims sometimes, but he prefers to go for a run. He's joined a gym over in Sandly now as well. It makes him happy.'

'Have you been for a swim yet, Anna?'

Tessie saw her blush, and she knew it wasn't the humidity in the air causing her to flush.

'I can't swim, Tess.'

Hey, don't feel embarrassed about that.

'I'll teach you if you like.'

Anna's eyes brightened. 'Really?'

Tessie smiled widely. 'Sure. Why not? It's not that hard, really. It's more about confidence than anything else. You don't have to worry about fancy techniques or styles, just basic swimming. It's important.'

Anna placed her hand over her belly. 'I'm going to make sure this one learns how to swim.'

Tessie nodded. 'Yeah, then they can come swimming in the sea with me.'

Anna placed her cup on the floor by her feet. 'I'd love to do something like that.'

'Well then, that's what we'll build up to. You won't have to go in deep or anything. You can just swim near the shoreline. A lot of swimmers do. Not everyone goes right out. I'll teach you about the do's and don'ts of sea swimming once you're ready for that.'

'Swimming pool first then.' Anna smiled down at the calm water.

'Definitely. You can get in now if you want.'

Anna laughed out loud.

'I'm being serious. There are water aids here. Plus, there's a shallow end, which is exactly where you will be. I wouldn't let you go, and you'd only learn how to kick today anyway, or we can leave the lessons till later in the year once the baby is here if you'd prefer.'

Anna looked far too excited to wait. 'I want to try now.'

'Do you own a swimming costume?'

Anna glanced down at her peach tracksuit. 'Can I get in the pool in my underwear?'

Tessie laughed. 'As long as you're comfortable.'

Anna stripped off to her black bra and matching full-brief knickers and walked over to the shallow end.

Tessie swam down to meet her. She pointed over to some ring-shaped arm bands. 'Slip them on your arms. Right up to the top.'

Anna sat down on the edge of the pool, dangling her legs in the water. 'What are the flat ones for?'

'They're kickboards. You hold it in front of you and kick your legs out behind you, but we won't be using those yet. You're going to hold on to the side and kick. You don't really need the armbands yet either, but they'll help you feel more confident. At any time, you can put your feet down and stand up at this end. I don't want you getting out of puff. A little at a time will be fine for now.'

'Does it take a long time to learn how to swim?'

Tessie raised one wet shoulder to her cheek. 'Everyone's different. We're not going to rush anything. You're pregnant, and I'm no swimming coach. Let's just make sure you know enough so that you know how to stay afloat.'

Anna smiled warmly. 'I'd like to float on my back like you were doing when I came in. It looked so peaceful. Can I learn that tonight instead? I'm a bit worried about doing too much while pregnant now. I think I got a bit ahead of myself.'

'We can do that. You can hold a floating device to your chest, and I can hold you from underneath.'

'Yes, can we try that?'

'Okay. Grab that red kickboard and that orange neck cushion. You can hold the board on your chest and rest your head back on the cushion to keep your ears out of the water. I want you to keep the armbands on, and we're staying in the shallow end.'

Anna did as she was told and made her way into the water. 'Ooh, it's not as warm as I thought it would be.'

Tessie grinned. 'Your body will get used to it in a sec. How are you feeling? I've got to say, you don't look as nervous as beginners tend to look.'

'I'm more excited than scared.'

'Good for you, Anna. I think you're the bravest person I know anyway. This just confirms it. Do you even get scared?'

Anna laughed as she slowly lowered herself to dip her shoulders beneath the water level. 'I've been scared plenty of times in my life, Tess.'

Tessie watched Anna's ice-blue eyes gazing softly at the water.

'My ex used to scare me quite a lot,' she added quietly.

Tessie reached over to her and held her hand.

Anna smiled warmly at her. 'It's okay, Tess. That's in my past now. Meeting Jake scared me, but in a good way. I never knew love like that existed.'

Tessie's heart warmed as she thought of Henry and Nate. 'I've been lucky, Anna. Henry was so kind and loving, and now I have Nate. They're different in many ways, but they're both kind and that's a huge deal.'

Anna nodded her agreement. 'Jake's kindness towards me blew me away at first. I wasn't quite sure what to do with it.'

'Jake's always been misunderstood. Here, hold the float tightly and rest your head backwards. I'm going to hold your back. Place one hand on the side and hold on. That will help you to relax until you get used to it.'

Tessie braced herself as Anna put her full trust in her.

'Ooh, this is weird.' Anna smiled widely as she allowed her body to relax under Tessie's guidance. 'I know what you mean about Jake. You really do have to get to know him. I don't think he allows many people in.'

Tessie was holding Anna up with ease, and Anna's relaxed body and floating aids were helping tremendously.

'I think you have to get to know everyone, really. People can surprise you.'

Anna was gazing up at the stars. 'The people here surprised me. You lot are so friendly.'

Tessie breathed out a laugh, making sure she kept her concentration. 'Pepper Bay is a friendly place. My mum always says it drew her in more than my dad did.'

Anna wriggled as she laughed. 'I do love your parents.'

'I love Stan. He's great, isn't he? I can see why you adopted him.'

'He's arriving in two days. Most of his stuff is already set up in his new home.'

'I love the little cottage you had built for him up here. It's so adorable. I want to live there. It definitely fits in with Pepper Lane. Have you given it a name yet?'

Anna's eyes sparkled. 'We spoke about it, and Stan wanted to name it after his late wife. Marsha Cottage.'

Tessie felt her heart swoon. 'Oh, how lovely is that. What would you call your cottage if you were given one?'

Anna giggled. 'I was given one.' She let go of the side and gripped the kickboard with both hands. 'I love the name Starlight. I love this place more than I can explain. What about you?'

Tessie stepped back, taking Anna with her. 'I don't know. I love living at the farm. I like how quiet it can be at times. I like hearing the animal noises.' She laughed. 'It's better than hearing a load of drunks.'

'Why's it called The Ugly Duckling?'

'I don't know. Apparently, it has always been called that from the moment it was built. There's lots of history on the old place, but no one seems to know the story behind the name. I know the story behind Pepper Pot Farm. It's always been in Nate's family, so the story has been passed down. How true it is, I can't say. The original owner of the land was married to a woman who was so tiny, he used to call her a pepper pot. So, when he turned the area into a farm, that's what he named it.'

Anna giggled up at her. 'You're like a pepper pot too.'

Tessie laughed. 'That's another reason I can only hold you up in the shallow end.'

She watched Anna's eyes turn back to the stars.

'Are you happy, Tess?' she whispered, as though her library voice was the only volume appropriate for a night-time swim.

Tessie didn't need to think about the question. The way her heart warmed every time she thought about her life told her the answer. 'I am, Anna. I really do love my life. What about you? I know you have this wonderful home now, a baby on the way, and are about to marry the man of your dreams, but are you really happy?'

They both giggled at each other.

'Incredibly happy,' sang out Anna.

'I'm so pleased,' said Jake, making them both jump.

'Jake, can you see me?' Anna wiggled one foot, as Tessie slowly guided Anna's body around.

'Oh, there you are.' Jake grinned widely.

Tessie beamed his way. 'What do you think, Jake? We'll make a swimmer out of her yet.' She noticed the confusion on his face.

'Swimmer? Anna, can you not swim?'

Tessie bit her bottom lip in.

Anna was looking at her. 'I was going to mention it, Jake. It just never came up. Tessie's giving me water confidence lessons tonight, and then once the baby is born I'm going to learn how to swim properly and, one day, swim in the sea with Tess.'

He smiled. 'Anna Cooper, you never cease to amaze me.'

Tessie watched him walk over to the edge of the pool and sit down. He was wearing a dark tee-shirt and light shorts. His long, toned legs swirled around in the water.

'Do you want to take over, Jake?'

'No, Anna looks very comfortable with you, Tess.'

Tessie smiled at him. 'I forgot you lived here and let myself in. I think I gave Anna a fright. She thought I might have been sleep-swimming.'

Jake laughed. 'I guess it's my fault as well. I didn't tell her about you and your random swim times. Do you remember that time you walked in on Josh and Joey canoodling in the pool?'

Tessie and Anna both laughed at the same time.

'I do,' said Tessie. 'But that wasn't the first time I walked in on them. They were always canoodling somewhere. It wasn't that difficult to bump into them.'

Jake nodded. 'That is true.'

'Canoodling.' Anna was laughing to herself. 'I like that word.'

'It's very fitting for those two.' Jake nodded.

'Jake, I think we're going to have to come in here every night from now on. This is so relaxing.'

'I think Tessie might have other things to do than hold you in the pool every night, Anna.'

Anna smiled widely as she glanced up at Tessie. 'He knows I mean him.'

Tessie smiled back. She glanced over at Jake. 'Well, if you don't want to do it…'

He cut her off. 'I'm sure I can manage.'

Tessie raised her head to look at the stars. 'This is why you just put the low lights on, Anna.'

Anna sighed deeply. 'It's so magical.'

'Tessie swims in here during storms too.' Jake was also looking up through the glass ceiling.

Anna's eyes widened. 'Not sure I'd do that. What if lightning struck and electrocuted me?'

Tessie grinned at her. 'That's what makes it exciting.'

Jake stared back at the pool. 'Anna, are you in your underwear?'

Tessie breathed out a laugh. 'She didn't know she would be swimming tonight.' She nodded at him. 'Get in here and take over. I need to get home. Nate might wake up and start worrying I've drowned. I left him a note on the side of the bed letting him know where I went, just in case he woke up and got in a panic when he couldn't find me anywhere.'

'He called a minute ago. That's what woke me up.' Jake slid into the pool fully clothed. 'He just got woken up by his phone ringing too, so I guess he thought, why not wake Jake up as well.'

'Was he asking if I was here?'

'No, he knew. He read your note. He was calling to tell me that my solicitors won't be needed after all. Monty had just called to say that Dana had just called to say she'll take the two grand and call it a day. Seems like everyone's awake tonight.'

'Maybe she couldn't sleep,' said Anna. 'Being mean to Nate might have been playing on her mind.'

Tessie locked eyes with Jake as his hands took over from hers to hold Anna. 'Yeah, that'll be it.' She couldn't help but scoff.

Jake grinned at her, then turned his attention towards Anna. 'Hello.'

Anna smiled warmly up at him. 'Hello.'

'Lunch at Edith's tomorrow, Anna.' Tessie walked up the swimming pool steps, leaving them to their night.

'Yes, definitely, Tess, and thank you for tonight. It's been lovely.'

'You're welcome.' Tessie headed off to the changing room. She glanced over her shoulder and saw Jake lower his head to gently kiss Anna's mouth. It warmed her heart, and she couldn't wait to get home and snuggle under Nate's arm. Her favourite place.

35

Nate

I can't believe my little sister is getting married. Where have all the years gone? I wish our dad was here. He would be so proud of Joey.

Nate glanced around at the light-wood panelled room where the double wedding of Jake and Anna, and Josh and Joey was about to take place. Pink satin-covered chairs lined either side of a small walkway that was sprinkled with red, pink, and white rose petals. There were no name tags on chairs, and no allocated bride and groom sides. The only guests were Stan, in a smart navy suit, Molly and Freddy, in their colour-coordinated outfits, Ruby Morland, who had the largest fascinator, her nephew, Scott Harper, the Walkers, and the Sparrows.

Nate was standing next to his grandmother in the first row. He smiled warmly at her long, soft, burgundy dress and lace shawl. He'd never seen his grandmother look so glamourous before.

Tessie's hands came over his arm from the row behind him.

'Hey, they're coming in.'

He turned to eye-up her dark-pink dress one more time. All morning, he hadn't stopped looking at her. Her beautiful locks were under the strictest amount of control, tossed and curled and pulled up into a tight roll with just a few strands roaming freely around the side of her lightly made-up face.

Tessie smiled warmly at him, then turned to watch their daughters walk towards the blonde lady waiting to officiate the wedding at the front of the room.

Nate swallowed down the lump in his throat at seeing his girls dressed like princesses in light-pink, three-quarter length, satin gowns.

Tessie took as many photos as the professional photographer in the room.

Daisy and Robyn beamed happily over at their parents as they passed them by.

Nate could see Elaine wiping a tear from her eye across the way.

The Reynolds brothers walked in together and stopped at the front. One on either side. They were wearing similar suits to the dark-blue one that Nate had on. They all wore dusty-pink cravats and a matching rose in their lapel.

Holding hands, Anna and Joey entered the room and walked towards the grooms. They purposely stood next to the wrong man, making everyone laugh.

Anna turned to the guests. 'Well, they look so much alike.'

Nate placed his hand over Tessie's as it came to rest on his arm as everyone sat down.

Anna and Joey swapped places, and the wedding began.

Tessie took more photos of the backs of their beautiful white dresses.

Anna's was plain silk and draped loosely, and Joey's was fitted and held lace that had been taken from her mother's wedding gown that she had retrieved from the loft at Pepper Pot Farm.

Nate rolled back the water that had formed in his eyes as his little sister said her vows to the love of her life. He was so pleased for Joey. All of her dreams had come true.

'Josh Reynolds, from the moment I laid eyes on you when we were kids, I hoped I'd marry you one day. Even your constant singing didn't put me off. You have always lived in my heart, and you will continue to do so in this life and the next.'

Nate watched his grandmother lift her handkerchief to gently dab her eyes, then saw Daisy hold Josephine's free hand.

Anna was holding Jake's hand.

'Jake, never in a million years did I expect to find you. You have been in every romance book I have read, every dream I have had, and every beat my heart has made long before you came into my life. To me, you are every star that fills the sky above Starlight Cottage. You are all the rainbows and every ray of sunshine.' She paused and smiled down at her pregnant belly poking out.

Jake placed one hand on their baby.

Anna smiled up at him. 'You're everything.'

Jake leaned forward and kissed her and got told off by the registrar because it wasn't that part yet.

The guests laughed, and the ceremony continued.

'Joey Walker, you are my light in the window during the darkness. Always was, always will be.'

Joey's big smile spread across her face.

'I love you, Jo,' Josh added.

It was Jake's turn to speak, and he looked as though he had no words until Anna reached over and took his hand in hers.

'Anna, I don't have anything amazing to say, because every time I look at you, you take my breath away. Just standing in your presence renders my brain useless. I... I wish I had the words to tell you how much you mean to me.

How I wish I had found you sooner. How blessed I feel that you love me.'

Anna raised his hand and gently kissed his knuckles. Her dog, who was wearing a big pink bow around his neck, left Stan's side to sit in between her and Jake, giving Jake's free hand a quick lick.

If Jake had any more words, he couldn't get them out. His eyes had glossed over, and his mouth had closed.

The wedding came to an end, and it was time to head over to the barn for the reception.

Nate turned in his seat to talk to Tessie. He kissed her forehead as she wrapped her arms around him.

'I wish it was us getting married, Nate,' she said quietly.

'We can ask about it before we leave. Find out what we have to do.'

He watched her eyes widen. 'Really?'

Nate laughed through his nose and then laughed again as Tessie snorted out a laugh.

'Are you kidding? What do you mean, really? Of course really. My heart's doing a happy dance right now.' He raised her hand and placed it over his chest. 'See.'

Tessie giggled. 'Are we really going to do it?'

'We were always going to do it. It was just a matter of when. We'll take the next available slot.'

* * *

The old barn smelled of freshly cut wood and sweet pea scented bunting. Glass storm lamps were filled with flickering fake candles and sat upon straw bales that were placed around the walls. A long table covered in a cream cloth lined the middle of the large area. Small summer posies and string-tied golden cutlery filled the table top, along with wooden placemats, white crockery, and crystal glassware.

Lively chatter filled the air until Joey stood and clinked her fork on her half-filled glass of orange juice.

'Have you got another speech, Jo?' called out Freddy.

Joey poked her tongue out at him. 'No. I have a suggestion.'

Everyone was smiling up at the look of delight spread across her face.

'What you thinking, Jo?' asked Nate, laughing at her silly grin.

'I'm thinking it's a beautiful day, so we should walk down to the beach and have a wedding day paddle.'

Josh was the first to stand. 'I'm up for that.'

Everyone agreed and headed towards Pepper Lane.

Nate was holding hands with Tessie on their walk. The bright sun was shining in the sky, the seagulls were flying overhead, and the peace and tranquillity of the nearby sea filled everyone with warmth and happiness.

He glanced over his shoulder to see his sister walking towards him as they passed by Edith's Tearoom.

'Don't think I haven't noticed you two giving each other secret smiles for the past couple of hours. What's going on?' asked Joey.

Nate smiled at Tessie, and she gave him a slight nod. He looked at his sister. 'We're getting married as well, Jo. We pencilled in a date at the registry office before we left.'

Joey laughed, not taking him seriously. 'Way to go with the big proposal, Nate.'

'No, really, Jo.'

Joey's face flushed with excitement. 'Oh my God, really? That's the best news ever.'

Nate and Tessie shared a loving look.

Joey tried hard not to squeak like a mouse. 'If I'm still away on my honeymoon, I'll come back. I wouldn't miss this for the world. We can always get back to our honeymoon later on.'

'It's in a couple of months, just after I finish my course in London, so you should be back. Depending on how long Josh is taking you away for. Do you know where he's taking you yet?' asked Tessie.

'I know we're going to Malta first, but after that he's keeping it a surprise. I have to pack clothes for hot and cold places. That's all I know.'

Josh placed his hand on the small of Joey's back. 'What's with all the whispering over here?'

Joey was far too excited. She started some sort of jazz hands manoeuvre and got tangled in her words.

Josh was trying not to laugh at her. 'What?'

Nate thought it best to explain. 'We're getting married in a couple of months.'

Josh placed his hands around their backs. 'That's great news.'

Tessie's face was practically glowing. 'And we were talking about your honeymoon as well, and now I'm wondering where we would go, Nate.'

Nate watched her eyes lose their shine.

'We don't have any money left once the house is built,' she added.

Nate stopped walking and frowned at her. 'Hey, I don't care about honeymoons, Tess. We'll be married, that's good enough for me. That's all I care about.'

Tessie's smile warmed again, filling his heart. 'Perhaps we could go somewhere next year. I've always wanted to go to Scotland.'

Josh gasped in their faces. 'Well, that's easily settled. I have a friend who owns a castle in Scotland. He's never there and often lets people stay. I'll have a word with him, and you can stay there. Frank can take you in the helicopter and bring you home or you can go in my plane. That will be more comfortable. It's up to you. It won't cost you a penny.' He straightened up and held out one palm towards Nate. 'Hey, sorry. I wasn't trying to push this on you. I was…'

Joey cut him off. 'It's a great idea, Josh.' She turned to her brother. 'Tessie wants Scotland, and there's a castle up there going spare. Gran will say the universe is working for you, Nate. What do you say?'

Nate could see Tessie from his peripheral vision. She was looking hopeful. 'Okay, thanks, Josh.' He reached out and shook his hand.

Josh smiled and gave his bride a slight tug away towards the shingles. 'Come on, leave the lovebirds to it. Race you into the water.'

Nate laughed at his sister as she hitched up the bottom of her wedding dress and ran onto the beach. He turned to a beaming Tessie. 'Looks like we're going to Scotland.'

Tessie cupped her hands together in front of her chest. 'Thank you, Nate. The girls will love it.'

Nate grinned as he breathed out a laugh. 'They're not coming on our honeymoon.'

'What honeymoon?' asked Elaine.

Nate and Tessie jumped at her sudden appearance.

'We're getting married soon, Mum,' said Tessie.

Elaine let out the biggest scream and proceeded to tell everyone who was in earshot.

Cheers and congratulations rippled across the beach.

Robyn and Daisy hugged each other before running into the sea, and Ed placed his arm around his wife in an attempt to calm her.

'I can't believe our baby is getting married.' Elaine smiled at Ed.

Ed shook Nate's hand. 'Welcome to the family, son. Although, you've been one of us for a while now anyway.'

'I'm glad you're going to take my baby seriously, Nate.' Elaine turned to Tessie. 'I think it's time I gave you this. Call it an early wedding present, love.' She slipped a small silver ring off her little finger. The old red stone that was surrounded by cubic zirconia jewels had sat on her finger since she was a girl, and Tessie had often twiddled with it when sitting on her mother's lap.

'Ah, Mum, that's the only jewellery you've got from your childhood.' Tessie looked down at it being placed in her hand.

Elaine nodded. 'It's one of the things I brought with me from my old life, and I only did that because my grandmother gave it to me the week before she died. That's my grandmother on my father's side. She was my favourite person growing up. She's who I named you after, love. It belonged to her grandmother, and she told me to one day pass it on to my own daughter or granddaughter if I wanted to. She never had any daughters of her own, and I was her only granddaughter.'

Tessie and Nate smiled at the old ring.

'That's lovely, Mum. I'll treasure it.'

Elaine nudged Tessie's fingers to a close around the ring. 'Or you could sell it if you ever need some more money.'

Tessie laughed. 'I'm not selling it, Mum. It means so much to you.'

Elaine waved the comment off. 'Oh, Grandmama told me to sell it if I didn't want it or if I needed the money. I saved it for you. I always knew I'd give it to you on your wedding day.'

Nate grinned at her. 'No offence, Elaine, but I don't think it would buy much nowadays, but with a little bit of polish, I can get it looking as good as new again, I reckon.'

Elaine and Ed shared a look that made Nate and Tessie narrow their eyes.

'It's not really costume jewellery, love,' whispered Elaine. 'It's antique. Made by a man whose jewellery is sought-after by collectors all over the world. All those jewels are real. It's insured for two million pounds.'

Tessie choked on air. 'Do you mean to tell me that I've finally got rid of all that money I had, and now I've got more?'

'We'll leave you to it.' Ed tried to lead a reluctant Elaine away.

Whilst Tessie was hugging her parents, Nate took a step away to stare over at the length of beach that divided Pepper Bay and Sandly. He gazed up at the cliff, then back down to the spot where he had held Henry in his arms. A vision of Henry standing there smiling at him appeared.

'Can you see Henry?' whispered Tessie, approaching him from behind.

Nate could feel her arm pressed up against his. 'I was just imagining him standing there.'

'Was he smiling?'

'He was always smiling.'

'Yes, he was.'

'I wish I knew if I had his blessing.'

Tessie took a step forward, but didn't let go of his hand. He watched her blow a kiss towards the cliff. 'You can go now, Henry, if you want. I'm going to be all right now. Everything is fine. You don't have to worry about me anymore. But remember, I'll always love you.'

'We both will.' Nate took a step to her side.

Tessie looked up at him with so much affection. 'He'll always be a part of our lives, Nate, but he's gone now. He's settled. Now you must find your peace too.'

Nate's eyes glossed over as he stared deeply into hers. 'You are my peace, Tess.'

Tessie went to place her free hand over his heart but stopped and unravelled her fingers.

Nate stared down at the old ring sitting in her palm. 'I'm starting to think I'm cursed with money. I've got a multi-millionaire as a best friend. His brother has just married my sister, and there's you with your secret stash that keeps on growing.'

Tessie gave a half-shrug. 'It's not the worst curse to have thrust upon you. Anyway, you're protected against curses, Nate Walker.'

A faint crease appeared between his eyebrows. 'I am?'

Tessie giggled over at Josephine paddling in the sea with Stan. 'My grandmother might have been aristocracy, but yours is a witch.'

Nate laughed. 'Ah, so that explains why I often find salt on the doorstep.'

Tessie slipped the ring onto her little finger. 'Money and sorcery, Nate. Sounds like something from a fairy tale.'

He looked around him at all of the love he could see. His daughters were splashing each other and the dogs. Ed and Elaine were holding hands whilst paddling. Freddy and Molly were trying to pull Scott and Ruby further into the sea. Jake was sitting at the shoreline with Anna in his arms as the gentle waves washed towards their feet, and Joey and Josh were knee-deep in water, wrapped in each other, kissing under the cry of the seagulls.

'It is like a fairy tale, Tess.'

'Where do you think we fit into that?'

Nate smiled and tenderly kissed her cheek. 'We're the ones who get to live happily ever after.'

* * *

If you enjoyed this story, why not come back for another visit to Pepper Bay with Scott and Dolly.

Lemon Drop Cottage

At first glance, Scott Harper is a shy artist who keeps himself to himself, but he isn't the man everyone thinks he is. Scott has a secret. One that has kept him firmly away from any chance of having an intimate relationship. The only woman in his life is the one he talks to online but has never met. It's easier that way, for them both.

Dolly Lynch has just taken over her aunt's shop in Pepper Bay. Between looking after her teenage son, running around for her old aunt, moving home, and opening a new shop, she barely has time to herself, so she really appreciates the moments she spends talking online with a man she's never met. Little does she know he's the same man who lives just up the road in the cutest cottage she has ever seen.

Lightning Source UK Ltd.
Milton Keynes UK
UKHW012051130922
408830UK00002B/38